Season of the Turtle

A novel by
Alley Robinson

authorHOUSE

AuthorHouse™
1663 Liberty Drive
Bloomington, IN 47403
www.authorhouse.com
Phone: 833-262-8899

This is a work of fiction. All of the characters, names, incidents,
organizations, and dialogue in this novel are either the products
of the author's imagination or are used fictitiously.

Published by AuthorHouse 04/07/2021

ISBN: 978-1-6655-2168-0 (sc)
ISBN: 978-1-6655-2173-4 (e)

Library of Congress Control Number: 2021906824

Print information available on the last page.

Any people depicted in stock imagery provided by Getty Images are models,
and such images are being used for illustrative purposes only.
Certain stock imagery © Getty Images.

This book is printed on acid-free paper.

Dedication

This is a work of fiction, and every character in it is fictional. The settings, however, are real, including beautiful Oak Island, on the southern coast of North Carolina.

I want to thank the Oak Island Sea Turtle Protection Program for the summers of learning, hard work, friendship and fun. I dedicate this book to my dear friend, turtle partner and tireless copy editor, Joni; to my first "turtle mama," Sylvia; and to the best turtle team *ever*.

Prologue

Nest 7, The Lay

The sea turtle crawled out of the waves and through the spreading foam, hesitating as she looked around, wary of predators and other disturbances. She was very tired. This was her second crawl of the night. At the first attempt, a fox had come up to her in the moonlight, sniffing the edges of her shell and pawing at one of her flippers. Nervous, she had turned and made her laborious way back to the water.

This time, in the quiet hours before dawn, she met with no difficulty except her own awkwardness on land. In the sea, she dove and turned and swam tirelessly, completely at home in her liquid environment. On land, she moved with difficulty, three feet in length and nearly three hundred pounds, and weighed down with her burden of new life. But the instinct of millions of years kept her moving, searching the beach where she was hatched almost two decades before. As she made her slow and cautious way, ghost crabs skittered away from her in the moonlight. They would return for the baby turtles later, but they were no danger to the mother.

Just over the low ridge of a sand dune, she found a likely spot and began to dig, flinging sand with her large flippers, rotating her body to create a pit. At last it was deep enough to suit her, and she dug a smaller egg chamber with her hind flippers. She was ready.

With the rear of her body poised over the chamber, she began laying her eggs. Two, then three more, then another two or three; each rubbery egg cushioned by the mucus secreted from her body. Her craggy face awash with "tears," she continued until more than a hundred eggs were nestled tightly together in the chamber. Then she used her rear flippers again, pushing the loose sand over the nest and all around, disguising its presence from predators.

Near exhaustion, but satisfied her work was done, she crawled even more slowly toward the waves, never to see the nest again, trusting in her progeny's instincts to take them, in their time, on their own path to the sea.

Chapter 1

Nest 7, Day 50

Aubrey stumbled through the sand, weighed down with supplies and equipment. "Why does it have to be so hot?"

"Gee, I dunno," said Kate sardonically. "Maybe 'cause it's the middle of July in North Carolina?"

Aubrey stuck out her tongue at her friend, although Kate was ahead of her going through the dunes and couldn't see. She paused to kick off her flip-flops and pull off her baseball cap. She kicked the shoes to one side of the path, where she would stop to don them on the return trip. She tightened the straight auburn hair she wore in a ponytail, pulling the tail through the back of the cap as she replaced it.

The heat and humidity just added to the general feeling of discontent she'd been experiencing lately. Bad enough to have just turned thirty-six, to have a defiant teenaged daughter, an arrogant ex-husband and a house that needed repair. Now, she was here at Oak Island beach in the middle of summer, hauling rolls of plastic edging, a hoe, broom and various other items to a sea turtle nest in the hot, sandy dunes.

Just then they crested the low rise that separated the parking area from the beach, and a sea breeze lifted her hair and spirits. Kate was below her, trudging the downhill slope of the dune, and Aubrey could see the sparkling ocean, happy swimmers in the surf and massive merchant ships in the distance. Beach-goers, a mix of locals and tourists, crowded the sand. The din of human voices and the constant clamor of gulls vied with the roar of the surf to make a pleasant distraction from her gloomy thoughts.

That's better, she thought. *I can't believe this is my first trip to the beach this year.*

When she and Sunny had moved from Wilmington to Oak Island nearly five years ago, they had come to the beach almost every day. Sunny, ten years old at the time, had been a loving and enthusiastic child, excited to be so close to the ocean.

"Mom! Look at all the shells! I'm going to decorate my room with them," she had declared. Her room in Aubrey's two-bedroom bungalow was still filled with the objects Sunny had created – a shell-encrusted mirror frame, a matching pair of shell-filled glass table lamps, and dozens of smaller items. A few years ago, the mermaid bedspread and curtains had been replaced with an island print comforter and dark brown shades, but the bright yellow paint on the walls remained. Looking into that room the past few days had been painful for Aubrey.

Sunny had earned her nickname almost from birth. Amelia Rose Benson had been the sunniest, happiest baby Aubrey could imagine. She and Craig had started calling her "Sunshine" when she was just a few months old. By the time she was walking, they had shortened it to "Sunny," and by now, no one in her life ever called her Amelia.

Aubrey wasn't sure when Sunny had decided life with Mom was "lame," but that's how she had described it last month when she had again asked to be allowed to live with her father.

"But, Sunny," Aubrey had opined, "now that school's out, you'll want to hang out at the beach with your friends."

"Oh, Mom, that's so *lame*. I see those kids all year. I want to hang at Dad's pool. I have friends there, too, you know."

Aubrey *did* know, and refrained from pointing out, once again, that she didn't approve of the friends at Craig's Wilmington condo. There was no denying that Craig's place was three times the size of Aubrey's, and that Sunny had her own bathroom there. At home, Sunny's bathroom was also the guest bathroom, and Aubrey was constantly after Sunny to keep it neat.

Sunny had begged and nagged and argued to be allowed to move in with her father, until Aubrey had given in. "Just for the summer," she had insisted, wincing at her daughter's squeal of delight.

Sunny had been in Wilmington two weeks now, and Aubrey was astonished at how much she missed the girl. She tried to stay in the loop with phone calls and text messages, but it couldn't make up for the eerie quietness of a house with no teenager in it. Being at this noisy beach was a pleasing change.

"You're pathetic," she muttered now, and Kate glanced over her shoulder.

"You say something?" she asked.

"No," Aubrey answered. "So, this is Number 7?"

They were on the beach side of the low dunes that separated the seaside homes of Oak Island from the ocean. Kate paused by a white pole and sign that identified the spot as a turtle nest under the jurisdiction of the Oak Island Parks and Recreation Department and the North Carolina Wildlife Resources Commission. It also described the fines associated with disturbing sea turtles or their nests. Handwritten with a felt tip pen was the number "7" and the date the nest was laid, June 1.

Because sea turtle eggs hatch at about fifty to sixty-five days, Kate and Aubrey were at the nest to prepare it for the hatching to come. In addition to putting up the sign, the OISTPP staff had marked the nest with a tiny stick in the center and squared off four wooden stakes with string around the stick.

Aubrey had been Kate's assistant for the last three years and had undergone the annual spring training at the rec center, so she knew what to do. Together, she and Kate installed green plastic edging around three sides of the staked nest and down the slope to the beach. This created a runway from the front of the nest along the twenty feet of edging on both sides toward the ocean. Nest 7 was about two feet into the dunes, sparsely surrounded by sea oats and grass, so they curved the runway slightly to bring it around the thickest vegetation. They brought more edging to put down when the nest showed signs of hatching, but this start would do for now. It was back far enough from the open sand, where people walked and children played, to prevent tripping anyone.

While they worked, onlookers began to gather. Many asked questions about the nest, and Aubrey usually deferred to Kate, only replying if Kate was occupied. Kate, ever patient, answered every question. Yes, the nests on this beach are all loggerhead turtles, so far. No, they don't necessarily hatch in the order in which they were laid. Yes, the mother turtles who lay their eggs on this beach were once hatchlings here themselves. They return every few years to make their nests in the same area, usually three or four nests in a season, and sometimes more than one nest per crawl. No, the mother turtle doesn't come back to check on the nest; she lays the eggs and goes back to the sea and on her merry way.

Personally, Aubrey thought the loggerhead mothers had the right idea: pop them out and get on with your life. Don't stick around to get your heart broken by your own offspring.

A little girl in braids, just like those Sunny used to wear, asked if the turtles were about to hatch, and Aubrey gave more than her usual your-guess-is-as-good-as-mine reply. She paused in smoothing sand up around the outside of the edging and sat back on her heels to answer.

"Well, they could hatch tonight, but probably not. It's a few days early. We hope they'll hatch in a few days, but it could be a week or more. Those little critters come out when they're good and ready, you know?" She winked.

The little girl nodded, smiling at Aubrey's cheerful tone.

Aubrey continued. "And because we can't be sure when it will happen, we get as ready as we can get, and then just wait."

"How big are they when they hatch?" asked the woman who appeared to be the child's mother.

A big man in a tee-shirt, rolled-up jeans and a patrol cap, standing several feet behind the woman, seemed to be listening intently, although she couldn't see his eyes behind the dark glasses. When a pair of teenagers stepped between them, he moved to one side and continued watching.

"About the size of a small cookie," Aubrey said. She raised her voice for the benefit of the others listening. "If you're here when they boil, be sure to stay well away from the water for several feet on either side of the end of the edging. It'll be dark, and you wouldn't want to step on the little guys."

"And no lights, please," Kate chimed in. She was very protective of her turtles, and her usual laid-back manner vanished when anyone disobeyed the rules of turtle watching. "That means no cell phones, flashlights or cameras."

Someone asked why no lights, and Kate answered pleasantly. "They get very distracted by light and can end up going the wrong way. Most of the homeowners along here," she indicated the large beach houses on the other side of the low dunes, "know to turn their porch lights off during turtle season. Protecting turtles requires a lot of community cooperation."

"Excuse me, ma'am?" Aubrey jumped when she realized the big man in the patrol cap had moved silently up beside her. He pulled off his cap. "Sorry, ma'am. Didn't mean to startle you."

"Yes?" She was unaccountably annoyed. Maybe it was the "ma'am," or just the sneaky way he moved.

"You said they 'boil.' What does that mean?"

Aubrey explained, "Sometimes a few come out early, and there are often a handful of stragglers, but when the biggest share come up together, it looks like they're boiling up out of the sand. So, it's called a 'boil.'"

He nodded and replaced his cap. "Thank you." He turned, and she noted he wore a large backpack across his broad shoulders. Unlike the other onlookers who crowded around, he moved several feet away before dropping his backpack and settling down on it to watch.

Despite the interruptions, it didn't take Kate and Aubrey long to finish their preparations. They paused to answer a few more questions, then made their way back down the beach and across the dunes to the car park. As they unlocked their vehicles, Kate called to Aubrey that she would see her in three days at 8 p.m. to start their watch.

"Say, Aubrey," Kate added. "What did that big guy want?"

Aubrey shrugged. "He asked what a boil is."

Kate looked puzzled. "Is that all?"

"Yeah. Why?"

"You had such a scowl on your face. I thought maybe he was coming on to you."

Aubrey shook her head. "I just don't like the look of him. That backpack. Do you suppose he's homeless?"

Kate laughed. "That's a little 'judgey' for you, Aubrey. 'Homeless' doesn't equal 'criminal,' you know. Or even 'bum.'"

Aubrey bridled. "I know that," she said, and bade Kate goodbye. As she drove away, she considered why Kate's remark had rankled. She sometimes felt the teacher-student relationship she had once had with the older woman had morphed into a parent-child relationship. Kate was only fifteen years older, but, with her shorter, broader stature and curly mop of gray hair, she was sometimes mistaken for Aubrey's mother. Aubrey wasn't entirely comfortable with that.

Face it, she thought. *You're not comfortable with much, these days. Your child, your house, your job, your ex-husband. That big guy on the beach. Your whole complicated life.*

Chapter 2

Nest 7, Day 55

"Oh, crap. He's here again," Aubrey said. Jerking her head toward a large figure walking slowly through the dark, along the shore from the east.

Kate, from her beach chair on the other side of the nest, squinted against the light flashing from the Oak Island Lighthouse, about two miles east of their current location.

"Are you complaining about the big guy again?" She snickered. "You're developing an obsession. Maybe you should inventory your feelings. 'Methinks the lady doth protest too much.'"

"It's not an obsession," Aubrey insisted. She lowered her voice. Tourists and locals loved the beach at night, and there were people lounging in beach chairs or on towels just a few yards away. "And try to remember you're a biology teacher, not a shrink. 'Inventory your feelings,' my ass." She leaned forward, peering at her friend in the dark. "And, by the way, the correct quote is 'The lady doth protest too much, *methinks*.'"

"Well, you'd know about that. I'm just a crude, horny old scientist."

Aubrey laughed, aware her friend was not old and rarely crude. As for "horny," Aubrey could hardly testify to that.

"But," Kate continued, "you don't know anything bad about our large friend over there."

"I know he's been hanging around here the past two days, ever since we started sitting the nest."

"So have others." She nodded toward the loungers. "These folks aren't out here to get a moon tan, you know."

"I know," Aubrey leaned forward and whispered. "But that's part of what's weird about him. He stays far away from everyone else, and the nest. He just watches. It's creepy."

"Maybe he's got a thing for tall, skinny redheads with bad attitudes."

"Ha! Try again."

"Did you ever consider that maybe he's shy? Sometimes men that big just don't want to impose their size on other people."

Leaning back, Aubrey humphed. "What makes you such an expert?"

It was Kate's turn to lean forward. She glanced around and whispered, "I ran into him this morning, when I came to check on the nest. He was looking out at the ocean, and I didn't want to startle him, so I just said 'good morning' as I passed."

"And?"

Kate shrugged. "He said 'good morning' and asked if I was checking on the nest, and offered to help. I said thanks, but I didn't expect any change from last night, just wanted to make sure. He came along, and we talked for a few minutes."

"And?" Aubrey was getting impatient.

"And he's a veteran. Last served in Afghanistan. He moved here from Georgia and he's looking for a job."

Aubrey sighed. "Out with it, Kate. If a job was his only problem, he'd have no problems. It's tourist season and everybody's hiring."

"Okay. You were right. He's homeless. And you know how hard it is for the homeless to find work, even here."

"And maybe he's also not very bright. Or he has a record of some –"

"Excuse me, ma'am."

They had become so engrossed in their whispered colloquy that neither had noticed the man slowly close the gap on the beach until he was standing next to them in the dark. Aubrey put her hands over her face and muttered, "Oh, crap."

Kate scrambled to cover. "Oh, hi, there. Nice to see you. I, uh, we …"

The big man bent and laid a ball cap in Aubrey's lap. "I think you dropped this."

Aubrey opened her eyes and picked up the black-and-orange Orioles cap. "Yes," she croaked. She couldn't look at the man she'd just been disparaging. "Thanks."

Without a word, he moved away and resumed his walk along the beach. When she was sure he was out of hearing range, Aubrey spoke again. "Oh, man, that was awful. Me and my big mouth."

Kate reached across the nest and patted Aubrey's knee. "Make it up to him," she suggested.

"How?"

"Ask your ex to give him a job in his construction company. I'll bet he'd be good at it, and Craig wouldn't worry about the way he looks. In fact, he'd probably think the rougher the better."

Aubrey laughed. "I'm not exactly tight with Craig these days, you know. And I don't want to owe him any favors. Especially now that Sunny's living with him."

"You're probably right. I just hate to see one of our vets in trouble."

"I know. But there's got to be some reason why he clearly has nothing. There's something wrong with him. Bet on it." She sighed and leaned her head back, looking up at the stars. She spotted the triangle of Mars, Saturn and Antares in the southern sky over the ocean. She loved the uniqueness of Oak Island's south-facing beach.

Another hour went by, passed in desultory conversation in the faint starlight. People came and left, until only Aubrey and Kate remained, along with a young Greenville couple who were leaving tomorrow and had hoped to see turtles. A nest had hatched last night, but they had missed it by half an hour. Around 10:30, even they gave up and said goodbye.

A brisk breeze kept the bugs from lighting, and the sound of the waves lulled Aubrey into semi-sleep. From behind closed lids she saw the glow of Kate's red light checking the sand covering the nest for any changes. Kate snapped the light off.

"Well, whaddya say, kiddo?" she asked. "Shall we call it a night?"

Aubrey rose from her low chair and began gathering her things. She shouldered her vinyl bag with the image of a loggerhead turtle and folded her beach chair. Only as she turned to follow Kate toward the car park did she notice the solitary figure, briefly revealed by the distant flash from the lighthouse: a large man in a patrol cap, sitting on the sand several yards west of where she stood. Rather than feeling threatened by his presence, she felt oddly protected, watched over.

She raised her arm in a goodnight salute but couldn't see whether he responded. Then she hurried to catch up with Kate.

They were stowing their gear in their vehicles in the orangey light of the small car park, when Kate said, "Oh, I forgot to tell you. A couple of my students from last year will be joining us, starting tomorrow. They get public service credit for taking part."

"Yeah, I noticed some teens in the 'newbie' training session," Aubrey responded. "Hope they stick it out to the end. Remember that kid last year? He showed up twice and spent the whole time complaining about how boring it was." She shut the lid of her trunk and opened her car door. "Anyone I know?

"Um, let's see. Heather Carson and Brett Solingen. Know them?"

"No. I'll ask Sunny when I get –" She caught herself, remembering with a sinking in her stomach that Sunny was not waiting for her at home. "When I talk to her tomorrow."

Kate waved, and Aubrey got into her car. She sat for a few minutes with the engine running, wishing she had somewhere to go besides her empty house. Her father had died three years ago, in Wilmington, and her mother lived in Maryland, in the house where Aubrey had lived as a teen. Aubrey didn't visit her as often as she should. She didn't like her stepfather, a loud, opinionated bigot, so different from Aubrey's cheerful mother and gentle father.

She would never understand why her parents had divorced. They had seemed to get along just fine, but when Aubrey came home from her first year of college at Penn State, they sat her down and calmly explained that they were separating, and Pop was moving back to his hometown of Wilmington, North Carolina.

She remembered her naive young self, arguing with them about the decision. Her mother had finally said, near tears, "We have a right to be happy, Aubrey. Neither of us has been happy for a long time."

She hadn't said it aloud, but she had truly thought at the time that happiness was for the young. Her parents were content, or seemed so, and that should have been good enough. It couldn't be about sex; they were almost fifty, for crying out loud.

Pop had moved to Wilmington to take care of his elderly mother. "Meemaw" had been almost eighty and, though spry, was beginning to flag mentally. She had lived another nine years in the loving care of Aubrey's father, and he had only survived her by four years.

She missed Pop like crazy. He was the reason she had convinced Craig to move to Wilmington with baby Sunny right after they had graduated from college and only weeks after her mother had remarried. It had worked out well for them; Craig had started a successful business and she had spent time with her father and Meemaw.

It had been a good thing that they were there when her grandmother had died. Her father had needed her emotional support, and she had needed his when she had learned Craig was sleeping with another woman.

"Honestly, Pop," she had said at the time. "It's such a cliché. Sleeping with his secretary! Doesn't he know she could sue him for sexual harassment?"

Craig had offered to move out of their home, but she had already decided to move herself and Sunny to her father's house. It was a wise choice, as it turned out. When Pop was diagnosed with stomach cancer that fall, Aubrey took a year off from teaching high school

English, Creative Writing, and Drama to nurse him. She had done her best to shelter ten-year-old Sunny from the ugliness of his sickness and death, arranging for hospice care for her father and sending Sunny to spend lots of time with Craig. And there was no denying that the child's cheerfulness and devotion had lifted Pop's spirits through the six months of his illness.

But the treatments had exhausted Pop's savings, and then some. After his death, Aubrey had been forced to sell the house he'd inherited from her grandmother to pay off his debts, and had just managed to keep enough for a down payment on a small place for herself and Sunny. That's when they had moved to Oak Island. Her former professor and good friend, Kate Mitchell, was living on the island and teaching at South Brunswick High School.

Kate had taught Aubrey in college in Aubrey's requisite science class. They had become friends, and Kate had traveled with Aubrey on spring break to visit Pop and Meemaw in Wilmington, and had loved the area. A few years later, after Kate had fallen in love with one of her students and gotten her heart broken, she had decided to quit teaching college and had moved south. She and Aubrey had remained good friends and were now colleagues.

Aubrey pulled into the carport of her little house on a quiet street off Oak Island Drive. The house was dark, and she cursed herself for not remembering to leave on a few lights. Inside, the silence was oppressive. Aubrey turned the TV on just for the noise, and went to her room to take a shower. Her bathroom was small, but the shower was large and the fierce water pressure soothing. She washed away sand and bug spray and melancholy, but was left with her nagging guilt about her remarks overheard by the big guy on the beach.

Does he sleep on the beach? she wondered. She loved the beach but was grateful to have a house to come to, even a lonely one.

Too distracted to sleep, she watched television for an hour, curled up in her pajamas on the worn old sofa, sipping iced tea and crunching the ice. The old movie wasn't enough to distract her from the pinball machine of her thoughts. She mentally critiqued the three-week Honors English class she had recently finished teaching for the high school's "Summer Institute." She worried about Sunny and whether Craig was watching out for her, and why Sunny had not responded to her offer to pick her up for church yesterday. She stewed over Craig's twenty-two-year-old girlfriend, whose picture, in a very tiny bikini, had appeared on Sunny's Facebook page.

When Sunny had pointed it out to Aubrey, they had shared a scornful laugh about it, before Aubrey had dutifully reminded her to be respectful of Maya, whether she liked her or not. She had to admit that she had been secretly pleased when Sunny had said she did *not* like her, not even a little bit.

Aubrey turned off the TV and the living room lights, went to her empty bed and said her nightly prayers. She prayed for the man on the beach and that she hadn't hurt him too much with her thoughtless remarks.

Slipping under the covers, she reminded herself that she really didn't like him. In the next moment, she recalled the feeling of protection she had experienced as they were leaving the beach. It was odd, the way he could make her feel uncomfortable and safe, all at the same time.

She fell asleep with the image of his dark silhouette in her mind.

Chapter 3

Nest 7, Day 56

As usual, Aubrey and Kate arrived together, shortly before dusk, and tidied the nest and runway. Tonight's sunset was spectacular, and Aubrey, dropping into her beach chair with a sigh, remarked on it.

"Did you ever see anything so beautiful?"

Kate paused in spraying herself with insect repellent and looked over her shoulder. "Mmmm. It is gorgeous, with the colors reflecting off those clouds." She put the spray away and sat in her chair. "You know those clouds mean rain, right?"

Aubrey groaned. "Oh sure, go ahead and spoil it, Madame Scientist. That's all I needed to hear today."

Kate sat forward. "Uh-oh. What happened?"

Aubrey looked around to verify that none of the onlookers were in earshot. She spoke softly. "I got papers from Craig's lawyer. He's proposing full custody."

"*What?*" Kate sputtered and pulled off her cap to run her fingers through her short, curly hair in a familiar Kate-gesture. "I thought you had an agreement?"

Aubrey nodded. "I had primary custody, and he got her every other weekend and certain holidays."

"And now he's decided he wants to have her all the time?" Kate sat back, throwing up her hands. "What changed?"

"When we first separated, he was too busy with his business and chasing women to have a young girl underfoot. According to my conversation with Sunny today, his business is running smoothly, and his latest girlfriend has moved in with him."

Kate expressed astonishment. "So now that he *has time* to be a father, he wants to take her from you?"

Aubrey's eyes filled, and she was glad to be wearing dark glasses. "And what's worse, she doesn't object."

"Sunny wants to stay with her dad? I thought this was just for the summer?"

"That's what she said." Aubrey cleared her throat. "Now she seems conflicted. I asked her on the phone if she wanted to be with him all the time, and she kind of hemmed and hawed around, but she didn't say no. And of course, I couldn't see her expression."

"Oh, Aubrey, I'm so sorry," the older woman sympathized. "What a jerk he is."

Aubrey stood and picked up the broom to smooth the sand on an already level runway. "I spent the whole day working in the yard and crying. I really can't afford a lawyer."

"You have to get a lawyer, Bree. What's your choice?"

"It's not official yet. Craig's lawyer said it's just a proposal. It hasn't been submitted to the court. Maybe he'll change his mind."

She worked her way down the runway, carefully and unnecessarily plying the broom. When she reached the end of the edging, she smoothed the sand out for a few feet beyond, then stood looking around, leaning on the handle.

There he was, moving along the twilight beach, just above the reach of the waves, with his big-man's stride and the erect bearing of a soldier. Seeing him, she blushed, reliving her embarrassment of last night. She moved back up to the nest and tossed the broom down.

"He's back," she said to Kate. "I wonder what he does all day?"

"I'd guess he looks for work," her friend replied evenly. "Isn't that what you would be doing?"

"Well, yes," Aubrey answered. "But I'm not –" She was about to do it again. What was it about this guy? She wasn't usually this unsympathetic. "Oh, never mind." She flung herself, scowling, into her chair, while Kate laughed.

"Hey, Ms. Mitchell!"

Aubrey looked over her shoulder at two teenagers running up behind her. Kate stood, smiling.

"Hi, Heather! Hi, Brett!"

They came to a stop just behind Aubrey, showering her with sand. Brett apologized and Aubrey laughed it off. Why was it so easy to be understanding with these two? Was she just more used to dealing with children?

Kate introduced the two kids, and Aubrey asked if either knew her daughter. Brett did not, but Heather thought she remembered her. She looked around. "Is she here?"

Aubrey shook her head. "Not right now. She's staying at her dad's in Wilmington for a few weeks." She was not ready to accept that Sunny might be gone longer than a few weeks.

Brett, a skinny, dark-haired boy with a wide smile and black-framed glasses, squatted to examine the edging around the runway. "This looks pretty good, but we could make it stronger if we used landscaping pins."

Kate knelt beside him. "We don't usually need it any stronger, and we have to be able to remove it without a trace when we're through with this nest. But if we have a really strong wind, your landscaping pins might be a good idea." She looked over at Aubrey. "I'll stop at the hardware store tomorrow and pick up a dozen."

Heather rolled her eyes. "He's always building stuff," she explained. "He wants to be some kind of engineer."

"An *architectural* engineer," Brett put in. "I want to help houses and buildings be safe from hurricanes and earthquakes and stuff."

Heather rolled her eyes again. She was a pretty girl, short, with frizzy blond hair and thighs a bit plump below the tight shorts she wore.

"How old are you, Heather?" Aubrey asked.

"I'm sixteen, Ms. Benson, but I'll be seventeen in November. I'll be a junior this year. I can't wait!"

Aubrey smiled at her enthusiasm. "How about you, Brett?"

He looked up from his examination of the runway and nest. "Oh. I'll be a junior, too."

Heather added, "Brett's just fifteen. He skipped a grade in middle school. *Brainiac.*" She made it sound like a reproach, but Brett just grinned at her. They clearly knew each other, whether or not they were friends.

Kate stood and dusted sand from her knees. "Well, a brainiac is just what we need on this team."

The sun was almost below the horizon now. Heather spread a towel to sit on next to Kate, and Brett sat by her in the sand, his skinny arms wrapped around his knees, his eyes on the stars overhead. A slim crescent moon rose above the line of clouds. Heather complained about not having a car. Her mother's car was in the shop and her father needed his tonight, so they'd require a lift home. Brett chattered about the stars and the coming school year, and Kate interjected the occasional remark.

Aubrey pulled out her cell phone to text her daughter.

Hey Sunshine! How's everything?

Hi mom I'm watching tv in my room

Just wanted to know if you'd like to come to church with me this Sunday. I can come get you if Dad doesn't feel like driving you.

I'll think about it and let you know

OK, sweetie. Call you tomorrow. Sleep tight!

Night mom

Aubrey dropped her cell phone in her turtle bag and leaned back in her chair, staring up at the stars. She thought about Sunny and how she had changed in the last year or two. She used to love church and Sunday school, reading, swimming, tennis and having her friends over for barbecues and endless games of corn hole.

In her mind, Aubrey could hear the squeals of the kids as they threw the small bags of dried corn at the hole in the target. Sunny had once explained that she loved the game because anyone could play, and some of her nerdy friends played better than her athletic friends. Aubrey had always been proud that Sunny had friends of such diversity, and she had never heard her daughter say an unkind word about anyone.

Since entering high school last year, Sunny had become more secretive with her mom and more exclusive about her friends. There were one or two Aubrey thought were especially shallow, but she tried not to be judgmental. Her father had always claimed that tolerance means being tolerant of ignorance, as well. Aubrey didn't always agree.

Take, for instance, the big guy down the beach. He hung around, hardly ever speaking. She had to believe his silence indicated he was mentally challenged or damaged in some way. Yet she knew and loved people who were not of typical intelligence. So, why did this man make her so uncomfortable?

She remembered reading Tacitus for a philosophy course in college. He'd written, "It is human nature to hate the man whom you have hurt." She knew she had hurt that man last night, and she was utterly ashamed of herself for her remarks, even if she'd meant them.

She also considered Matthew 7:1, "Do not judge, so that you may not be judged." It was not her right to pass judgment on anyone, let alone a stranger, yet he had gotten under her skin from the first minute. And now that she had embarrassed herself in front of him, revealed a side of herself that was small-minded and cruel, she resented him even more.

Why, with all she had going sideways in her life, did she spend so much of her time thinking about this man who meant nothing to her? She shrugged him off and turned her attention to the conversation between Kate and the teenagers.

Kate was explaining how the mother sea turtle, impregnated at sea, crawled ashore on the beach near where she had been hatched many years earlier. "We don't know exactly where the homing instinct comes from, but we know many species that possess it in one form or another. We've studied birds, butterflies and so on. But in many ways the sea turtle is unique."

As Kate spoke, Aubrey felt someone approaching from behind her. She glanced over her shoulder and noted the distant menacing clouds on the horizon. She also saw the "big guy" in the faint glow that remained of sunset in the western sky. He met her look and paused, pointedly looking away. She returned her attention to Kate, but from the corner of her eye, she saw him drop his backpack and crouch beside it, listening to Kate's impromptu lecture.

"Oh, my," Kate said. "I didn't mean to rattle on that away. Looks like I drove everyone off."

Heather made no response, but Brett assured Kate that he'd enjoyed hearing what she'd had to say. Aubrey jabbed her thumb behind her. "More likely *that's* what chased 'em off," she said.

She sensed rather than saw Kate's stricken expression, and realized too late that one might assume she was referring to the soldier. Raising her voice, she hastened to add, "That big cloud bank looks pretty threatening."

"You're right," Kate affirmed, scanning the eastern sky. "We might be in for some rain, gang."

While the pewter clouds gathered, further darkening the sky, Kate gave the young people instructions. "When the nest boils, I need you two to be my counters." She handed each a little metal "clicker" and, using her flashlight, showed them how they work. She drew a line in the smooth sand, bisecting the two walls of edging, one about five feet from the nest and the other about five feet from the first, and let them decide who would be at which line.

"Then we compare counts," she concluded. "And hope they come up the same."

A smatter of raindrops dotted the gathering, then stopped. The few onlookers that remained conferred with the members of their parties and, soon, only Kate, Aubrey, the students, the big guy and a couple of determined tourists still lingered.

One of them, a gray-haired woman in an orange swimsuit cover, approached Kate. "I hate to leave if they're about to hatch," she said. "Do you know what time it will happen?"

Kate's smile was just visible in the moonlight. "No, ma'am," she said patiently. "We don't know what time or what night."

The woman's companion, a tall, thin woman in a white tee-shirt, joined in. "You don't know if it's going to happen tonight?" Her tone indicated there was some deficiency in Kate's knowledge.

"Nope," said Aubrey. "Might be tonight. Might be tomorrow night. Might be next week."

The two women went away in a huff, muttering something about finding another nest where the "staff" is more experienced.

Aubrey waited until they were out of earshot before she laughed. "Honestly, Kate. How can you be so nice to people who are so rude?"

"They're not rude," Kate insisted. "They're just uninformed."

Aubrey rolled her eyes. A low voice spoke from behind her.

"You probably get all kinds of crazy questions." The big guy was standing a few feet behind Aubrey's chair.

Kate laughed. "Well, yes, but they're not really crazy. Sea turtles are outside most people's experience. So, they ask things that seem silly to us."

"Like?"

Aubrey glanced behind her. "Like, won't our being here keep the mama turtle from coming to check on her nest."

Kate shrugged. "Folks just aren't used to mothers who lay their eggs and walk away, never to know if they even hatched."

"Sounds like a fine plan to me," Aubrey muttered under her breath. Louder, she added, "Tell them about the question one woman asked last summer."

"Oh, now," Kate protested, then laughed. "Okay. She wanted to know how we got the mother turtles to walk up here between the lines of edging to lay her nest."

Brett and Heather laughed hesitantly, and the soldier chuckled.

"Kate's a saint," Aubrey said. "She never loses her patience, at least, not with the questions they ask. She did go all 'Terminator' on one guy last year, during our first boil of the season."

"Really, Ms. Mitchell?" Brett asked, peering into the dark at her.

"Well, he *stepped* on a turtle! The fool didn't stay out of the water, as I asked –"

"Ordered," interjected Aubrey.

"*Asked* him to do, and more than once. So, he plants one of his big feet right on top of a baby turtle who was headed the wrong way. *Idiot.*"

"It was a shame," Aubrey agreed. "We need to save every little turtle we can."

"How many of them make it, once they're in the ocean?" the man asked. "Any idea?"

"It depends on your definition of 'making it,'" Kate explained. "Only one in a thousand survives to sexual maturity." She turned to Brett and Heather. "To the age where they can reproduce."

The teens nodded sagely. The man said, "One in a thousand. Not good odds. No wonder you went off on the guy who stepped on one."

Kate leaned forward. "I *know*. *Right?* What if that was the one who would have made it?"

"Uh, Kate," Aubrey put in. "I don't teach logic, but –"

"Oh, I know, I know. That doesn't make sense. But ..."

The man squatted next to Aubrey's chair. "But the bad odds make it extra important that we save every turtle we can."

"We"? Aubrey thought. *Who made him part of this?* Even as she thought it, she realized that was uncharitable.

"Exactly," Kate agreed.

Kate always said that the more people who felt invested in sea turtle survival, the fewer people who did things destructive to the species. Such as dumping plastic bags in the ocean, where sea turtles, thinking the bags are jellyfish, ingest them and die. At Kate's urging, Aubrey had stopped using plastic straws, declining them at restaurants and other eateries. Kate had said that once you've seen a plastic straw pulled from a turtle's nostril, you never view straws the same way again.

Aubrey could see her friend's wide smile in the moonlight. *Oh no, now his interest in turtles has won Kate over.*

Two things happened at once to claim everyone's attention: it began to rain in big, warm drops, and the nest boiled.

Kate, distracted by the conversation, had not checked the nest surface for several minutes. In that time, a few baby turtles had climbed through their sandy nest to the surface. Once they were out, most of their siblings followed. When Kate spotted what was happening, three dark little runners were already dashing down the runway, and the surface of the nest was alive with wriggling little bodies – a true boil.

"Kids, start counting! Bree, help me with the edging!" Brett and Heather crouched by the runway, a few feet from each other. As instructed, each teen knelt by a line in the sand and held their counters, ready to click as a turtle crossed the line. Meanwhile, Kate and Aubrey raced for the dunes just beyond the nest, where each grabbed a roll of edging. When they started back toward the end of the runway, the big guy took Kate's roll. She thanked him and headed back to the boil.

The roll of plastic edging was heavy, and it took all Aubrey's effort to shove it into the sand a few feet at a time, continuing to unroll it as she made her way toward the water. The soldier finished his first, but the end was still several feet from the waves' reach. When he knelt by Aubrey, she let him take over, while she scurried to get the hoe. As she went, she glanced at the runway and saw many small, dark shapes against the dark sand, moving quickly.

Wiping rain from her eyes, she grabbed the hoe and ran back to the end of the runway, where the man was finishing the second roll of edging. Starting at the open end, she began digging a trench about six inches deep into the sand, to lead the eager hatchlings to the water. Again, the soldier stepped in and, seizing the hoe, took over for her, working quickly.

"Just short of the waves." she told him. He nodded.

The rain had stopped for the moment, and a new batch of onlookers had caught the flurry of activity and were standing around the runway, watching the little turtles.

"No lights!" she shouted, moving up along the runway. "And stay out of the water!" She brushed the wet sand from her hands and pulled on the purple latex gloves she kept in the pocket of her shorts.

A cell phone camera flashed, and she shouted again. "No lights! That means no flashlights, cameras or cell phones!"

She found the lead turtles halfway along the runway and walked alongside them. The big soldier brought her the hoe. "Anything else?" he asked, raising his voice over the roar of the waves.

"Stand by," she said, adding, "if you don't mind."

She used the hoe to draw a line in the sand a few feet from the water's edge and paralleling the waves. "Please don't cross this line!" she shouted to the handful of people standing near the end of the runway.

She saw the lead turtles reach the trench, tumble in, and scramble along the bottom, still heading to the sea. A man nearby took a flash photo, and two of the turtles hesitated, turning, as their siblings clambered over them.

"I said no lights!" she barked at the wrongdoer.

Barely visible in the dark, he shrugged and shouted back. "I can't take a good picture without a flash," he said.

"I don't care! You're distracting the turtles!"

"Look," he yelled back at her, "I'm a photographer, and I—"

A huge, dark shape loomed beside them, and the soldier's low, firm voice said, "The lady said no lights, *sir.*"

The photographer took a step back, then turned away and muttered that he'd gotten what he needed anyway. Aubrey's attention returned to the turtles in the trench. Peering into the dark, she could see the first one had reached the end of the trench and was climbing up the shallow end, just a couple of feet from the reach of the closest wave. It was a determined little mite and made a beeline for the water. Aubrey suppressed a cheer; she didn't want to attract the onlookers crowding around.

One by one and two by two, the tiny turtles emerged from the narrow trench and made the final rush to the water. Most made a direct run, but now and then one turned east, distracted by the signal from the Oak Island Lighthouse a couple of miles away. Aubrey picked up each errant wanderer in her gloved hand and turned it in the right direction. Flippers beating like little oars, they made the joyful transition from sand to sea.

Aubrey carefully walked the water's edge, peering down into the waves, looking for any tiny, dark shapes washed back by the waves. The now-familiar voice spoke behind her. "There's one," he said, pointing.

She spotted the stranded hatchling, scooped it up, and turned it toward the oncoming wave before putting it down.

"And there."

She squinted. "Hey, you're good at this," she said.

"Lot of experience looking for movement in the dark," he said. "There. See?"

She did. They worked together, Aubrey picking up any turtles he spotted. There weren't many, as most had made it into the sea without incident. When Kate called out that it was all over, Aubrey gave the man her extra red light, and they walked the wet sand up and down, looking for any more beached hatchlings.

"I think we're good," she said, turning her flashlight from red to white. They headed back to the nest.

Kate was grinning in the flashlight's beam. "A good boil," she said. "The kids counted eighty-four!"

"*Wa-hoo!*" Aubrey shouted. "That's great!"

"I'll come back tomorrow morning, to see if there are any stragglers, but you don't need to –"

Kate was interrupted by a brilliant flash of lightning, an almost simultaneous thunderclap, and Heather's scream.

"Wow! That was close," Brett observed unnecessarily. He seemed more intrigued than frightened, but Heather was clearly terrified.

"Can you clear up here, Aubrey?" she asked. "I need to get these kids home."

"Sure," Aubrey answered. "You go." She knew Kate would not risk endangering the children.

"I'll help her," the big guy offered.

As he reached to hand her the extra flashlight, she was sure his hand was shaking, which seemed out of character. She looked up at his face, but he turned away and began pulling up the runway edging.

Kate and the kids ran for the opening in the dunes that led to the parking lot. Aubrey and the soldier rolled up the extra edging they had put down that evening but left the original runway.

"We might have a few stragglers overnight, and the runway will help, even if it's short." She looked at the waves. "Besides, the tide's coming in, so the water will be closer to them for a while."

On her knees, Aubrey scrambled to fill in the nest hole. This would keep the remains of the nest safe from predators and prevent it from filling with water. She used her finger to write "84" in the sand, then realized the rain would soon wash it away. *Never mind,* she thought. *The turtle patrol will know the count soon enough.*

Another lightning strike presaged a sudden downpour that drenched the two as they carried the tools and boxes of edging to Aubrey's car. The loud thunderclap that followed drowned the man's shout.

"What did you say?" she shouted back, unlocking her car trunk as she turned to look at him. He was bending to pick up the rake that had dropped from his hand. In the wet light, his face looked tense, wary. He shook his head and lifted the trunk lid.

"Thanks," Aubrey said, as they stowed the items away. "You were a big help tonight."

He nodded. "Better get going," he said. He stepped back to let Aubrey go past him to the driver's door. She opened it and slipped inside, grateful to be out of the rain.

Out of the rain. She looked at the tall soldier, squinting at her from under the dripping brim of his patrol cap, backlit by the flickering lights of the parking lot. *Damn.* She held the car door open slightly.

"Get in," she said, jerking her head to the right.

"What?"

"Get in. And hurry up, before we both start growing gills."

He hesitated, then jogged around her car and opened the passenger door. He tossed his backpack onto the floor in front of him and got in. Inside, he seemed to fill her car. Annoyed with herself, she already regretted the impulse that had led her to make the invitation.

"Where are we going?" he asked, closing the door.

"Where do you think? My house." Now she was annoyed with him, as well. Lately she had been questioning her ability to make good decisions, and he was one more decision she had clearly flubbed.

"Are you sure that's a good idea?"

Oh, yeah. Annoying. "No. But I don't seem to have *good* ideas anymore."

The lightning and thunder had abated for the moment, but the rain was heavier. At her house, they dashed for the side door off the carport. The carport roof leaked so badly it was almost like no roof at all. She left her flip-flops on the concrete stoop, to deal with in the morning.

Inside the little utility-laundry room, he once again seemed to fill the entire space. He stood with his back to the door, waiting for her to brush the sand from her legs with the towel she kept on a hook for that purpose. She handed the towel to him and moved into the kitchen, while he began meticulously removing the sand from his backpack and his bare feet and legs.

She had a pot of coffee brewing in her coffeemaker by the time the man entered the kitchen. He stood in the doorway, one hand holding the backpack over his shoulder. With the other, he pulled the cap from his head. His curly dark hair was short on the sides and a bit longer on the top, and the slight shagginess around his ears showed he needed a haircut.

"My daughter's away for a couple of weeks," she said. "You can sleep in her room. Let me show you."

She led the way through the dark living room to the short hallway. As they passed an open door, she said, "And you can use this bathroom." At the end of the hall, she opened the door to Sunny's room and snapped on the light. The yellow walls glowed in the sudden illumination. "The sheets are clean," she said, adding, "I have coffee brewing if you want some."

He edged past her into Sunny's room and placed his backpack gently on the bed. He looked around, a slight smile on his face, then turned to Aubrey.

"Sure. Coffee sounds nice."

He followed her back to the kitchen, where she took two mugs from the cabinet and set them by the coffeemaker. Leaning against the counter, she asked, "Have you been on Oak Island long?"

He shook his head. "Just a few weeks."

"What made you choose this area?"

He rubbed the back of his neck, staring at the floor. "I came to see a friend, but he was gone."

Aubrey could see her questions made him uncomfortable. Just then, the coffeemaker gave its death-gasp that signaled completion, and she filled their mugs. She put one on the round kitchen table in front of the chair nearest him.

"Sugar? Milk?"

"No, thanks." He sat. "This is great. Thanks."

"Are you hungry?"

He smiled, looking down at his mug. "No. Appreciate it. I had dinner."

Did he think she was offering him food because he was homeless? She shrugged. "I'm always hungry after a boil. I don't know why."

"It's the adrenaline rush. After it passes, you need energy."

She wanted donuts or cookies. What she found were graham crackers. Sighing, she sat in the chair opposite him, munching and sipping and completely at a loss for conversation. It seemed that everything she said to him was either offensive or amusing. Or amusingly offensive. She was relieved when he stood and carried his empty mug to the sink.

"There's plenty of coffee. Help yourself."

"Thanks, but I've had enough." He rinsed the mug and set it in the sink. "It was great. If you don't mind, I'll turn in."

"Fine. Sleep well." She studied his back as he walked down the hall. She couldn't help noticing how his damp shirt clung to his muscular back. Or the snug fit of his jeans and the square set of his very wide shoulders.

Oh, crap, she thought. *I need a boyfriend. When big homeless guys start looking attractive ...*

Chapter 4

Nest 7, Day 57

H e left a note by a fresh pot of coffee.

Thanks for a great night's sleep and the hot shower. Sheets are in the washer. You're a nice woman. Tom Clayton

She pushed the note aside and poured a cup of coffee, not that she needed it. Too keyed up to sleep, she'd had three cups the night before, watching late-night television in the living room. Shortly after she had turned on the TV, she had heard the shower running in the guest bathroom.

Two hours later, she had turned off the set and headed for bed. The door opposite her own showed no light at the bottom. She took a quick shower herself, just to get the rest of the sand off, pulled on the oversized tee-shirt she favored for sleeping, and crawled into bed. Then she had gotten up and turned the lock on her bedroom door.

Now she wondered, had he really had "a great night's sleep"? She could have sworn she'd heard him call out in the wee hours of morning but had convinced herself it was thunder that had wakened her and had gone back to sleep.

She picked up the note again. His handwriting was clear, with straight lines and firm strokes. No errors in grammar, spelling or punctuation. Maybe he was brighter than she had thought. So, not mentally challenged. That didn't rule out mentally disturbed. She wasn't judging him; she just didn't care for the man.

She looked at the clock. Almost eight. She had showered and dressed before leaving her room that morning, in case he was still in the house. She had expected he would still be there and was a little annoyed that he wasn't. It seemed rude of him to leave without saying goodbye. Then she had found the note. And he had put the sheets in the washer, along with a towel and washcloth. So, not really rude, just … *dismissive.*

It was another hot, muggy day. Without Sunny in the house, Aubrey wasn't sure what to do with her day. She knew Kate wouldn't really need her at the nest this morning but, having no better plan, she decided to go there anyway.

"Hey, pal!" Kate greeted her cheerfully in the 70th Street parking lot. "What brings you here this morning?"

"Nothing else to do," Aubrey said somewhat forlornly.

"Oh, sorry, hon." Kate gave her an understanding hug. "Sunny'll come to her senses soon, I'm sure."

"Maybe. At least it's cooler at the beach."

Kate tossed the tools in her small truck. "Actually, I was just leaving. Want to grab some breakfast at Russell's?"

"I don't know. Oh, hell, why not? Meet you there."

Over shrimp and grits, Kate told Aubrey there had apparently been no more turtles overnight. After a boil, they always smoothed the sand on the runway near the nest, so they could clearly see from their tracks if any more turtles had hatched. Except for rain speckles, the sand was unmarked this morning.

Then they talked about Sunny, of course. Aubrey couldn't believe Craig would really sue for full custody, after all this time. "Why does he want her around all the time? He already has a teenager to raise."

"Aubrey! Craig's new girlfriend isn't actually a teenager, is she?"

"Practically. She's twenty-two." Aubrey shrugged. "Maybe she needs a companion closer to her own age, so Craig offered her Sunny. Although, really, Sunny's too mature for her. Maya's not that bright."

Kate laughed, shaking her head. "There you go again, dissing someone's intelligence. Just like with that soldier."

With careful indifference, Aubrey asked, "Have you seen him this morning?"

"No, I haven't, come to think of it." Kate paused in buttering a biscuit. "And I usually do. But why are you asking? You don't like him anyway."

"I never said I didn't like him. I just don't trust him." Even as she said it, Aubrey realized her statement wasn't as true as it had been a few days ago.

The women finished their breakfast and paid their checks. In the crowded parking lot, Kate told Aubrey they would excavate Nest 7 in three days.

"See you Friday," Aubrey said, getting into her car.

As she drove away, she wondered why she hadn't told Kate about Tom Clayton spending the night at her house. Then she wondered how he had so smoothly made the transition from "the big guy" to "Tom Clayton" in her thoughts.

"Here's another one!" Kate sang out. "That's three live turtles, so far!"

It was Friday, and Heather and Aubrey, holding up a towel to keep the hot afternoon sun off the little turtles, escorted them down the runway and safely into the water. Then Aubrey returned to the nest, where Kate was elbow deep in the hole she had so carefully dug by hand. Brett was keeping track of the numbers of empty shells, as well as what Kate called "dud" shells, where no turtles had developed.

"Uh-oh," Kate said. She held a turtle close to her face, squinting through her sunglasses. "A dead one. Shame." She put it in a separate spot, between the piles of empty shells and the smaller pile of dud shells.

Aubrey stared at the still little form, willing it to move. She dropped to her knees and prodded it with the tip of her gloved finger. Nothing.

Once again, she felt sea turtle moms had the right idea. This little one's mother would never know the heartbreak of seeing one of her offspring lying dead on the sand, never having made it to the surface, let alone the water.

Kate found a second dead turtle, then a third. When she reached the bottom of the nest, she verified the count with Brett and jotted the data in her notebook. Aubrey carefully picked up the dead turtles and placed them in the bottom of the hole, one at a time. Then Kate added the dud shells, and followed those with the empties. She covered all with the wet sand until the hole was filled, then smoothed dry sand over all of it.

Heather helped her use the broom to make the entire area – nest, runway and all – seem like any other patch of beach. This would make it less likely that predators or vandals would find the nest and dig for the remains.

"C'mon, kids," Kate said to Brett and Heather.

Leaving the discarded sign and stakes to be picked up by the rec center staff, they gathered up their coiled lengths of edging and other equipment and headed up the beach. Aubrey remained, kneeling by the hidden burial site.

A big shadow fell across the sand, and a low, quiet voice asked, "What's wrong?"

She looked up at Tom Clayton, towering over her like a colossus. "Three dead turtles," she said in a choked voice.

He didn't ask why that made her cry, just quietly knelt beside her. A few minutes later, she stood up and pulled off her gloves, stuffing them into her pocket. She extended her right hand to Tom, who stood as he took it in his.

"Thanks for all your help, Tom. Good luck."

Then she walked away from him, heading for her car.

If anyone had told her that she would be walking the beach four days later, looking for Tom Clayton, she'd have said they were crazy.

Yet here she was, walking through the evening downpour in her blue plastic poncho. She thought she knew where he camped most often, near an unfinished home construction site about half a mile west of the pier.

Sure enough, there was the house, looming like a wooden skeleton in the wet evening light, its exposed walls and bare roof just beyond the sea grass dunes. And there was a large huddled form on the sand on the other side of the dunes from the house. He was tented over with a green canvas poncho. He surely couldn't hear her approach over the sound of waves and pelting rain, but he lifted his hooded head and stared open-mouthed as she reached his side.

"Aubrey! What the hell are you doing out in this?" he asked, speaking loudly over the noise.

"Come on, Tom," she shouted. "And close your mouth before you drown."

She got him to come by simply turning and walking away, ignoring his shouts, so he had to follow her to make her listen. Halfway to her car, he lost patience and grabbed her arm, turning her toward him.

"Aubrey!" He stood close, speaking in a quieter tone. "Look, I appreciate what you're doing, but it's an all-round bad idea."

"Probably. But we're doing it anyway." She started to turn away, but his hand tightened on her arm, holding her there.

"I mean it. Listen." He hesitated. "I heard you lock your door the last time, and I don't blame you. It was the smart thing to do. But it made me realize that you had no reason to trust me. You still don't."

"Maybe. But I'm trusting you anyway." She pushed his hand from her arm. "Now let's go before I get any wetter, if that's even possible."

He loped back to his pile of belongings but caught up with her as she reached her car. She took her poncho off and tossed it in the back seat, and he followed suit.

She glanced into the back at his poncho. "Is that new?" she asked, starting the car.

"Yeah. I got it after – well, you know, after the other time it rained."

He didn't speak again until they got to her house. As they dashed to the door, he looked up at the leaky carport roof and said, "This thing is more car *wash* than car *port.*"

She laughed as she opened the door. "It's the old story: I can't fix it in the rain, and when it's not raining –"

"It doesn't leak."

"That's right." She shrugged. "I have to admit, when I bought this house, I never asked the reason for the stack of new shingles in the shed. I guess the previous owner was a procrastinator, too."

He laughed, and the sound surprised her.

She led him inside and they went through the ritual of wiping sand from their feet; first her, then him.

"I haven't had dinner yet," she said. "How about some scrambled eggs?"

He glanced at the digital clock on her stove: 8:07. He gave her a dubious look and asked, "You haven't had dinner?"

She stared him down. "That's right. And I'm hungry." This had the added benefit of being true. Rather than eating, she had been pacing the house the past two hours, worried about how he was managing in the rain, but she wasn't about to tell him that.

While she scrambled half a dozen eggs and Tom made toast, the noise of the rain got louder, with wind gusts battering the house. She was surprised to notice that he seemed jittery. He spoke little while they ate, and she filled the silence with inconsequential chit-chat, hoping to put him at ease.

But when they were washing the dishes, a sudden clap of thunder rattled the windows. Tom dropped the plate he'd been drying, and it broke.

"I'm sorry," he muttered. He knelt to pick up the three large pieces and, as he handed them to her, she saw his hands were shaking. She chose to say nothing, not wanting to embarrass him further.

They moved to the living room, where Aubrey turned on the TV. The storm was expected to move out of the area by dawn, but rain would be heavy overnight, with plenty of lightning.

Tom sat on the sofa, but he seemed restless. "Mind if I take a shower?" he asked.

"Go ahead," Aubrey answered.

She had been taught as a child never to be in water during a thunderstorm, but he was an adult and could make his own decisions. When the sound of the water went on for longer than usual, she wondered briefly if the shower was his attempt to muffle the storm sounds. *But he's such a big guy,* she thought. *Could he really be afraid of storms?*

She turned off the television and went to her room. As she passed the guest bathroom, where the shower still ran, she paused with her fingertips touching the door. Should she ask if he was okay? She imagined knocking, and the shower stopping, and Tom pushing the shower curtain aside and …

She hurried down the hall to her room, horrified to realize she'd been picturing him in the shower, water sluicing across those wide shoulders and running down his chest. Again, she thought, *I need a boyfriend. Soon.*

As she undressed for bed, she heard the shower stop and, a few minutes later, his tread in the hallway and the sound of his door opening and closing. She jumped into bed and grabbed the novel she'd been reading, trying to transport her imagination to 19th-century Scotland, and away from the steam-filled bathroom down the hall, and the door across from hers.

Aubrey woke, heart pounding in the dark of early morning. Was it thunder that had wakened her? But storms rarely disturbed her once she was truly asleep. She held her breath. Over the sound of the storm, Aubrey heard an unfamiliar noise, like an animal in pain, perhaps caught in a trap. She got up, wondering if the sound had woken her guest. She opened her door a few inches and saw his was closed. The sound came, louder now, and she could tell it had come from behind his door. She stepped into the hall and raised her fist to knock, but hesitated. When the sound came again, she knew it was Tom, and she opened his door and went in.

"Tom?"

No response. He was a huddled shape under Sunny's dark bedspread. As she moved closer and reached out to touch him, he muttered "Get out. Get out."

Face flaming, she turned to go, then realized the command was part of his nightmare and not directed at her. She suddenly remembered last night, when it had stormed at the beach, and his shuttered expression. Had he been clamping down on his fear?

"No! No!" He shouted, thrashing under the covers. Then he made the sound she'd heard earlier, a keening moan, as though something caused him great pain.

She surprised herself by moving closer, then carefully climbing onto the bed to curl up behind him. When he moaned again, she reached her arm across the broad expanse of his back and rested her palm on his shoulder. Remembering the nightmares Sunny had as a small child, she gently patted his shoulder, murmuring, "It's all right. You're safe. Don't worry. You're safe."

In only a few minutes, he stopped the moaning and thrashing, and lay quietly trembling. She pressed closer to his back, spooning him, feeling the warmth of his body through the covers. Soon, even the trembling ceased, and he seemed to drift into a deep sleep. She waited until she was sure, then slowly drew away and rose from the bed.

She backed away on tiptoe, watchful for any sign of waking, but he slept on. Staring at his sleeping form, a feeling of great tenderness washed over her. This feeling, at least, had a benevolent source: she clearly missed her daughter.

As Tom poured her coffee the next morning, he made no mention of his night terrors. She assumed he had no awareness of the incident, and she wasn't about to tell him. Still, she felt somehow guilty, as if she'd learned a secret about him that gave her an unfair advantage.

They sidled past each other in the kitchen. She offered cereal. He declined. She got more coffee. He rinsed his cup. The silence was painful.

He started to speak just as she burst out, "I lost a baby."

"What?"

Aubrey put her hands to her cheeks, willing the heat to subside. "I'm sorry. I just meant, that's why I get so upset about the dead baby turtles. Anyway, that's my self-diagnosis. When my daughter was two, I had a stillborn son. They let me hold him for a time, and for some reason, the dead turtles remind me of him. So still. So – I don't know. Such a waste, I guess."

She couldn't look at him. Why on earth had she chosen to share such an intimate detail of her history with this man she barely knew, and didn't even like? Just because she knew about his night terrors didn't mean she owed him anything. Vulnerabilities weren't baseball cards you could trade back and forth. You give me your battlefield trauma; I'll give you my deepest sorrow. And now they were both embarrassed, as well.

"That's terrible." His voice was low and husky, as if her pathetic outburst had moved him. "I'm sorry."

That was all. No effusive declarations of sympathy. No digging for details or passing judgment. Not even the logical question asking why she had chosen to divulge that information at this moment. Just a simple expression of sympathy with all indications of being sincere.

"Thanks." She still couldn't make eye contact. "I just … wanted you to know."

She risked a glance. He was nodding, his expression somber but not funereal. He was holding his backpack. "I guess I'll take off."

"Can I give you a ride somewhere?"

"Thanks, but I'm good." He shouldered his pack.

"Tom?" she asked. "Do you have a cell phone?"

He grimaced. "I did, but I lost it a few weeks back. Why?"

She shook her head and stared into her coffee. "No reason. Take care of yourself."

"You too. And thanks again."

She didn't answer. Didn't even look up until he was gone.

Chapter 5

Nest 75, Day 53

I t was getting close to 11 p.m., and any interest in their new nest by tourists and locals had waned. An individual or couple drifted past now and then, but the big draw was a nest that had boiled an hour earlier, farther west along the beach. Aubrey and Kate had the nest and their section of the dark beach mostly to themselves.

It was a clear, breezy night, full of stars and free of bugs. People walked past from both sides, but few paid any heed to the two women sitting quietly at the edge of the dunes. The boom-and-shush of the waves covered the sporadic exchange of remarks.

Aubrey had been uncharacteristically silent most of the night, just staring at the white foam breakers racing rhythmically up the dark sand. She occasionally glanced in both directions along the beach, looking for a large silhouette against the others that strolled or jogged in the distance.

"Where are your little helpers?" Aubrey asked Kate. She wasn't about to ask Kate about the one "helper" who was really on her mind. "Did they know we've got a new nest assigned to our team?"

"I texted them both before I did the prep. But Brett is on a tour of Washington, and Heather's staying with her grandmother in Decatur. They'll be back next week. Speaking of gone, why didn't I see you at the faculty rally Tuesday?"

Aubrey reached behind her ball cap and tightened her ponytail. "I was out of town. I was busy. I was sick. You choose."

"It wasn't that bad, you know. We got a lot of good information."

"Hey, I went to the orientation. The rally wasn't mandatory, so I bailed. Was that wrong?"

Kate laughed. "So wrong. You're doomed to Teacher Hell."

"Kate, teachers don't go to Hell. Not even bad teachers. They suffered enough on Earth, and they go straight to Teacher Heaven."

Kate slouched in her beach chair, smiling. "And what's that like?"

Aubrey thought for a moment. "Well, first of all, there are *no* parents. And no administrators. All the students are brilliant and attentive, and they think you are the grand wisdom fountain from which they gratefully drink."

Kate was into it now. "And no student has a cell phone or a tablet, so they pay attention and *never* contradict you."

Aubrey sighed. "Sounds like Heaven, all right. Let's not think about it." She hesitated, then took the plunge. "Kate. I haven't been to the beach in a week or more. Have you seen our big soldier?"

Kate lifted her head and squinted at Aubrey in the moonlight. "As a matter of fact, I saw him the day I was prepping this nest. Why the sudden interest?"

"Well, I haven't seen him in a week or so, and I just wondered if he's okay."

Kate settled back. "He had a job for three days at some plumbing supply place, moving boxes of materials around, or something like that. They had a couple of guys out sick, and needed the job done in a hurry. I'm sure he didn't make enough to get a place to live, but he probably ate better for a few days."

"That's nice," Aubrey said, feigning indifference.

"I told him the Dairy Queen was looking for somebody, according to the sign in their window."

Aubrey laughed. "I can't see Tom in a hair net."

"*Tom?*" Kate noticed immediately. "We know his name now, and are no longer calling him 'the big guy'?"

Aubrey hesitated, and Kate leaned forward. "Okay, kiddo. Spill."

So, Aubrey told her almost everything. The two separate rainy nights Tom spent in Aubrey's house, the good manners, even the night terrors. She left out the part where she had spooned Tom's sleeping form until he had fallen asleep.

Kate was flabbergasted. "Are you nuts? I told you to take it easy on the guy, not to invite him for a sleepover!"

"Kate. Shh."

Kate's voice changed to a furious whisper. "You go from one extreme to another! Can't you just be nice to someone without putting yourself in danger?"

"Easy, Kate. You'll scare any hatchlings back into the sand."

Kate threw up her hands. "Honestly, Aubrey. Listen, I like your Tom just fine, but we really know nothing about him. He could be a serial killer. Or a rapist."

"And I'm such a boring victim that he decided to let me go unharmed?"

Kate's tone became that of a kind caregiver counseling an irrational patient. "Aubrey. You don't have to be a psychologist or sociologist to understand that many women are just naturally drawn to nurturing. And you don't have to be hetero to have those feelings, either. When I was in college, I fell in love with a beautiful girl who was very damaged. I thought I could help her, of course. After she beat me up, I learned she actually suffered from an untreated bipolar disorder. She was way too damaged for a layperson like me to mend."

"Kate!"

"Yup. Now, I know fine people with below average intelligence, and others with definite mental or emotional issues, and they deserve our respect and kindness. But that doesn't include taking a stranger into your house to fix him."

Aubrey knew Kate was right. Tom's night terrors had made him more vulnerable, and thus more human, and the woman and mother in her longed to soothe and heal.

"Okay. I promise to be more prudent." She looked down the beach to where the crowd around the newly hatched nest was beginning to disperse. "Looks like our audience is coming back. But, Kate, one last thing. Did Tom mention me at all when you saw him the other day?"

Dark as it was, she could see Kate roll her eyes. "No, he didn't. But if you want to write him a note, I can pass it to him in study hall." She mimicked popping gum and tossing her hair.

"Ha!" laughed Aubrey. "Join this century, please. I once made a remark to Sunny about passing notes in class, and she had no idea what I was talking about. Nowadays the kids text each other."

"Not in *your* classes." Kate knew that Aubrey kept a wire basket on her desk, and every student entering had to leave their phone in it until class was over. "How is our sunshine girl, by the way?"

Aubrey tilted her head back, studying the star-dotted sky. "She seems fine. I'm the one who's struggling with this arrangement."

"Have you talked to her lately?" Kate asked.

"This morning." Aubrey sighed. "She was all excited about meeting some new friends at the pool and didn't have time to talk to old Mom."

"Aubrey, you know Sunny loves you and –"

"What time do you think this one's gonna go?" A man with a cigar interrupted Kate.

"I'm afraid there's no way for us to know that, sir," Kate answered politely, smiling. "We don't even know if it will happen tonight."

A woman approached. "Will you stay here all night?"

"No. Just until we're pretty sure it's not going to hatch tonight." Kate preferred to be vague about their schedule, not wanting anyone to return to the nest after they left.

"Well, I think it's wonderful what you people do to help the little turtles," the woman added. She took the hand of the cigar smoker and led him away.

"Thank you, ma'am," Kate said, with double meaning.

Aubrey turned to her friend. "You were saying?"

"Hi, Kate!"

It was dark, but Aubrey recognized a young woman she had met last year, another turtle nest parent Kate had worked with in the past.

"Lynn!" Kate jumped up and hurried to greet her friend.

Aubrey struggled not to feel abandoned. She hated feeling this way – needy and pathetic and clingy. She could understand why Sunny, with typical teenage rebellion, might prefer to live with her anything-goes father instead of her stricter mother. But Sunny seemed determined to reject Aubrey again and again. That morning, when Aubrey had called her, Sunny had been in such a rush to join her friends, she had all but hung up on her mother. And there was no getting around it: it hurt.

It seemed everyone was walking away from her. Kate just now. Sunny this morning. Even Tom had been in a rush to leave her house the mornings after she'd sheltered him.

She bowed her head and willed the tears to go back where they came from. *Here we go,* she thought, *another pity party for poor little Aubrey. So, stop it.* But she couldn't suppress a small sob of heartbreak.

A large, warm hand covered hers where it grasped the arm of her chair. She turned her head and saw Tom crouched beside her, studying her face. For some reason, the comfort he offered only made the tears come faster. She remembered putting her arm around him that night at her house and wished to her soul he could do the same for her now. She settled for turning her hand over to clasp his fingers.

She heard Kate's voice, a short distance away, saying goodnight to Lynn. Aubrey gave Tom's hand a quick squeeze and withdrew hers to wipe her eyes. When Kate returned to her chair beside the nest, Tom engaged her for a minute or two, which gave Aubrey a chance to pull herself together.

Another hour passed with no activity at the nest. Every fifteen minutes or so, Kate or Aubrey would shine their flashlights briefly on the surface of the nest, looking for any divot, or drop in the level of the sand.

A friendly young woman asked, "If the problem with lights is that they distract the turtles, why can't you have lights while you're just waiting for them to hatch?"

"Good question," said Kate. Sounding like the teacher she was, she asked the half-dozen people gathered, "Can anyone tell me why?"

No one spoke until Tom said quietly, "If you have light, it takes your eyes a little time to adjust to the dark."

"Exactly!" Kate said. "If the turtles started coming, we would need a couple of minutes to turn off any lights and let our eyes adjust. Who knows what might happen in the meantime? That's why we sit here in the dark."

Aubrey felt oddly proud of Tom's wise answer. Surreptitiously, she touched his arm, smiling when he turned to her, and pleased when he smiled back. She realized she'd been hasty in her early assumptions about Tom and was now having her eyes opened.

They were opened further two days later. Aubrey and Kate, along with several tourists, were still waiting for Nest 75 to boil. Brett and Heather had returned from their respective vacations, and Tom had joined them every night, along with a handful of eager observers. Always, when the women decided to leave the nest and go home, they would discover Tom had quietly vanished into the night.

A little boy about six years old seemed drawn to the tall soldier, sitting on the sand a few feet from the others. He approached Tom and shyly asked how they knew there were turtles under that patch of sand.

Aubrey knew that Tom had heard this question answered more than once. When he looked at her, mutely asking permission to respond, she nodded, smiling.

"Well, there's a special squadron that does a recon on the beach about O-six-hundred every day. You know what time that is?"

The boy's face broke into a grin. "Yes, sir! My daddy's a soldier! That's six o'clock in the morning."

"That's right. I like to call them the 'Dawn Patrol.' They scout the sand for the tracks of the mama sea turtles. They know just what those tracks look like, and that there's a pretty good chance each set of tracks leads to – guess what?"

"A turtle nest!"

"Affirmative, soldier. And they follow the tracks to the nest and mark it for these good people –" he gestured to Aubrey and the others – "to be here when it's close to time for the little turtles to bust out of their shells, break cover and make a dash for the water."

The boy stared at Tom with his mouth open, clearly fascinated by the story and Tom's military manner of speech.

"What happens when they hatch?"

Again, Tom looked at Aubrey and Kate.

"Go ahead," Kate told him. "You're doing fine."

He turned to the boy. "The little turtles dig their way out of the sand with their flippers." He demonstrated with his arms. "Sometimes they need to rest a while after they make it to the surface, before they head to the water."

"Do they go fast?"

"Once they're out of the sand, they really hump it, for as small as they are." He stood and pointed to the runway. "They come right down here and go as fast as they can along the track. Just about this fast." He and the boy started walking along beside the runway, the child's smiling mother watching from a few feet away.

"You know, Aubrey," Kate observed, "that man has all the makings of a teacher."

"Tom?" Aubrey asked, surprised. She laughed. "It would be like that Schwarzenegger movie. We could call it *Kindergarten Soldier.*"

"He sure doesn't scare that little guy. And he has a natural affinity for teaching."

Brett, sitting on the sand next to Kate's chair, cleared his throat. "So, he was a soldier?"

Kate answered, "Yes. In the Middle East."

The boy nodded. "So was my dad."

Sensing tragedy, Aubrey said, "Did he make it home all right, Brett?"

"No," Brett said, looking away. "He was killed in Afghanistan. By a sniper. Two years ago."

Both women expressed sympathy. Aubrey said, "I lost my dad after I was grown, and it was one of the hardest things I've ever been through. Losing a parent at your age must be the worst thing imaginable."

Heather was sitting near Aubrey, and she thought she heard the girl say, "Well, maybe not the *worst.*" But when Aubrey asked her to repeat it, Heather just shook her head.

Aubrey thought, *You never know what's going on with these kids. They can seem so shallow at times, but there are dangerous undercurrents we can't always see.*

She heard the little boy's mother telling him it was time to go and looked over in time to see the child grinning up at Tom and saluting him. The big man saluted smartly in return, then stood watching as the mother and child walked hand in hand up the beach.

She had misjudged Tom; he was clearly a thoughtful, intelligent man. Of course, she had to admit that Kate had a point – just because he seemed bright didn't mean there wasn't something wrong with him psychologically. But Aubrey didn't think so. Night terrors aside, she could no longer picture Tom as dangerous or even peculiar. Of course, it still troubled her that he was unemployed and homeless.

Anyway, she agreed with Kate that inviting Tom into her house had been a foolish lapse in judgment, and she had no intention of repeating the mistake.

Kate's red light blinked on, then off, then on again as Kate did a double take. "Okay, guys! We have turtles!"

Aubrey saw two tiny black spots in a shallow indentation near the edge of the nest. One looked like a head and the other a flipper, too far apart to belong to the same turtle. Heather squealed with excitement and Kate turned the light off. Several onlookers gathered along the runway near the nest.

Tom ran to the spot just above the nest where Kate had placed the box with the extra rolls of edging. He hoisted the box and glanced at Aubrey, who nodded and followed him to the foot of the runway.

Wordlessly, he started unrolling one of the forty-foot lengths and inserting it into the sand. Aubrey pulled on her gloves, just in case, and began extending the other side of the runway with the other roll. She heard Kate issuing instructions to the students and requests to the watchers.

"Please," she said. "No lights. No cell phones. No cameras. Stay a couple of feet back from the edging so the volunteers can do their jobs. And please, don't touch the turtles. We wear these gloves to protect us from salmonella."

Tom finished quickly and came to help Aubrey with her side. Kneeling next to him in the sand, Aubrey was much too aware of his warm, bare arm as it grazed hers. Tom seemed not to notice. They were nearly finished when Kate approached them through the darkness and said, "Sorry, guys. I think we have a couple of advance scouts, and that's going to be all." She headed back to the nest.

A few minutes later Aubrey heard Brett, above the excited chatter of the onlookers, call out "One," echoed faintly by Heather a minute later. Then she heard "Two" and another echo in Heather's soft voice.

Tom rose, found the hoe, and used it to draw the line near the water. He started to dig the trench, but stopped when Aubrey said, "We probably won't need the trench, Tom. If two turtles are all we have, it's easy to keep track of them and get them in the water."

The two little turtles cleared the end of the runway and Tom and Aubrey walked along with them to the edge of the waves. The one closest to Tom was carried off by the next wave, but Aubrey saw the other get pushed back by a wave and begin crawling sideways, parallel to the water. She seized the wriggling turtle and turned it in the right direction. The next wave carried it off.

Tom and Aubrey stood watching at the edge of the water to make sure the turtles weren't washed back again. Satisfied, they walked back to the extended runway and waited, but, as Kate had predicted, there were no more turtles that night. An hour later, the observers drifted off, and the team began packing up to leave. Tom rolled up the edging extensions and put them in the cardboard box.

"You can just leave them by the nest," Kate said. "Nobody's going to take them. Thanks for your help."

She turned to the teens. "Am I taking you two home tonight?"

Heather said, "Yes, please, Ms. Mitchell. Dad needed his car tonight, and Mom's car won't be out of the shop till tomorrow."

"No problem," Kate said. "Coming, Aubrey?"

Aubrey looked around for Tom, but he had faded into the dark, as usual.

"Fine," she muttered quietly, shrugging. "I only wanted to say goodnight."

Chapter 6

Nest 75, Day 57-58

S ea turtles, Aubrey knew, are very unpredictable when it comes to hatching. Their last nest had boiled, produced eighty-four turtles all at once, and no others until the excavation. This nest was clearly going to be a different matter. There had been the two the night before, now here were two more dark spots. At least tonight they had emerged during a higher tide, and Kate told them not to bother with the extra edging.

Once the two new babies had dragged themselves from the sand, crawled past Brett and Heather, and made their way to the end of the original runway, there remained only a few yards to the water, with Tom and Aubrey escorting them. The crowd, larger than the previous night, cheered and got too close and had to be reminded to stay back.

And, as before, that was it. There were still five or six onlookers hanging around when the team started their preparations to leave. Kate asked the teens if they needed a ride.

"I do," Brett said. "Heather's got her dad's car, but she's got something to do on the way home and can't drop me off."

He sounded a little sullen, and Aubrey hid a smile.

"Actually," said Heather, "I have my mom's car. Dad had something to do tonight." She went on to explain that she'd been unable to find parking at the nearest spot and had been forced to park two streets further west, so she needed to walk in the opposite direction. She seemed a little nervous about going off by herself on a dark beach at nearly midnight.

Tom spoke up. "I'll walk you to your car, Heather. I'm going that way myself."

They all called out goodnights to each other, except for Aubrey. It wasn't until she got in her car that she realized she was annoyed that Tom, who always seemed to disappear at quitting time, had been available to walk Heather to her car.

Good grief, she admonished herself. *You cannot be jealous of a teenager.*

The nest boiled the next night. Kate's friend Lynn, whose nest had boiled the night before, was on hand to help, along with Bernie, a member of Lynn's team. Kate was glad of the extra help, as she had suspected tonight was the night, and Heather had not shown up.

"What's wrong with Heather?" she asked Brett, who shrugged.

Half an hour later, following another spectacular Oak Island sunset, Kate spotted a large divot in the surface of the nest. Aubrey and Tom got the extended runway in place and dug a trench from the opening to a foot from the tideline. Within minutes, a handful of dark spots dotted the sand of the divot – tiny flippers and heads.

"Turtles!" Kate cried. Aubrey drew lines for Brett and Tom as counting markers, and Kate handed them the clickers. Aubrey and Lynn donned latex gloves in the event it was necessary to handle some turtles and waited beside Kate for the boil to begin.

Like a pot boiling over, the sand over the nest erupted with dozens of turtles. Onlookers cheered and applauded, and Kate shouted her usual litany, "No lights, no cameras, no cell phones!" Aubrey and Lynn, on opposite sides of the runway, kept pace with the lead turtles. The crowd – now numbering two dozen or more, as word of the boil was shouted along the beach – pressed forward. Aubrey found it easy to stumble as onlookers interfered with her progress along the path.

"Get back, please!" she shouted. "Let me through!"

Her attention on dark dots on dark sand, she tripped over a large body crouched in front of her and nearly fell. When the "obstacle" grabbed her arm and steadied her, she realized it was Tom, in position to count. She patted his shoulder in thanks and kept moving, shouting her entreaty to the excited crowd.

The lead turtles tumbled into the low trench and clambered over each other as they continued their progress. Lynn, first at the trench, and carrying the hoe, drew the line in the sand parallel to the tideline but several feet back, behind which onlookers could stand. She, too, was shouting commands at the top of her voice.

"Behind this line, please! Stay out of the water!"

The tiny turtles spilled out of the end of the trench and fanned out, rushing toward the water. Most were unerring in their flight, but occasionally a turtle would try a sideways sprint or even curve back toward the beach, and Lynn and Aubrey would bend to turn them in the right direction. It was like trying to keep dozens of tops spinning at once.

Aubrey was exhausted by the time she heard Kate shout, "That's it!" It took several more minutes for the last turtles to run down the lane, into the trench and across the wet sand to the water, and another half hour of combing that stretch of beach to make sure no turtles had been washed back.

They jogged back to the nest, where Kate waited with Brett and Tom. All three were beaming, and Aubrey looked from one to the other before asking, "What?"

Kate's voice caught in her throat. "A hundred and *eleven*."

"No!" said Aubrey, thrilled.

Kate nodded while Brett and Tom punched each other's arms. "A new record for me, and for you," she said, "best team *ever!*"

The three women hugged each other, squealing, then hugged Brett and Tom. Tom stepped back, grinning, while the others chattered and talked over each other. Several onlookers stepped up to congratulate them, and a few even snapped pictures of the proud nest parents.

Aubrey noticed Tom in the faint glow of her flashlight. He was standing a short distance apart, staring at the ocean, and she moved to stand beside him. With excitement making her bold, she slipped her arm around his waist. Her heart leaped as he put his arm across her shoulders and hugged her briefly. Then he stepped away to gather up the tools. The crowd dispersed, calling back their thanks and congratulations as they moved away into the dark.

"How about a drink to celebrate? My treat!" Kate said. "If we go to the Lazy Turtle, Brett can have a milkshake. And they don't care if we track sand across their floor."

Lynn made a face. "I love the Lazy Turtle, but I have to go home. I promised Jeff I'd get home early tonight, and I've already blown that. It's nearly eleven."

Kate said, "And Bernie already left, so it's just the four of us. Come on, guys, we have to celebrate!"

Aubrey saw Tom hesitate and wondered if money was an issue. But he'd mentioned earlier that he'd worked a few hours on a fishing boat in Southport that morning, so he couldn't be broke.

He glanced at Aubrey, hesitated again, and said, "Sure. What do you say, Brett?"

"Yeah!" Brett said. "Mom knows I get home late on turtle nights, and she trusts Ms. Mitchell."

Kate, still high from the successful boil, laughed and said, "I'll have a word with your mother about her poor judgment. Let's go, turtle team!"

She and Brett jumped in her truck, while Aubrey and Tom got into her car. He made polite replies to her excited conversation, and she was relieved they only had a few blocks to drive.

At the Lazy Turtle Bar and Grill, Kate bought beers for the adults and a chocolate shake for Brett. They sat at a table outside, overlooking the water, and talked and laughed and told stories about their favorite onlookers and most memorable turtles of the night. Tom was quieter than the others, but he had a tale to share, as well.

"That little boy from the other night was back," he said. "Did you see him, Aubrey?"

Aubrey turned to the big man sitting next to her on the bench. "No, I missed him! Did he get to see the turtles?"

Tom grinned. "He sure did. He sat right beside me while I counted and watched them go by. I never saw a kid more excited."

"I'm so glad," she said, touching his forearm. "He was a cute little guy."

"It's good what you folks do here. Not only help the sea turtles but answer all those questions. When people, especially kids, learn to care about something, it sticks with them their whole lives."

Aubrey was moved. For Tom, this was practically a speech. She started to tease him about it, then changed her mind.

"Thanks, Tom," she said, and was echoed by Kate.

"I'm going to keep on helping with sea turtles," Brett said. "Even when I'm in college, I can come back home for the summer and help."

"That's great, Brett," Kate said. "And speaking of home, I'd better get you to yours."

"Hey, now," Tom objected. "The next round was going to be on me."

"Buy one for Aubrey," Kate said. "I'm beat. I think I hit that proverbial wall."

She and Brett left the table and walked around the building toward Kate's truck. Aubrey expected Tom to move to the other side of the table, but he sat quietly, his arm lightly touching hers where it rested on the wooden surface.

"Want another beer?" he asked.

She shook her head. "I'm not finished with this one. And one beer is all I allow myself when I'm driving. You go ahead."

"Not me," he said. "But I might get a cup of coffee."

Later, even Aubrey could not have explained why she said it. "Coffee's free at my house."

He looked at her for a long minute. "What are you saying, Aubrey?"

That made her nervous. She laughed and shrugged. "You've

stayed at my house before. I just thought ..." She stopped, not sure what she thought.

"It's not so easy staying at your house."

"It isn't?" Under his intense scrutiny, her heart began to race.

"No."

"Weren't you comfortable?"

"No." There was another long pause, with Tom staring into her eyes. "I was in the wrong bed."

"Tom ..." Now her breath came too fast and her hand beside his began to tremble. "Can't we just ... take it one step at a time and see where it goes?"

"I'm not pushing, Aubrey. I just want you to know how it is."

She nodded. Her glance dropped to his mouth, and she blushed. She was practically asking him to kiss her, although she was too embarrassed to meet his gaze. His arm lifted and settled gently across her shoulders, and he slowly pulled her closer. She closed her eyes.

His lips were warm where they met hers. Not demanding or aggressive, but somehow seeking an answer. She gave him one, slightly parting her lips and tilting her head. Her hand cupped his jaw, then slipped to the back of his neck, her fingertips feathering the short hair at his nape. The kiss deepened. She felt his powerful arms bulge as he tightened his clasp.

They heard the door open behind them and they separated quickly. The waitress's voice said apologetically, "Sorry, folks. Closing time."

Aubrey stood, reaching beside her for her handbag. Tom gathered the bottles and looked around, but the waitress stepped up and took them from him. He thanked her, dropped a few dollars on the table, and followed Aubrey around the corner of the building.

Aubrey felt Tom's scrutiny on the drive to her house, and grasped for a topic of conversation, but her mind was blank. After a long silence, she jumped when he spoke.

"How'd you get the name 'Aubrey'?"

"My mother –" Her voice was a croak. She cleared her throat and tried again. "My mother was a Bread fan. She loved that song."

"No nicknames?"

"My dad called me 'Red' half the time. My hair was bright red when I was born. It darkened over the years. And some people, like Kate, call me 'Bree' sometimes. I've always thought Aubrey didn't really suit me. Kind of a dainty name. I was a tomboy, and –" She realized she was babbling nervously, and pressed her lips together.

"I think it suits you," he said. "It's beautiful. Haunting."

She licked her lips, wishing he wouldn't stare at her like that. By the time they pulled into her carport, her fingers were numb from gripping the wheel too tightly.

She fumbled with the key, and Tom took it from her hand and opened the door, then stepped back to follow her into the house. After their usual sand-removal ritual, they continued to the kitchen. He put his backpack in a chair and stood watching as she started a pot of coffee.

Aubrey was too shy to look at him. Wiping water drips from the counter, she cleared her throat and asked, "Do you want to grab a shower while we wait for the coffee?"

He answered, "I'll let you go first."

"Okay." She had kissed him, invited him to her home with a fair understanding of what was to follow. Now that he was here, she wasn't sure she could go through with it. "Well, put your things in Sunny's room. I'll meet you back here."

Silence. She dared a glance in his direction. He stared at her for a long moment with an unreadable expression, then nodded and picked up his backpack. She followed him down the hall, pausing while he opened the door to Sunny's room and went inside. She opened her own door and closed it behind her.

Had she really changed her mind? It surely wasn't a sudden attack of prudery – she had long believed that consenting adults who cared about each other were free to be intimate. In the shower, the water heating her skin and teasing the intimate places, made her realize she still wanted him; wanted his presence and his body. So, what was left?

It had to be fear. Fear that sex would take her in directions she wasn't ready to go. Fear that it would engage her heart even more thoroughly and make her vulnerable. And, finally, shamefully, fear that he would find her unsatisfactory and unattractive.

After her shower, still musing, she combed her hair, got out her favorite scented skin cream and smoothed it on. She dug in a drawer, pulled out a lacy teal nightgown and matching peignoir and put them on. Blow dryer in hand, she looked in the bathroom mirror to dry her hair.

What the hell am I doing? she thought. *I just told Tom he's sleeping in the other bedroom, and now I'm telling myself the opposite.* She put the dryer down and pulled the nightgown and peignoir off. After stuffing them back in the drawer, she pulled on her usual faded, oversized tee-shirt.

She heard water running in the guest bathroom, and left her room, hurrying past the bathroom door on her way to the kitchen. The coffee was ready, so she got two mugs. She filled hers, leaving Tom's empty so it wouldn't get cold. She sat at the kitchen table and thumbed through a catalog left there from the day's mail.

The shower stopped, and she heard the rattle of the shower curtain being drawn back. Against her will, her imagination presented a picture of Tom stepping out of the tub, water glistening on wide bare shoulders and muscular arms. Her pulse hammered. She stood, seeking a distraction before her imagination could go further. She tried to pour Tom's coffee, but her hand shook as she did and she overfilled his cup, spilling some on the counter. She grabbed a paper towel and mopped it up.

She heard the bathroom door open and glanced toward the hallway. Steam rolled out the door, followed by Tom in jeans, barefoot and bare-chested. He turned toward the bedroom, but then glimpsed her over his shoulder and about-faced to the kitchen instead.

His short black hair was wet, and beads of water sparkled in the dark hair on his chest. She turned her head, wanting something, *anything* to look at other than Tom.

"Is that for me?" he asked.

"Hmm? Oh! Yes." She grabbed the brimming mug, spilling hot coffee onto her fingers. She yelped and quickly set it back down.

He was next to her in an instant, seizing her hand and steering her to the sink, where he turned on cold water and held her scalded fingers under the stream.

He was too tall, too big, too close and much too naked. Her face was just a few inches from his bare chest, and she smelled soap and shampoo and warm, wet man. When she tilted her head and stared up at him, she saw a tiny raw patch on his chin, where he'd scraped himself with a razor. With the hand not under the running water, she reached up to touch the place. His eye caught the movement and he released her, stepping back out of her reach.

One more rejection was one more than Aubrey could take. She kept her face turned away as she shut off the water and dried her hands, but however she hurried, she couldn't get out of the kitchen without him seeing the tears on her cheeks.

"No," he said. He blocked her path and pulled her to him, wrapping both arms around her and pressing her cheek to his chest. "I can take anything but that," he said, his mouth against the damp hair at the top of her head. "You can change your mind, even tell me to get out, but you can't cry."

He held her tight, her arms pinned to her sides by his embrace, but her mouth was free. She turned her head and kissed his bare skin. With her tongue, she tasted the dewy curls of black hair. He held still, barely breathing, but when her lips found the flat male nipple in its puckered nest, he gave a strangled cry and scooped her easily into his arms.

She looped her arms around his neck as he carried her down the hall. He stopped at her bedroom door and looked down at her. His jaw was clenched, his eyes fierce. "Tell me *no*," he demanded. "Tell me to stop, while I still can."

She pulled herself up with her arms tight around his neck until her lips claimed his. Their mouths met and clung with urgent need. Somehow, he found the doorknob and carried her into the dark bedroom. He sat on the edge of her bed, still holding her, still kissing her.

Aubrey sat on his lap, dizzy, disoriented. One force alone

prevailed – the need to touch him, kiss him, take him into her. She felt his rising need throb against her hip and moved reflexively against it. He gasped and shifted her onto the bed, stretching out beside her, continuing to press kisses on her lips, cheeks, eyes.

Her hands moved over his bare torso, needing to learn every inch of his body, the taut skin, silky hair, rock-hard muscles. She was momentarily distracted by the feel of a puckered scar, like a deep trench, across his lower back, and opened her mouth to ask, but just then his big, rough hand slid beneath her shirt and found her bare breast, and she forgot everything else.

By the light from the open door, he managed to rid her of the tee-shirt; she unsnapped his jeans but couldn't wrangle the zipper down. He chuckled, his mouth busy at her breasts. She retaliated by snaking her hand inside the front waist of his jeans.

With an anguished hiss, he rolled onto his back and fumbled with his zipper. "Son of a bitch," he muttered. "This may kill me."

Laughing, Aubrey rose to a crouch beside him, doing her best to help him ease the zipper down without painful consequences. "That'll teach you," she said. Then the zipper teeth parted and what had been trapped was now free.

"Holy shit," Aubrey said, eyes widening, as Tom arched his back to drag his jeans down over his hips. He had to ask twice for her help before she could tear her gaze away long enough to pull the jeans from his legs.

Naked, he snatched the jeans from her before she could toss them aside. He dug in the tiny inside pocket for the two foil-wrapped packets hidden there.

"Nothing like planning ahead," she said.

"I've been carrying these for a week," he told her, covering his rigid flesh with the thin latex shield. "Just hoping."

"Just hoping someone would come along?" she asked archly.

"Just hoping *you* would come *around,*" he answered. "Now. Come *here.*"

He pulled Aubrey down beside him. Despite his expert kisses and artful play with her breasts, Aubrey was distracted by her concern over what would happen next.

They say bigger is better, she thought. *But damn.*

Then his teeth tugged lightly at her nipple, and she forgot to worry. She began to appreciate being in bed with a big man. The size of his body crouched over hers made her feel powerless and safe at the same time. She ran her hands over his chest and shoulders, stroked his ribs and back. But when she felt his warm hardness against her hip, she gasped in alarm.

He seemed to understand. "Don't worry," he whispered. "It won't happen until you're ready."

"How do I get ready for *that?*" she asked, laughing shakily.

"Like this." His hand slid down her belly and lightly stroked the inside of her thighs. When his long fingers caressed her warm center, she parted her legs, but he went no further. Propped on one elbow, he kissed her mouth, down her throat, between her breasts. He washed her nipples one at a time with his tongue, until she squirmed, raking his hair with her fingernails.

Lips followed tongue and teeth followed lips. Her hips rose and fell of their own volition, seeking his hand. She wanted him, wanted his touch inside her. At last he stroked her, but lightly, teasingly. It was almost unbearable.

"Please, Tom," she moaned.

As his teeth grazed her nipple, his fingers went deep, triggering an explosion of pleasure in her. When her vision cleared, he was watching her, smiling gently. "Now, you're ready."

Poised above her, his knees between hers, he lowered himself to kiss her again. His lips against her ear, he whispered, "I'll go as slow as I can. Tell me if it's too much, and I'll stop." Slowly, tenderly, he eased into her, the strain of his carefulness showing in his face and the trembling of his body.

Aubrey was delighted to discover pleasure in place of the discomfort she'd expected. She wrapped her legs around his waist and arched against him, wanting more. Shuddering, he sank into her until he was fully rooted in her heat. She squirmed, gasping, unsure whether she could contain all of him, but the sense of repletion was intoxicating.

She could tell he was holding himself still, not wanting to hurt her. His muscles were taut, his back bowed away from her, his face buried in the crook of her neck. "It's fine, Tom," she whispered. "It's wonderful. *You're* wonderful."

He raised his body by the length of his arms and, hesitantly, began to move. The sensation was exquisite, powerful. She clutched at his arms, digging her fingernails into his skin. She looked up at his face and saw him watching her attentively. Unable to form words, she smiled and nodded.

The motion quickened, and she closed her eyes to concentrate on the feelings he aroused in her. All her senses, the world, the universe, narrowed to that space where her flesh encompassed his. There was no thought, no sense of time passing. Over and over, Aubrey's body grew taut as a drawn bow, vibrated, went deliciously slack, then began to grow taut again.

The moment came when Tom's body strained, heaved, and he pressed deep enough to hurt. Almost before she could feel the pain, his body, too, went slack. Groaning, he rolled away from her.

The sense of emptiness was acute and, although she knew he was not to blame, she felt bereft, abandoned again. Stifling a sob, she rolled onto her side, toward him, and flung her arm across his heaving chest. He turned slightly toward her and gathered her against him, stroking her hair.

Then she did cry. She cried for Sunny, who didn't want to be with her. She cried for her lost son and broken marriage. And for the dead turtles. And for good people like Tom, who were judged and marginalized by people who should know better. People like her. No wonder she'd been rejected. She'd earned it. She pressed her face against his chest and sobbed aloud.

"Aubrey!" He kissed the top of her head. "What's wrong? Did I hurt you?"

She shook her head. He reached for the bedside lamp and snapped it on.

"Then what's up?" he asked.

She started to speak, then swallowed and shook her head again. He put his thumb under her chin and tilted her face up to his. She realized then that she had rarely seen his face in good light without his dark glasses. Framed by black lashes, his eyes were light blue with dark blue rings around the irises. How could she not have noticed his beautiful eyes? Another failure. More tears.

"Aubrey, I told you I can't take it when you cry." Still cradling her, he dragged up a corner of the sheet and started wiping her face. "Now, tell me what's going on."

In a choked voice, she started with the least important. "M-my ex-husband's girlfriend is living with him. She's twenty-two."

"What do you care? You don't want him." He paused. "Or I am reading this wrong?"

"No, you're right. I don't want him. But do you know how it feels to be a thirty-six-year-old woman, replaced by a twenty-two-year-old girl?"

He released her chin and she buried her head in the curve of his shoulder. "No," he said seriously. "Can't say I do. How long have you been divorced?"

"A little more than four years."

He hesitated. "You mean ... she was *eighteen*?"

"No! It's not like that. He just met her about six months ago."

"So, this guy you don't want, who you divorced four years ago, has a young girlfriend, and it makes you feel 'replaced'?"

Aubrey smiled against his skin. When put that way, it did seem illogical. "You're right. The fact that she's young and gorgeous shouldn't make me feel old and unattractive. I just –"

"*Unattractive?*" He rose onto his elbow, displacing Aubrey from her cozy spot on his chest. "Aubrey, do you own a mirror?" He cupped her cheek, then ran his hand down her throat to her breasts, his gaze following, while the look on his face make it clear he found her anything but "unattractive."

She tried to pull the swath of sheet over herself. "Well, now's not

the time to start taking inventory. Anyway, that's not the main –"
She gasped.

"Go ahead," he mumbled, with his mouth at her breast. "I'm listening."

"Maybe you can listen while you're doing that," she said breathlessly. "But I can't talk."

He sighed and settled back down beside her. "Go on," he demanded.

"As I was saying, they're not my real problem. It's my daughter, Sunny. She's living with them. For months, she's been saying how much she hates Maya, but since school let out, she's been after me to let her stay at her dad's condo for the summer. In a moment of weakness, I agreed. Now I miss her like crazy, and she won't always take my calls, and the last time we talked, she had to hurry because she and Maya were on their way to the pool."

"What's his name?"

Aubrey lifted her head. "You mean my ex? Craig."

"I mean the boy who lives in Craig's building. The one Sunny has the crush on."

Aubrey frowned, annoyed. "Sunny doesn't have –" She stopped. Was that it? Sunny liked some boy that hung out around the pool in Craig's building? She felt a small glimmer of hope. "That would mean –"

"That it's not about you. Imagine."

"Hey!" She slapped his chest, laughing, and he pulled her on top of him.

She lay quietly, happy at last, her chin resting on her folded arms, so she could stare at his face. His beautiful face.

"So, was that it?" he asked. "I would swear there was more bothering you."

She thought, *Yes, there's more. Not long ago I thought you were a bum, or a maniac, and now I think I'm in love with you, and I'm ashamed that I could have been so terribly wrong.* But she couldn't tell him that. Maybe she could have told him before they made love, but now it would sound like the sex had changed her mind.

Not that it hadn't been mind-blowing, life-altering sex, but he probably already thought she was shallow and hardhearted – she was beginning to think so herself – and her confession would surely just confirm that.

"No," she said at last. "That was it, really. Anything else is minor."

"Good," he said, and lifted his head to kiss her quickly. "Now, let me up for a minute, would you?"

She rolled off him and watched him stand and walk to the bathroom. He was gorgeous to look at from any direction. She gave a low whistle and, without looking back, he said, "Stop that."

She laughed, then gasped when he turned on the bathroom light and she saw plainly the scar she had only felt before. It was about eight inches long, slanting across the lower right side of his back. He closed the bathroom door behind him.

What had torn him that way? Now she had another reason to cry, and felt the familiar sting of tears. Something had hurt him, and she found that she wanted to take that long-ago hurt away. She was sure he would find that amusing, and she added it to the list of things she couldn't tell him.

She got up and straightened the bedcovers. She was slipping under the sheet when the bathroom door opened, and he approached the bed. Looking at him took her breath away. He stopped by the bed, and Aubrey reached up to touch him. He sucked in his breath and closed his eyes.

The second time was better than the first. For one thing, Aubrey was better prepared and not afraid. Furthermore, the experience lasted longer and involved positions that gave her more control. When it ended, she was shattered but sated.

She relaxed in his arms, too drowsy to curb her tongue. "If you're looking for work," she said, "I'm sure you could make a fortune as a gigolo."

He laughed quietly. "Not interested," he said.

"I can tell you've had plenty of experience." She kissed his throat and the underside of his jaw.

He was silent for a minute, then said, "I was pretty active in my younger days. When you're my size, it seems like women come after you. Hey, stop laughing." He put his finger against her lips. "I meant, when you're tall and so on. But, yeah, I guess they were after the other thing, too. Some of them anyway. It's one of the 'advantages' of being big, if you can call it an advantage."

"Don't you?"

He slid his hand down her arm to lock his fingers with hers. His hand made hers feel very small.

"Not after a while. You get to feeling like an object. Most of those women didn't care if I even had a brain, let alone what thoughts might be running around in it."

"I see what you mean. In that way, it's a *dis*advantage. Like being stunningly beautiful can be for a woman."

He brought her knuckles to his mouth and spoke against them. "Well, I couldn't say. You tell *me*."

Her heart flip-flopped in her chest. "You know, Tom, for a quiet man, you can say some really powerful things."

"That's another disadvantage of being big," he said. "For some reason, people tend to think you're stupid. They never think you might be quiet because you're shy. You know, not every big guy is Lennie Small."

He looked into her face and laughed, and she realized her expression had given her away; she hadn't expected a Steinbeck reference from him.

"In an infantry unit," he explained, "you spend a lot of time just sitting around. Some guys play cards or talk. Or nowadays, play video games. I read."

"Okay," she confessed. "I'll admit that when I first met you, you were so quiet, I thought you might be a little slow." She shrugged. "Not that there's anything wrong with that, of course."

He laughed again, and she blushed, recognizing she had just uttered the classic bigot's disclaimer. "Well, dammit, you know what I mean." He grinned, clearly enjoying her discomfiture, and she started to sit up.

"No, don't leave," he said, gently tugging her against him. "I like teasing you, but I don't mean to hurt your feelings."

She settled against his broad chest. "I guess my problem is that I've been learning a lot of uncomfortable things about myself lately."

"Such as?"

"Such as, I have many more prejudices than I like to admit. And I'm not as nice as I'd like to be."

He wove his fingers into her hair and turned her face to his. "Are you interested in my opinion on the subject?"

More than anyone's, she thought, but only said, "Yes."

"I think you're one of the nicest, kindest people I've ever met."

Her eyes welled up again. "I am?"

"Yes. I've seen how you are with people. Sure, you can be a little impatient with some of them. But mostly you're understanding and friendly. You invited me into your home twice, because you didn't want me sleeping rough in the rain." He smiled. "And I don't think sex was on the table back then. You were a little scared of me."

"And I didn't even know how much there was to fear then," she said, nudging her knee between his legs to make her point.

His eyes widened. "Soon," he said, pointing to the two empty foil packets on the night table, "I'll need my pack from the other room."

"Okay," she said happily. "I'll just torment you a little."

And she did. Several minutes later, sweating and breathing hard, he seized her roving hands by the wrists and held them over her head, rolling her onto her back, pinning her with his body half covering hers.

"Okay. That's enough for now. If we keep going, I'll have to get my pack, and I'm feeling lazy. Tell me what you're doing tomorrow."

Aubrey craned her neck to look at her bedside clock. "You mean *today.* A little housework, a little gardening. Going over the reading list for my honors English class to make sure I've read all the books." She giggled.

"What's funny?" he asked with a half-smile.

"Talking about housework and school in this position."

"Oh. Sorry." He released her wrists and she wrapped her arms around his neck. He nuzzled the curve of her throat. "Mmmm. Aubrey, you smell so good."

She slid her hands down his back and rediscovered the deep scar she had seen earlier.

"Tom ..." She took a breath to ask him about it, but he anticipated her.

"I was a sergeant in a forward unit in Afghanistan. We were in three jeeps on our way back to base, when we hit a couple of IEDs. My jeep flipped over. The driver and the guy in back were killed. I was trapped underneath with a big piece of metal in my back."

She held him tighter, her cheek pressed to his. She felt his breath in her hair. "Oh, Tom. Is that why you have the nightmares?"

He went very still. "It wasn't a dream? You really got in my bed that time, and held me?"

She nodded. She heard him swallow, then clear his throat. A moment later, he went on.

"All the others bought it. One guy kept calling me while he died. 'Sarge! Sarge!' Then he went quiet. When they found me, they thought I was dead, too. I was in the base hospital for three months before I was transferred stateside. And all the time, these damn nightmares. It got better. Now it's only loud noises that set me off. Fireworks. Thunder."

"Oh, sweetie, I'm so sorry." The endearment had slipped out quite naturally, but Tom didn't react. "How awful for you."

"Worse for the others," he said. "I got a free ride home and a Purple Heart. They went home in boxes and their families got folded flags."

She had no response to that. She could only hold him tighter and offer him the meager comfort of her body. They fell asleep with their foreheads pressed together and his big hand on her breast.

Chapter 7

Nest 75, Day 59

Aubrey scrambled six eggs while Tom buttered the toast. Tom was showered and dressed, ready to go to a job interview at a paint store in Southport. Because Aubrey offered to drive him, he had time to eat breakfast first. He was explaining how he'd come to be in the area.

"In the hospital, I met this guy who had a handyman business in Supply. He gave me his card and told me if I ever needed a job, to look him up. Several months later, when I decided I wanted out of west Georgia, I took all my cash out of the bank and put it in a duffel bag in the trunk of my car."

He looked up from his task to see Aubrey's surprised expression.

"Yeah, I know. Stupid. I never even thought about getting robbed. Most guys don't mess with me." He shrugged philosophically. "I made it to Myrtle Beach and decided to spend the night at a hotel, clean myself up and drive to Supply the next morning. During the night, somebody stole my car. It was a junker. Don't know why they picked it, except it was easy to hotwire."

He carried the plate of toast to the table. Aubrey put about most of the scrambled eggs on his plate and the rest on her own. She set their plates on the table and saw him looking at them.

"I have a tremendous appetite this morning," he admitted, grinning. "I don't know why."

She laughed and hugged him before sitting down.

"But I'm wondering why you gave *me* so much more."

"You can't handle all that?" She put a napkin in her lap and folded her hands.

"Oh sure. No problem." He sat down opposite her and waited for her to begin.

"I usually start with a prayer, if that's okay," she said.

"Yes, ma'am," he responded, bowing his head.

She kept it short. "Heavenly Father," she prayed. "Thank you for this food, for the turtles last night and for the day to come. Bless Tom as he looks for work. Amen."

"Amen," Tom echoed softly.

"Anyway ..." Aubrey prompted.

He shrugged. "Anyway, the police still haven't found the car. I had some money left in my wallet after paying for my hotel room. My insurance will cover the value of the car, but I also put in for the money that was stolen, so it seems they're dragging their feet over paying me anything."

Aubrey spoke around a bite of toast. "Credit card?"

"Never had one." He grinned at her. "Just a country boy, ma'am." He piled eggs on a section of toast and took a large bite.

"Shouldn't you be getting some kind of support from the Army? I mean, you got out because of that injury."

He looked out the kitchen window as he chewed and swallowed. "I guess I could. But it feels wrong. I'm fit and able to work. It's not the Army's fault I was stupid with my money."

Aubrey sensed it went deeper than that. Was survivor's guilt keeping Tom from turning to the Army for help? She wanted to ask, but realized it was none of her business. Sunny sometimes accused of her of being too controlling, so here was another chance to improve herself.

"We all make mistakes, Tom. Don't be too hard on yourself."

He smiled at her, swallowing the last of his breakfast and reaching for his coffee. She carried their plates to the sink, and he followed with their coffee mugs. They went to their separate bathrooms to brush their teeth and met in the kitchen minutes later.

He wore a tan tee-shirt tucked into blue jeans. He needed a haircut, but he was clean, lean and very muscular. "Do I look all right?" he asked.

"Not a fair question," she said, looping her arms around his neck. "I know what's underneath."

He kissed her quickly, then set her back from him. "That's the kind of remark that could make a guy late for his interview," he said.

She dropped him at the paint store and drove to the nearest grocery to pick up a few items. While she shopped, she called Sunny's cell phone, but got no answer. When the call went to voice mail, she left a message.

"Hey, sweetie. Just checking in. Call when you get a chance."

She hung up, thinking this message was an improvement over the last one, when she'd said, "Sunny, please call me. If you remember, letting you live with Dad was conditional on you keeping in touch. You personally, not your father. And a brief text is insufficient. So, *call me.*"

She was proud of herself for sounding less demanding. She parked in front of the paint store and waited for Tom to emerge. While she waited, she called Kate. Kate reported that she had been to Nest 75 that morning, and no more turtles had hatched after they left. They exchanged other bits of news, then Aubrey said, "Kate, I think you should know that my relationship with Tom has gotten physical. He spent the night last night and, well, I really like him."

There was a long pause. "Well, if you trust him, that's good enough for me. If you remember, I liked him from the beginning."

Aubrey laughed, delighted. "I do remember. I always said you were the smart one."

Just then, Tom came out the paint store. His mouth was set in a straight line, but he smiled when he saw her waiting. She said goodbye to Kate and disconnected.

"How'd it go?" she asked, as he got in.

He shrugged. "Well, he didn't turn me down, but he didn't offer me a job. He said he'd give me a call if anything opened up."

"Doesn't sound too hopeful." Aubrey started the car.

"It wasn't. When they get to the part about what work I've been doing for the past year, they tend to lose interest."

"Why?" She caught herself. "I mean – that's really none of my business, and –"

Tom laughed. "It's nothing sinister. When I got home from Afghanistan on extended medical leave, I planned to return to my outfit as soon as I could. But I took some time locating my mom, and when I found her, she was in the final stages of cancer. I resigned from the Army to take care of her. Eight months later –"

It wasn't easy crawling over the console to put her arms around Tom, but Aubrey managed.

"Hey, now," he said, patting her back. "You and this crying thing – have you always been this way, or am I responsible?"

She sniffed. "It's something new I'm trying out to see if I like it. What do you think?"

A lady came out of the store, glanced at them, and hurried to her car.

Tom said, "I think it attracts too much attention. If you want a hobby, model trains can be fun. Or stamp collecting."

"You could be right." She kissed him and crawled back into her seat. She fastened her seatbelt and put the car in gear. "Anyway, I'll check into that model train thing."

At home, Aubrey invited Tom to wash his clothes in her laundry while she vacuumed and dusted. After she shut off the vacuum cleaner, she heard the washer going, but Tom was nowhere in sight. Following the sound of banging, she found him in the carport, repairing the roof. The shingles that had been in the shed were stacked just outside the door, and Tom – all six-and-a-half feet of him – was on the rickety ladder that had also occupied the shed.

"Tom?" she called softly, so as not to startle him.

"Yeah?"

"I'm going to take hold of this ladder, and I didn't want it to be a surprise."

He laughed. "Okay, Aubrey. Thanks."

She put one foot on the bottom step and held the rails. Her head was level with his knees. She had a sudden flashback to a day when she had held a ladder for Craig while he put up a shelf in their first apartment. That had been a good day. They had been young and in love, full of hope, and she had been pregnant with Sunny, although they hadn't known it yet.

Where had it gone so wrong? Oh, sure, he had cheated on her, probably years before she knew about it, but she hadn't been a perfect wife. Their marriage had been dead for some time before she found out about Craig and his secretary. Somewhere along the line, she had stopped believing in him, stopped admiring him. The truth was that she had turned away from Craig, and he had turned to other women, and she wasn't sure which had happened first.

How can you be a good wife when you no longer respect your husband's character? Some of the qualities she had admired in him when they were first in love had become flaws in her maturing eyes. His drive had degraded into blind ambition, where shortcuts superseded ethics. She had heard him make promises to clients and employees that she knew he didn't intend to keep. And the frankness and self-esteem that had once seemed so refreshing had grated on her until she had simply stopped listening to him.

She had once heard someone say that women provide the moral compass in a marriage, and it had rankled at the time, but perhaps only because she was guilty of keeping her moral compass to herself. She had simply kept the peace and made her own life within the wider circle of her husband's. If she had held him to a higher standard, if she had illuminated for him some of those early missteps, would he have become a better man?

"Coming down!"

Aubrey jumped. She had been so lost in thought that she hadn't noticed when the hammering stopped, or that she had been resting her forehead against Tom's muscled calf. She quickly let go of one rail of the ladder and stepped aside to let him climb down.

"All fixed?"

He smiled, looking up. "I think there may be other gaps that aren't as obvious. We'll find out next time it rains."

He looked down at her and pulled her to him, kissing her long and hard. Then he said, "Thank you."

Her head still tilted back, she leaned against him. "You're the one who fixed the roof."

"Small potatoes compared to what you've done for me. You trusted me enough to invite me to your home. Three times. You fed me, took me to that job interview. And then there's last night."

"I should thank *you* for last night." She grinned. "Twice. And again, for this morning." She wrapped her arms around his neck. "So, thank you, thank you … and thank you."

Another kiss, then Tom whispered, "Maybe you'd like a reason to thank me again."

"Great idea." She took his hand and led him in the door, through the laundry room and into the kitchen. Just as they passed the counter, her cell phone rang. Aubrey glanced at the display.

"I don't believe it. It's Sunny!" She picked the phone up eagerly. "Hi, sweetheart! I'm so glad you called." She smiled at Tom, who smiled back and gestured that he was going back outside.

"Mom!" said Sunny. "What's new? Anything?"

Aubrey heard the side door close behind Tom. "Not much, baby. I still miss you like crazy. How about with you?"

Sunny chattered happily about her dad's great condo and the huge pool. She had been shopping with Maya that morning and had picked out a great new jacket.

"And tomorrow we're going to Thalian Hall to see a musical!" she enthused. "Dad's busy with some work thing."

Aubrey heard Craig's voice in the background. Impulsively, she asked to speak to him. Sunny hesitated, but Aubrey reassured her. "There's no problem, sweetheart. I just have a question to do with Dad's business."

Muffled whispers, then Craig's voice on the line said, "Hey, Aubrey. What's up?"

Aubrey took a deep breath and plunged in. "Hi, Craig. Listen, I have a friend who's looking for full-time work, and I wondered if you have any openings."

"Building or office work?"

"He would want building work, I'm sure. Something in Southport or Oak Island would be best."

"Hmm. Does he have any construction experience?"

Aubrey thought of Tom's neat repairs to her carport roof. "Some, I think. He's strong and able-bodied."

"Well, I would have to meet him first. No promises."

It was on the tip of her tongue to retort that his promises weren't worth much anyway, but for Tom's sake, she held her temper. "Of course, Craig. That's reasonable. Are you free this afternoon?"

"I have a couple of local projects to check on after lunch, but if he could meet me at home about three, I could give him a few minutes."

"Great! Thanks, Craig."

When Sunny was back on the line, Aubrey explained to her that she was helping a friend find work, maybe with her dad's company. As a result, she would be at Craig's condo at three, and she and Sunny could have some time together. They chatted for a few more minutes and said goodbye.

For the past several minutes, Aubrey had been listening to the sound of a lawn mower without recognizing it as her own. When she stepped down into the carport, she saw Tom coming around the corner of the house, pushing her old mower ahead of him. He was wearing his dark glasses, patrol cap and no shirt, and for several seconds she just stood in the shade, admiring him. Then she stepped into the light and, noticing her, he shut off the engine.

"You don't have to do that," she said, crossing the lawn to where he waited, smiling.

"Are you kidding? This is a real treat. I like yard work." He pulled his tee-shirt from his back pocket, where he'd partially stuffed it, and mopped sweat from his face and chest. A line from the balcony scene of *Romeo and Juliet* flashed through Aubrey's mind: "See, how she leans her cheek upon her hand! O, that I were a glove upon that hand, That I might touch that cheek!" Now here she was, wishing she were a tee-shirt!

He must have discerned some part of her feelings, for he stepped close and, looking down into her face, said softly, "Should I finish this later?"

"Yes. I mean, no." She shook her head and took a deep breath. "I mean, whatever you want is fine. I just came to tell you we should eat lunch pretty soon, then get cleaned up and drive into Wilmington."

He took off his sunglasses and squinted down at her. "What's going on?"

"I hope I wasn't too presumptuous. My ex has a construction company. He often has projects going in this area, and I thought he could use a good man." She swallowed. "Did I cross a line?" she asked.

"And he wants to see me?"

"It was an impulse," she said. "If you don't want to see him, I'll call him back and cancel."

He touched her cheek. "I suppose I should be embarrassed asking my girlfriend's ex-husband for a job. But I don't expect it was easy for you to ask him for a favor. And the fact is, I really need the work." He smiled. "Sure. Let's go."

"Oh, good. And I didn't tell him I'm your –" Aubrey stared at the grass cuttings on the top of her bare feet, then back at Tom's face. "*Am* I your girlfriend, Tom?"

His expression was serious, even stern. "I don't sleep with women

I don't care about, Aubrey. But if you prefer 'friends with benefits,' or even a one-night stand ..." He shrugged.

She squinted in the sunlight. "I don't know how good a girlfriend I'll be, Tom. I'm a little out of practice. But I'd like to try."

He grinned. "Okay. That's settled. Now, I can knock this out while you fix lunch, if that works for you."

"Is tuna all right?"

He put his sunglasses back on. "Sure. I'm not particular."

He reached down to pull the starter cord, but paused halfway and added, "About lunch."

Tom devoured two tuna sandwiches, along with some raw carrots and celery. Aubrey accepted his offer to clean up while she took a shower. She had just finished rinsing the shampoo from her hair when she heard his voice. She pulled the shower curtain open a bit to see him smiling and naked in the doorway.

"I thought I'd join you but didn't want you to think I was going *Psycho* on you."

She laughed and moved back to let him in. He ducked under the curtain rod and stepped into the tub. They took turns washing each other, and she watched his arousal grow. While he shampooed his hair, she took matters literally into her own hands and then, briefly, her mouth. That hurried things along, and they were still mostly wet when they stumbled to the bed and the drawer holding the blessed foil packets.

"No, Aubrey," he said, sheathing himself in latex. "I'm close to the edge now. If you help ..."

She, too, was near climax, and did the moment he entered her, and after. He was not far behind, and soon they were both lying side by side, breathing hard.

"Damn," he said. And again, "Damn."

When he finally caught his breath, he asked, "Are you okay?"

Aubrey wasn't ready to speak, but she found his hand and squeezed it. He brought her hand to his mouth and kissed her knuckles. "Good," he said.

He rolled to his side and kissed her, stroking her breasts, and she sighed happily. She wondered if he could be as happy, but she was too shy to ask.

"Should a man with no home and no job feel this good?" he asked. "I thought it would be easy finding work in this area, but I've been here six weeks and haven't found anything but one- or two-day jobs. I was feeling pretty low until you came along."

Aubrey rolled toward him and hid her face in his wide, warm chest. "Don't say that," she whispered. "I was hateful to you, at first."

"Not hateful," he insisted. "Just suspicious. Understandably."

How could she ever have thought him anything but good and honorable and caring? Again, she felt like crying, but he had seen too much of that from her. She snaked her arms around him and held him as tight as she could. *I love him,* she thought. *Should I tell him? Is it too soon?*

She pressed her lips together, held him and was held by him and all she could do was try not to weep. Finally, feeling in control of herself, she murmured, "We should get dressed now."

He sighed. "I suppose if we show up at his place like this, your ex will guess we're more than friends."

Aubrey laughed softly, disentangled herself from Tom and left the bed. Earlier, when he had removed his clothes from the dryer, he had laid them on the bed in Sunny's room. Aubrey had since collected them and hung them in her closet. Now she opened the closet doors and pointed them out. Then she darted up the hall to the guest bathroom and collected his shaving kit. When she returned to the bedroom, she held his shaving kit aloft and sashayed into her bathroom with it.

Tom, sitting on the edge of the bed, laughed and shook his head. "Woman, I swear, if you don't put some clothes on, we're going to be late leaving for Wilmington."

Aubrey approached him and put her arms around his neck. With Tom seated, his face was level with her breasts, and Aubrey went weak in the knees when Tom took a nipple into his mouth. She threaded her fingers into his hair and pressed him closer.

"Oh, Tom," she whispered. "I can't tell you what that does to me."

"I could tell you what it does to *me*," he said. "But I'd rather show you."

And he did.

As it turned out, they were only five minutes late. Craig opened the door, and Aubrey noticed his eyes widen when he saw the big man standing behind her. She introduced them, then asked if Sunny was at home. When Tom and Craig disappeared into Craig's home office, Aubrey knocked on the door of Sunny's room. Sunny immediately opened the door and, squealing, gave her mom a fierce hug before inviting her in.

Aubrey had been there before, but the size and décor of Sunny's room at the condo still impressed and, to some extent, *depressed* her. Of course, Sunny would rather live here; this room was bigger than their living room in Oak Island. It was painted a medium gray, with bright white trim and furnishings. The artwork and furniture were expensive and in excellent taste. It didn't look like a teenaged girl's room at all. There were no posters, no stuffed animals or trophies or keepsakes from adventures. The only reflection of Sunny's life was the desk in the corner, where her summer reading material was stacked next to a picture of Sunny with her mom at a breast cancer fundraising walk the previous year.

"It's a beautiful room, Sunny," Aubrey said.

To her surprise, Sunny shrugged and frowned. "It's okay, I guess. Maya wants to redo it. She likes salmon and teal. Dad won't let her do their room or his office, and she already did the guest room and the rest of the place. So, I guess this is next."

Aubrey avoided the neatly made bed with its raspberry cover and sat in the desk chair. "Don't you want it redecorated?"

"I don't care. I like the gray all right. And it's not that I *mind* salmon or teal. It just seems like I ought to have some say in it."

"Maybe Maya will let you make some of the choices in here," Aubrey suggested.

"That's just it. She won't! She acts like I'm just a visitor here. This was my room before she ever showed up."

Sunny threw herself onto her back on the bed, one arm across her eyes, both fists clenched. Aubrey was surprised at her tone.

"I though you and Maya were getting along. You sounded fine when I talked to you earlier. Did something happen?"

Sunny sat up, looking at Aubrey with tear-filled eyes. "Oh, Mom, it's so awful. They just told me." She burst into tears, her hands over her face. Aubrey moved quickly to sit beside her and take her daughter into her arms.

"Honey! What is it?"

"Oh, Mom. Maya was only being n-nice to me so I wouldn't freak out."

"Freak out about what?"

"They're getting m-married!"

Aubrey froze. Still holding Sunny and rocking her gently from side to side, she thought for a minute about this news. She explored her feelings as she might probe a sore tooth with her tongue, checking the intensity of the pain.

There was none. At least, none for her. She thought Craig was making a foolish error in judgment, but that was his problem. Mostly, she felt sorry for her daughter, to whom this news would, of course, be shocking. It was one thing for her dad to have girlfriends, and he'd had several over the last four years. But for him to marry again must be a distressing reality for any child to face.

"Do you want to come home, sweetheart?"

Sunny went quiet. She sniffed, edged out of Aubrey's embrace, and reached for a tissue from the dispenser on her bed table. She blew her nose and wiped her eyes.

Looking down, she said, "N-no. Not just yet. I want to stay for a while." She looked at Aubrey, and her reddened eyes were angry. "But I'm not going anywhere with Maya! She can go shopping by herself. And if she goes down to the pool, I'm not going. Not even if —"

She bit her lip and looked away again, and Aubrey remembered what Tom had said about Sunny liking a boy here. She wouldn't press her daughter right now, but she might have a word with Craig, just to alert him to the possibility.

On the drive to Wilmington, she had told Tom about Craig's proposal to take primary custody, and her worry that Sunny might prefer that. He had been skeptical, and she'd had to admit she didn't really know how her daughter felt about it. She wouldn't tell Sunny about what her father was suggesting until Craig did, but she'd give a lot to know what Sunny wanted.

Aubrey put her hands on Sunny's cheeks and looked her in the eye. "You don't have to go anywhere or do anything you don't want to do, baby. But you must show respect to Maya, because she's an adult and this is her home, too, and especially now, because she's going to be your stepmother."

"But I don't like her, Mom! You don't see what she's like –"

Aubrey gave Sunny's head a tiny shake. "It doesn't matter whether you like her, only that you show her the respect you would show to me or your father. Or your teachers."

Sunny pushed Aubrey's hands away. "So, I should be a phony, and pretend I like her?"

"You know very well what I mean, Sunny. *Showing* respect means answering when she speaks to you and not giving her an attitude. It means looking her in the eye and being polite." She seized Sunny's hand and resisted the girl's attempt to pull free. "Now, I know you're upset about this news, but –"

Sunny's jaw dropped. "Don't you even care, Mom? Dad's going to marry that – that –"

"No, Sunny, I don't care. Except for your feelings, I don't mind at all. My marriage to your father was over a long time ago. I've moved on." She patted Sunny's hand and stood up. "Now, show me this beautiful jacket you got this morning."

Sunny stood, reluctance in every move. "I put it back in the bag. I was going to tell Maya to take it back to the store. I don't want it anymore." As she talked, she pulled a bag from the closet, and Aubrey recognized the logo of a pricey downtown boutique.

"Oh, baby! It's gorgeous!" Aubrey raved, when Sunny showed her the leather-and-fabric jacket. "Try it on," she insisted.

She raved some more when Sunny put it on and posed in front of the big bedroom mirror, turning this way and that, zipping and unzipping the front. Sunny's usual smile returned as they talked about the jacket's features and how well the pewter color went with Sunny's auburn hair. When she was through modeling, Sunny removed the jacket and hung it in her closet, and Aubrey made no comment about her apparent change of heart.

"Why don't you show me the pool?" Aubrey asked. She hoped to catch a glimpse of whatever boy Sunny had her eyes on. But as they went through the living room, the door to Craig's home office opened and he and Tom emerged. Aubrey couldn't help noticing how Tom towered over Craig.

"Ah. There you are," Craig said. "I told Tom to report to a building site in Southport, where we've got a small office complex going up. He can start Monday. That should give us time to process the paperwork."

"Great!" Aubrey said.

"He said he doesn't have a, uh, 'fixed address' right now, but he thought you'd be okay with us using *your* contact info." Craig cocked an eyebrow at Aubrey, and his smirk was suggestive.

Aubrey blushed, but lifted her head and answered, "Of course. I can always find him if I need to."

Sunny clearly knew something was going on between her parents. She interrupted cheerfully, "I'm going to show Mom the pool, Dad. You coming?"

"No, thanks, honey. You guys go ahead."

Tom thanked Craig as they shook hands goodbye, and on the way down in the elevator, Aubrey introduced Tom and Sunny. With her usual frankness, Sunny said, "Wow! You sure are big! Were you ever a football player?"

Tom laughed. "In high school. I played tight end."

"I'll bet colleges were after you."

"Nope. I was stupid. My family needed money, so I quit school in my junior year and worked in the strawberry fields. I wasn't smart enough to realize that if I'd just held out until I graduated, I could have had better paying jobs where I didn't have to work so hard."

Sunny looked a bit chastened. "Sorry, Mr. Clayton. I didn't mean to be nosy."

Tom smiled. "Call me Tom. You weren't nosy. I got my G.E.D. in the Army, and some college credits, too, but I could've made it a lot easier on myself."

The elevator dinged on the ground floor, and they got out. Sunny took them both on a chatty tour of the pool, sauna and hot tub area. Aubrey noticed how often her daughter glanced around, as though hoping to see someone. She was beginning to believe Tom was right about Sunny's crush.

On the drive back to Oak Island, Tom asked Aubrey if he'd been right to use her as a contact until he had a phone and address of his own, and she insisted it was fine. Then he talked about Sunny.

"That's a great girl you've got there. Not many girls her age have that kind of poise. I assume that's from you."

"Actually," Aubrey said, "her dad has the self-confidence."

Tom shook his head. "Her dad's a jerk," he said. "He's dying to know what our relationship is, but he doesn't have the balls to ask."

"Or the right," Aubrey pointed out.

Tom chuckled. "He doesn't strike me as the type to worry about whether he has the right to something. Funny, I just can't picture you two together."

"At the end," Aubrey said, "neither could I."

"But you got Sunny out of the deal, so it was a net gain. She looks like you. Same beautiful hair." He smoothed her hair behind her ear and left his hand on her shoulder. "Only she has curls."

She glanced sideways, smiled, and returned her attention to the road. "She got my coloring and Craig's curls. And my body, I'm afraid."

"Why afraid? You've got a smokin' body."

Aubrey laughed. Regretting having revealed her insecurity, she tried joking her way out. "Oh, yeah. I'm too tall, too wide at the hips, and not enough boobage. Other than that, I'm perfect."

Tom tugged at the small gold hoop in her earlobe. "I'd say you're just the right height, your hips are amazing and, speaking of perfect – but we'd better not talk about the boobs until we get home. Also, could you drive just a little faster?"

Aubrey twirled a lock of Tom's hair around her fingertip. She enjoyed his silky black curls, the weight of his head on her chest, and the lazy pleasure of lying naked in bed in the gathering gloom of evening. She missed her daughter and wanted her home, but she had to admit there were advantages to being single.

"We should get up and fix some dinner."

"Mmmm. I have what I want right here." He scooped his big hand around one of her breasts and licked it like an ice cream cone.

She squirmed, tugging at his hair. "In an hour, we need to be at the nest."

"Great," he drawled. "A whole hour to do this."

His hand slid down her belly and between her legs to demonstrate what "this" meant. With his mouth above and his hand below, Aubrey was powerless to do anything except revel in the dual stimulation.

Moments later, she heard the foil packet being torn open, and shivered in anticipation. His mouth claimed hers for a long, fervent kiss, and she wrapped her legs around his thighs.

"I can't seem to get enough of you," he murmured. "Is it too much?"

She arched her back, taking him deep. "Much too … much," she said, gasping. "Please don't stop."

They were later than usual getting to the nest. Tom carried Aubrey's chair and turtle bag as they climbed over the low dunes and turned west toward the spot. In the last rays of sunset, she could see Kate's silhouette standing by the signpost, and the skinny figure of Brett next to her. Two other, bulkier forms were nearby, and Aubrey's first thought was that Heather was back and had brought more help, but as they neared, she saw the other two wore dark uniforms and shiny badges.

"What in the world?" she said, hurrying her pace.

The two uniformed Oak Island police officers moved toward them. One of them stepped between her and Tom; the other stood directly in Tom's path, one hand on his holster.

"Thomas Clayton?" he said.

"Yes," Tom answered. "What's this —"

"Put those things down, Clayton," the officer said. "And put your hands on your head."

Aubrey watched in shock and disbelief as Tom complied, and the officers pulled his hands behind his back and cuffed him. She grabbed the back of Tom's shirt as they started to lead him away.

"Please! What's this about?"

"Step back, ma'am," said an officer, and Kate put her arms around Aubrey, pulling her away from Tom.

While Aubrey watched in horror, the officers led him away, in the opposite direction from which she and Tom had come, until all she could see in the dark were the reflections of the lighthouse beams glinting on the officers' belts and the metal cuffs around Tom's wrists. Through the dark distance, she could hear them advising him of his rights.

"Tom!" Aubrey cried.

He didn't look back.

"Oh, my God!" Aubrey cried, and only Kate's grip kept her from sinking to the sand. "What's happening?"

"Listen, Aubrey," Kate said sternly. "Stop crying and listen." She looked over her shoulder at Brett. "Brett, please take a walk."

The boy sprinted away down the darkening beach. Kate lowered Aubrey to the sand. A small crowd had started to gather at the sight of Tom's arrest, and stood in small groups, whispering and pointing, but well back from where Kate and Aubrey crouched on the sand.

Kate took Aubrey by the shoulders and gave her a hard shake. "Listen to me!" she whispered fiercely. "Tom's under arrest for the sexual assault of a minor."

Aubrey stopped crying and stared at Kate open-mouthed. She slowly shook her head as Kate explained that the officers had arrived at the beach minutes after she and Brett. One of them had pulled her aside to ask if she knew a Tom Clayton and had added an unmistakable physical description. At her affirmation, he had asked if she was expecting him to show up, and she affirmed that, too. He had then gone on to explain that a warrant had been issued that evening for his arrest, on a charge of sexual assault and battery of a minor. He had refused to give her more information.

"No," Aubrey said. "It's not possible. Tom would never ..." She lowered her head and resumed sobbing.

A woman approached in the dark. "Kate," she said quietly. "Brett found me down the beach and said you were in trouble."

"Oh, Lynn. Thank God," Kate answered. "Can you take over here? I'm not expecting much action. Maybe a few stragglers.

"Of course. You go on. And I'll take Brett home."

"Bless you, Lynn," said Kate. She helped Aubrey stand. Brett gathered up Aubrey's things and followed them at a discreet distance as they made their way to the parking lot.

Aubrey wept and staggered, guided by Kate's strong arm around her waist. They passed several late-night walkers as they went and, this being the South, most asked if they could help. Kate thanked each one and assured them they were fine.

At Aubrey's car, Kate demanded her keys and Aubrey dug them from her pocket and handed them over with a hand that shook. Kate unlocked the car, opened the passenger door and bundled Aubrey into the seat. She turned to find Brett standing by with Aubrey's chair and bag. They stowed them in the trunk and Kate sent Brett back to the nest.

Kate drove Aubrey's car, with the younger woman slumped in her seat, still crying, the short distance to Aubrey's house. Once inside, she guided her to a kitchen chair and made her sit. She started coffee brewing, then searched the cupboards until she found the small bottle of bourbon she knew was there. Waiting for the coffee, she sat across from Aubrey and took a napkin from the holder on the table, passing it to her friend.

"How the hell did this happen?" Aubrey wailed, mopping her face with the napkin. "It can't be true! Tom would never –" She broke into sobs again, and Kate waited, patting her arm.

Once Aubrey was a bit quieter, Kate spoke. "We don't know what happened," she said. "The police wouldn't tell me anything. I did ask about bail, but they said we can't do anything until tomorrow, at the earliest. Tom will be held overnight and arraigned sometime tomorrow. The judge will set bail then."

"Oh, God, Kate! Sexual assault of a *minor?* Tom would never do something like that! I know him!"

Kate leaned forward and put her hand on Kate's arm on the table. "Do you, Aubrey?"

Aubrey gasped and pulled her arm from Kate's grip. "What are you saying? Do you really think Tom –"

Kate interrupted, "I'm just saying we really don't know him. I can't believe Tom did this, either, but you have to admit we really know very little about him."

Aubrey stared open-mouthed at her friend. "You. Of all people. You're always telling me to give people the benefit of the doubt."

"And I still believe that, honey. But I want you to be prepared if it turns out … *wrong.*"

Aubrey nearly spat out the words. "You mean if it turns out Tom's a pedophile?"

Kate held up her hands. "Please, Aubrey. Just slow down. We don't know the details yet. I'm not judging Tom, I swear."

Aubrey folded her arms on the table and laid her head on them. She couldn't believe this was happening. It was all so unreal – seeing Tom being cuffed and taken away, hearing what Kate described as the charge against him.

She heard Kate pouring coffee and setting a mug in front of her. She raised her head, grasped the mug in both hands and took a groggy sip, surprised to taste bourbon in the coffee. The jolt of the liquor and the spreading warmth roused her. She sat up straighter.

"We have to do something," she said. "We have to get Tom out of jail. And find a good lawyer. I'll go online." She started to stand, but Kate stopped her.

"Aubrey, honey, it's 9:30. Sure, look for a lawyer, if you want, but you can't do anything tonight."

Aubrey sank back into the chair. "This is all so horrible, Kate. Just when things were going so well. For Tom. For me. I – I think I love him, Kate." She looked at her friend through tear-brimmed eyes. "How could I love a man who would attack a child? It's just not possible."

Kate was silent for half a minute, then she leaned forward, speaking forcefully. "Dammit, Aubrey. You're right! It's not possible. We've been teaching a long time – over fifty years between us – and teachers get to be good judges of character. You weren't bowled over by Tom's looks, and for sure *neither* of us were charmed by his fancy patter! You didn't even *like* him at the beginning. Then you got to know him. Both of us did, and we know he's a *good guy*."

Aubrey stared at Kate while the tears dried on her cheeks. When Kate's speech ended, she smiled tremulously. "Oh, thank you, Kate. I was starting to think I was alone in this."

"I don't know who accused Tom, but I have my suspicions."

Aubrey nodded. "Heather."

Kate smiled agreement. "We haven't seen her since night before last, when Tom walked her to her car. I don't know why Heather would make up a story like this, but I'm going to find out."

"How?"

"I don't know yet. But you go see Tom tomorrow and find out what you need to do to get him out. I'm going to pay a friendly teacher-student call on Heather." She smacked her palms on the table and stood. "We're going to get to the bottom of this."

Aubrey jumped up and hugged her friend. "Let me drive you back to your truck. I'm okay now, thanks to you."

At the beach, she took Kate's hand in both of hers. "I don't know how to thank you, Kate. I never felt so lost, not even when I found out Craig was cheating on me."

Kate waved off Aubrey's analogy. "Craig's an asshole. Tom's the keeper."

Aubrey nodded. A few moments ago, she hadn't known what to do next, or where to start. Now she felt a compelling need to do something she had done too seldom in her life. As soon as Kate's truck disappeared down the street, Aubrey put her hands together on the top of the steering wheel and rested her forehead on them.

"Dear Lord," she said aloud. "Please help Tom. And help me know what to do. You know even better than I that Tom is a good man, an *honorable* man. His life hasn't gone too smooth lately ..."

She faltered as it occurred to her that she and Tom had both been having rough times. Then they met, and it felt as if everything had changed. Now this thing had happened, and she had been knocked for a loop.

She remembered her father telling her that she was stronger than any of life's storms. Strong enough to get through her parents' divorce and the death of her beloved grandmother. And, although Pop wasn't around to see it, strong enough to survive losing him and her marriage. With God's help, she would get through this, too.

She hastily wiped the tears from her cheeks with her fingertips, folded her hands beneath her chin and finished her prayer. "I can't do it without you, Lord. But with your help, Tom and I will weather this storm. If you see me stumble, give me a kick in the pants, and I'll get back on track. Thank you, God. Amen."

She turned the key to start the ignition, already stronger.

"Brace yourself, storm. I'm coming at you."

Chapter 8

Nest 75, Day 60

In all the years she'd lived in Brunswick County, Aubrey had never been to the county jail in Bolivia. She'd been close, because most of the county government offices were there, but she had never really noticed the jail. It was one of a cluster of buildings in the complex; the bleakest one, although she reasoned any building would look bleak surrounded by a tall, chain-link fence topped with coils of razor wire.

While waiting in the visitor's room, she pressed her cold fingers to her eyes. She didn't want Tom to see she had been crying. It had been one of the worst nights of her life. Unable to sleep, she had alternated pacing the house with bouts of lying in bed weeping. Although heartened by Kate's support, she couldn't help crying every time she thought of her big man lying on a narrow bunk in a jail cell.

Besides which, selfishly, she missed his physical presence. After just one night together, she missed having him in her bed. She wanted his solid warmth against her back, his big hand resting on her hip or cupping her breast.

She looked around her at the room. There were others waiting, but only a few, as it was not quite time for the visits to begin. An older woman sat knitting in a corner. A young woman bounced a baby on her knee. An old man paced the room with the aid of a cane, muttering about "rules" and "damn bureaucrats."

Aubrey understood his frustration, but she was thankful to be a rule breaker on this occasion. Last night, she'd learned on the center's website that visitation at the jail must be scheduled online at least twenty-four hours in advance. The thought of not being able to talk to Tom about all this for more than a day was unbearable. She had decided to drive to Bolivia and speak directly to the people in charge of visitation.

It had turned out to be a lucky decision. The officer at the desk in the Detention Center lobby was a former student who had been delighted to see Aubrey. When Aubrey had explained the situation, the young woman had been sympathetic.

"We can make exceptions if there's a good reason. I'll let you talk to your friend this morning, Ms. Benson. And on your way out, just ask me to schedule the next visit."

"I hope another visit won't be necessary, Jenny, but thanks."

Aubrey was prepared to wait as long as necessary, but it was just over twenty minutes before another officer showed her to a booth containing a computer screen and telephone, and instructed her in their use. She knew from the website that she would not be able to touch him, but when his face flickered onto the screen, she automatically reached for him.

"Tom!"

"Oh, God, Aubrey. I can't believe you're here."

"You look terrible," she blurted out.

At the same instant, Tom said, "You've been crying."

She shook her head. "That's not what I meant to say."

It was true, however, that he didn't look good. Wearing an orange jumpsuit too tight for his big frame, he looked haggard, as though he'd slept no better than she.

"I'm sorry about all this, Aubrey."

"Sorry? It's not your fault, Tom. Did they tell you who made the accusation?"

He nodded. "Heather. Kate's student."

Just as she and Kate had suspected. "Did they give you any details?"

He looked away from the camera. "I don't want to say it, Aubrey. It's ... ugly."

Aubrey straightened, staring at the screen. "Tom. I'm only going to ask this once. Not because I need to hear it, but because you need to say it. Did you do anything to Heather?"

Tom looked back to the camera. His expression was bleak, but his voice was firm. "No, Aubrey. I never touched her. If she says I did, she's lying."

Aubrey took a deep breath and let it out. She did her best to smile. "Then we'll get it all sorted out, Tom. And we'll get you out of here. I promise. You've got me and Kate on your side."

Tom's jaw clenched. "Listen, Aubrey. I don't want you mixed up in this. I'll just stay here until –"

"You don't get to choose for me, Tom. I make my own decisions." She smiled. "Now tell me what they said."

Tom's face looked carved from granite. "Heather told them I walked her to her car Monday night, which is true. She said when she got in her car, I shoved her down across the seat and tried to pull her shorts off. When she resisted, I hit her. Then she kicked me hard enough to make me let go, and she slammed the door and took off."

"They really believe a sixteen-year-old girl could fight off a guy like you?"

He shrugged. His posture was soldier-straight, as always, but she read defeat in every line of his face.

"There's more," he said.

"More?"

"I was arrested a month-and-a-half ago for assaulting a police officer. They released me on my own recognizance, and the hearing is coming up in two weeks." He lowered his head for a moment, then straightened and met her shocked expression. "I was going to tell you,

Aubrey. I just … I wanted to get my shit together first. Get a job, a place to live, maybe even a car. So I wouldn't seem like such a loser."

Aubrey didn't know what to say. She looked at Tom, looked away, licked her lips and looked back again. "Tom. Assaulting a cop? I don't understand."

"It was One July, the fireworks on Oak Island for … I don't remember why they do theirs on the first."

"It's Oak Island Beach Day."

He nodded. "Okay. Anyway, I wasn't expecting them. I'd only been in town a couple of days. The beach was crowded. When it got dark, I went looking for a place to bunk down. I was in a narrow space between two businesses. You know that hardware store with the picnic table outside?" She nodded. "Well, I thought I could stretch out on the table for a few hours, until the beach got quiet. But then the fireworks started."

Suddenly, Aubrey realized what the firework display would have done to Tom. "Oh, God. Tom. The fireworks."

He nodded. "If I'd known … but I wasn't ready. I just hunkered down with my hands over my ears. Someone grabbed me. I thought … I don't know what I thought. I was back there, in that damned jeep. I just threw a punch. I didn't know it was a cop until too late."

"Didn't you tell them? Didn't you explain?"

"Yeah. Well, not right then. The one I punched was bleeding, and two other cops landed on me. I swear I didn't resist, but they were plenty mad, and they weren't exactly in the mood for explanations. That's when I lost my cell phone."

"And you were arrested?"

He nodded. "It was Friday night, and the courts were closed over the weekend. Monday was the Fourth, so I didn't get a preliminary hearing until Tuesday. The judge was understanding. That's why I got the OR. The public defender thinks she can get me a reduced charge based on my service record and –" he looked away again – "a mental eval. She figures I'll get time served and maybe some community service."

Aubrey thought for a minute. "Who's the public defender?"

"Her name is Rachel McDowd. Nice lady, but overworked. Hard to get hold of."

"What time is your arraignment?"

He shrugged. "Sometime today, is all I know."

"I'll see what I can find out."

"Damn it, Aubrey! I'm telling you to stay out of it!"

On the screen, Aubrey saw a guard move behind Tom. Tom turned and said something to the guard that Aubrey couldn't hear, and the guard nodded and moved away.

"Tom, I –"

"No, listen," he said. "This is nothing to do with you." He took a deep breath and his gaze shifted away from her face. "We had a good time together, and you're a nice person, but that's all it was ever going to be. Just one night."

Aubrey's heart sank. Had she been wrong, after all? Another lousy judgment call? She remembered asking Tom if she was his girlfriend, and he had said he didn't sleep with women he didn't care about. Now it seemed …

Wait a minute. She wasn't wrong about Tom. But he was surely wrong about her if he thought she was going to buy this noble routine. Here was the kick in the pants for which she'd prayed. She almost laughed out loud.

"Nice try, Tom, but I'm not leaving you to handle all this yourself. Everyone makes mistakes – and I've made some lulus – but you're not one of them. You've got people on your side again, like in the Army, and we're not just about to give up!"

With that, she hung up the phone and punched the icon to end the session, closing the screen on his surprised expression.

Aubrey was in the courtroom when a judge set Tom's bail at $20,000, which seemed a staggering sum. Aubrey knew that a bail bond company could help, but she had no experience with them.

When the officers shuttled Tom out the side door, he glanced back at her, and her heart broke at the look of resignation on his face. She did her best to give him a bright smile and reassuring nod. She was relieved when his features lightened and he gave her a slight smile in return. As awful as this experience was for her, she couldn't imagine what it was like for him.

A friend from church was a retired property attorney. She called him and he gave her the name of a bail bond company in Bolivia, as well as the phone number of Rachel McDowd, the public defender assigned to Tom's first assault charge. Anxious to get Tom out, she went to the bond company's office first.

An hour later, she drove back to the courthouse. She had left a $3,000 check with the bondsman and used her smartphone to transfer the money from her savings account to her checking. The bond was in process, and all she could do was wait. Meanwhile, she called Rachel McDowd and left a message on her voice mail.

As she sat in the waiting area, Aubrey's stomach gurgled, and she remembered she'd had nothing to eat since the dinner with Tom the previous night. It was nearly two, but she decided to wait. What if they called her name and she was in the cafeteria, or in the vending machine area?

Her cell phone rang. Kate returning her call.

"How's it going?" asked her friend.

"Okay, I guess. Now I'm just waiting for them to bring him out. But, Kate, it's so awful. He seems so … down."

"Of course, he does. Just remind him he's got a couple of teachers on his side, and teachers don't give up."

"Did you talk to Heather?"

"No. I went to her house, but her mom wouldn't let me in. She's kind of screwy – her mom, I mean. Kept saying I'd have to wait until Heather's dad was home. But I saw Heather in the background. She stuck her head around the wall she was lurking behind. Aubrey, she's got a big, ugly bruise on the side of her face."

"Oh, God, Kate."

"Bree, all that means is that *someone* hit her. Doesn't mean it was Tom."

"I know it wasn't Tom," Aubrey said with asperity. She took a deep breath and continued more calmly. "But it doesn't help his case."

"True. Have you talked to the PD yet?"

"I left a message for her to call me. I'm making notes about what to tell her. I think – oh, Kate! Here he comes!"

She disconnected the call and stood as an officer led Tom into the waiting room. He was wearing the clothes he'd had on at the time of his arrest, and she wished she had thought to bring something fresh for him to wear.

She rushed to him, but his expression and the slight shake of his head warned her not to be too demonstrative. She settled for taking his hand to lead him outside. On the sidewalk, she wanted to hug him, but he quickly asked, "Where's your car?"

It wasn't far, and she unlocked the doors as they hurried toward it. He was still holding her hand, and he pulled her along behind him as he went to the passenger side. He opened the door, sat and tugged her down into his lap. He held her close, his face in her hair.

"Aubrey," he said, and again, "Aubrey. God, I needed this."

"Oh, Tom," she said, trying to hold back tears. "What a horrible day. I missed you so much."

With shock, it occurred to her that it hadn't been twenty-four hours since they were together at her house. He must have been thinking the same thing, for he said, "This time yesterday, we were in this car, on our way to Wilmington. It feels like a year ago."

"At least," she agreed.

He took her face in his hands and searched her eyes for a long moment, then kissed her. She felt her stomach flip and her blood race. Her arms were around his neck and her hands in his hair. The kiss was passionate, hard, and she could feel that he was, too. He groaned and murmured against her lips.

"I shouldn't involve you in this cluster f–" He stopped and took a breath. "Sorry. I mean, in this mess. It would be better for you if you just let me get my stuff from your house and go back to the beach."

"No way," she said, laughing shakily. "I signed a dozen papers at the courthouse saying you're living at my address. You don't want to get me in trouble, do you?"

He rested his cheek against the side of her head and sighed. "I'm afraid I've already done that, sugar. How much did you pay to get me out?"

She kissed the side of his neck and felt new stirrings beneath her thighs. "I think we'd better get home before we *both* get arrested." She slipped from his lap through the still-open door. While she jogged around the back of the car, he leaned across and opened the driver's door.

To stall, she told him about Kate's visit to the Carson's house, and Heather's bruised face, and about leaving a message with Rachel McDowd. They were out of the parking lot and on their way to Oak Island when he asked again about the bond money.

"I have to know, Aubrey. I'm going to pay you back, you know. Every penny. So how much?"

She took a breath. "Three thousand."

"Damn." He blew a long breath through pursed lips. "Did you have that much?"

"Yes, but it kind of emptied my savings, so I'm afraid we'll have to stick with the PD."

"She knows her stuff," he said. There was a long silence, then he added. "I could have stayed in jail, Aubrey. I was okay in there."

She glanced over and saw him looking out his window, his arms folded over his chest.

"No, you couldn't stay there," she insisted. "We need to work together to figure this out."

He was silent the rest of the drive home. When they reached her house, he took a shower in the guest bathroom while she made sandwiches. She knew he would have been given lunch at the detention center, but she didn't know whether he'd eaten it.

He sat at the table in fresh clothes and glumly ate the sandwich, responding only when Aubrey asked a direct question. She felt a little impatient over his return to his former reticence, but she reminded herself that he'd been through a lot since last night.

She knew he'd been humiliated and, beyond that, now felt indebted to her. A sense of obligation was the last thing she wanted from him. She wanted him to feel they were in this together, a team.

How do you make someone feel accepted? It was the sort of issue with which teachers often grappled, and she was sure she could put her experience to bear on the problem.

Tom got up and carried his plate to the sink, washed it and put it in the drainer to dry. "I feel like taking a walk. Alone," he said, without turning around. "Do you mind?"

She looked up, dumbfounded. "Of course, I don't mind. Why would –" She closed her mouth. This was not a time to be confrontational.

Within a few minutes of his departure, Aubrey's cell phone rang. It was Kate again.

"How's it going, Bree?"

"I told him I had to pay three grand to bond him out. It's a blow to his pride, but he's processing it." She sighed. "He was so glad to be out of that place, Kate. And glad to be with me. But it's hard for a man like Tom, you know?"

"I know. Hang in there. He'll come around. Meanwhile, I went to see Brett."

Aubrey carried her plate to the sink and stood with her back against the counter. "Did you learn anything?"

"Not much we didn't already know. He said the police have already talked to him. He talked with a few of her friends, and they said that Heather told them she got in very late the night Tom walked her to her car. She went straight to bed, but the next morning, her mom freaked when she saw the bruises on Heather's face and arms. She told her mom she'd been attacked, but she didn't know the guy."

"Didn't know him? Then what –?"

"But when her dad got home that night, she told her parents it was Tom. She didn't go to the nest that night, of course, but she told the police where it was."

"That means something," Aubrey conjectured. "That she said she didn't know her attacker, then blamed Tom."

"She also told the police she knew Tom would be at the nest because he was 'stalking' the pretty English teacher."

"What?" Aubrey was aghast. "*Stalking?*"

"That's what Brett said she told the police. Of course, we're getting all this third-hand, don't forget."

"Well, I can fix that impression," she said. "If anyone was stalking anyone, *I* was stalking Tom."

"I wish I knew more about Heather. She's kind of an unknown factor in this equation," Kate mused. "Her mom seems a little flaky, but it could be that she's just freaked out about Heather being attacked."

Aubrey snapped her fingers. "Well, we have a source on the inside, don't we?"

"You mean Brett? I already –"

"I mean Sunny. She's not close to Heather, but she can surely find out something."

"Well, why not?" Kate asked. "We've got nothing to lose by asking."

Aubrey said goodbye to Kate and called Sunny. From the sounds in the background, Aubrey could tell her daughter was at the pool.

"Hi, honey! Having a good time?"

"Sure. How about you? Anything new?"

Yes, my new boyfriend was arrested last night for attacking a child and I spent all day getting him out of jail. But all Aubrey said was, "Just getting ready for school to start."

Sunny groaned. "Don't remind me!"

Aubrey knew Sunny liked school, so she wasn't put off. "Say, hon, do you by any chance know a girl named Heather Carson? She's going to be a junior this year."

"Um. Well. She's a year ahead of me, but I know who she is. Barely. Why?"

"Oh, someone was asking if she would be a good mentor for one of the incoming freshmen, and I had to admit I don't know her." Aubrey bit her lip. She hated lying to Sunny, but she wasn't ready to bring her into this.

"She's kinda new. I think she just moved here last year. She hangs around with the nerds, so maybe she's smart enough to be a mentor. Did I tell you that me and Diane and Kim are going to be greeters at freshman orientation? We have to dress nice and wear these lame badges, but we get to show groups of ninth graders all over the school and try and make them not be so scared. I remember when I started at South last year. I was so freaked!"

"That's great, honey! You'll be terrific at that. Those freshmen will be so impressed. When you get home, I'll help you pick out something really cool to wear. Or maybe we can go shopping!"

"Sure," Sunny answered. "But I think I'm going to wear the skirt and blouse I bought at Macy's with Maya."

Aubrey swallowed her disappointment. "How are things going with her?"

"All right, I guess. She's being nice, but kind of phony." Sunny had lowered her voice, so Aubrey guessed Maya was somewhere nearby.

"Just remember what I told you, sweetie. You can last another couple weeks." She took a deep breath and returned to the reason for the call. "So, Heather's new and nerdy. Anything else?"

"There was a rumor going around a couple of months ago that she was, like, crushing hard on one of the football players. She was making kind of a fool of herself. I mean, like the guy's *uber* popular and he's gonna be a senior this year! Why would he be interested in her? But she kept, like, hanging around him in the cafeteria and stuff. I mean, get a grip!"

Aubrey was unable to keep from wincing at her daughter's overuse of the word "like," but she let it go this time. Normally, Sunny adhered to her mother's rules about grammar, but she was no doubt within earshot of other kids her age. Aubrey knew the passion for fitting in to which most teens devoted themselves.

"Do you know the football player's name, Sunny?"

Sunny didn't question her mother's reason for wanting to know facts seemingly irrelevant to the mentoring question. "No, but I'm sure Diane knows. She's a total jock freak. Want me to find out?"

Aubrey tried to sound casual. "Oh, if you happen to talk to Diane, you could ask her." She knew Sunny spoke to Diane by phone or text several times a day.

After chatting a minute longer with Sunny, she called Rachel McDowd's number again, and was surprised when the public defender answered her own line. Ms. McDowd seemed a bit harried, but she was friendly enough, and said she could see Tom the next day, but the appointment would have to be early and brief. Aubrey agreed to have him in her office in Bolivia by eight.

She hung up and checked the time on her phone. Tom had been gone nearly two hours. She looked out the kitchen window toward the street, then out the living room window into the back yard. No sign of him. In a moment of panic, she ran to her bedroom, relieved to see his backpack in the chair.

She could think of only one place to look for him. She grabbed her handbag and keys and went out to her car. Minutes later, she was walking along the beach toward the house under construction. He was sitting on a slight rise of sand just in front of the dunes, arms around his open knees, staring out to sea.

As she approached, he spoke without looking around. "This isn't going to work, Aubrey."

She sat beside him, her legs curled to one side, her shoulder leaning against his. "What isn't?"

"You and me." He looked at her, eyes hidden behind dark glasses. "You don't need this kind of trouble in your life."

"Like I said, that's my choice to make." She looked at his hands with his fingers laced together, so strong but so gentle. How could he ever hurt someone with those hands, especially a child? She put her hand over his, and he shifted his thumb to enclose her wrist.

"You've got to think of Sunny," he insisted.

"I am. How can I tell my child to stand up for what's right, and not to let innocent people be wrongly accused, if I cut and run when taking a stand becomes inconvenient? I can't be the only influence in Sunny's life, so I damn sure better be the truest."

He was silent for a long moment, and his voice was gruff when he said, "You are the truest person I know, Aubrey."

She felt joy like a sudden ache under her ribs. "Let's go home," she said.

Although he said nothing else, he held her hand on the way back to the car. Over a dinner of macaroni and cheese and a green salad, she told him about the appointment with Rachel McDowd.

"I'd like it if you were there when I talk to her," he said.

"Of course." She was pleased he'd asked. She'd been prepared to wait in the reception area, or even in her car, if he'd wanted to talk to his lawyer in private.

After they washed the dishes, Aubrey got ready for the beach, and they went to the turtle nest together. Kate greeted Tom with a big hug that seemed to surprise him. Brett was there, too.

Aubrey hadn't considered the possibility that Heather might have been there and was relieved she wasn't. It was awkward enough with Brett. He was clearly unnerved to be around Tom, but they all forgot the circumstances when five little turtles came out of the sand shortly after sunset. They waited in the dark for more, with a dozen onlookers hanging around.

Tom, after helping Aubrey guard the five hatchlings into the water, sat apart from the rest of the group. Kate answered questions from the visitors, and Brett roamed restlessly up and down the runway. Every time Aubrey glanced at Tom, he seemed to be staring at the boy, but his expression was unreadable in the dark.

In the car, two hours later, she asked him why he'd been so focused on Brett.

"Something's up with him," Tom said.

She started the car and waited for Kate to back out of the parking space next to hers. "What do you mean?"

"If I had a friend who'd been attacked by some guy, I couldn't just hang around with him later and not want to have it out with him."

"Oh, come on, Tom. Did you really expect Brett to confront *you*?"

"No, but I expected him to *want* to confront me. He acted uncomfortable and embarrassed, not angry and resentful. Why?"

She turned the car onto Oak Island Drive. There was little traffic at this late hour. "Maybe he doesn't care about Heather all that much."

"No. He's crazy about her. She's not interested in him, but he definitely likes her." He stared out the window. "I have the feeling he knows damn well I didn't attack Heather, and he's jumpy around me because he knows she lied."

She pulled into the carport, shut off the engine and turned to him in the dark car. "Really?"

"Yep. Basically, he's a decent kid, and he doesn't like covering for Heather, even if he is in love with her." He opened his door and climbed out, then got her things out of the back seat.

"So, maybe we need to lean on Brett a little more," Aubrey said, shutting her car door behind her.

Tom moved up beside her into the pool of light from the porch lamp. "Or maybe you need to stay out of it, detective."

"Oh, you're no fun," she said, trying to tease him into a better humor, but he wouldn't rise to the bait.

Inside, Tom fixed the coffee while Aubrey showered, but when she got back to the kitchen, he wasn't there. A moment later, she heard the shower running in the guest bathroom. She poured two cups of coffee and sat at the table, but when the bathroom door opened, he went the other way, down the hall and into Sunny's room, closing the door behind him.

Aubrey waited for several minutes, but he didn't return. At first, she was hurt. Then she was angry. He knew she was in the kitchen, waiting for him, and he was deliberately snubbing her. Was he trying to distance himself from her, to keep her from being any more involved than she already was?

The hell with that, she thought. *I'm in this business, and I intend to see it through.*

At least his bedroom door wasn't locked. He probably didn't expect her to be that bold. When she slammed open the door, he rolled onto his back and sat up, clearly surprised.

"Listen up, buster," she said, pulling her tee-shirt off over her head as she advanced on him. "I won't be stood up in my own house."

She climbed onto the bed, crouched, and wrapped her arms around his neck. "Remember what you said to me the other night? If you don't want me, just tell me to stop, and I'll leave you alone."

"If I don't want you?" He pulled her tight against him. "I never wanted anyone so much. I was just trying to –"

"I know. But we're past that point." She kissed him. "You're going to let me help you with this," she said. "And," she added, reaching under the covers, "you're going to let me help you with *this*."

"Oh, yes." He groaned. "Whatever you say, woman. Just keep doing that."

She did, amazed at how quickly he swelled and hardened in her hand. His hands clutched her breasts, squeezing in time with the rhythm of her strokes. Their mouths crashed together, clumsy in their eagerness. She seized his lower lip in her teeth, tugging. He pinched her nipples, twisting lightly, then harder, until she cried out in climax.

On his back, he took hold of her hips and dragged her on top of him. She writhed against him, desperate for greater contact. She pushed herself into a crouch over him and dug her nails into his wide chest. Hands under her buttocks, he lifted her up and impaled her on his rigid flesh. She squealed, tossing her hair, squirming now from the pressure. But when he circled her waist with his strong hands and began to lift her up, she pried his fingers loose and pressed down more firmly.

"No, Aubrey," he insisted. "Stop doing that." He was so much stronger than she, and he pulled her onto the bed beside him, breaking the contact. "Sorry, baby," he whispered, panting. "We forgot something."

"Oh, shit," she said, realization dawning. "Where are they?"

"My pack. Your room."

"I'll get them."

He brought the back of her hand to his mouth and kissed it. "Bless you," he said.

Aubrey darted across the hall and dumped his backpack out on the bed, pawing through the contents. She found the precious foil packets and raced back to his bed. She tore one open and slapped his hand away when he reached for it.

"I'm doing this," she said.

"Holy crap," he said, chuckling. "I'm in so much trouble."

She was out of practice, which made it take longer. By the time he was safely sheathed, his fists were clenched in the bedsheets, and he was sweating and breathing hard.

"Oh, you're going to pay for that," he said, flipping her onto her back. He pulled her long legs over his shoulders and bent to worry her nipples with his teeth.

She closed her eyes, smiling. *This is going to be so good,* she thought. She shivered, trying to relax her muscles. She felt his heat pressing against her, opening her, and her back arched reflexively.

"Tom!" She opened her eyes to see him staring intently down at her. How she loved his face, the carved planes of his cheeks and jaws, the fierce blue of his eyes. The way his expression said he wanted her, needed to be inside her, but would take care not to hurt her, at whatever cost to himself.

She clutched his arms and moved her hips. "More," she whispered. "More."

He gave her more – much more. And later, wrapped together in mutual satisfaction, they exchanged light touches, gentle kisses, quiet laughter over very private jokes. His muscled arm was her pillow; her narrow waist the resting place for his hand.

"I can't believe," he said, suddenly serious, "that last night I was lying in a jail cell, thinking my life couldn't get much worse. And that was after an amazing night and day with you. These last three days – it's been very high, very low, and now, back in the clouds again."

"I know." She reached over to stroke his cheek. "To be that happy, and then that miserable." She turned her head to look at him. "It makes it hard to trust the future."

"I'm sorry, Aubrey," he said. "My life right now –"

She pressed her fingers to his lips. "But I trust *you*, Tom. And I want you to trust me."

"I do trust you. No one has ever been this good to me. This kind."

It's not kindness, she thought. *It's love.* But she couldn't say that to him. It was too soon. *Don't be first,* she cautioned herself. *Wait.*

"I don't know about the kind part," she said. "I wasn't all that kind to you in the beginning, if you remember."

He chuckled, lightly cupping her breast. "I hope you didn't think you had to have sex with me to make up for it," he said.

"Of course not," she said lightly. "I had sex with you for fixing the carport roof."

"Well, that's only fair. It was a real mess. What will you give me for mowing half the lawn?"

She laughed. "Ask me when you finish it. Right now, we should get some sleep," she said. "We have an early appointment tomorrow."

She sat up and reached to the foot of the bed for the covers, drawing them up and over them both. He tucked her more firmly against his body and rested his cheek against the top of her head. His breath warm in her hair was the last thing she felt before falling asleep.

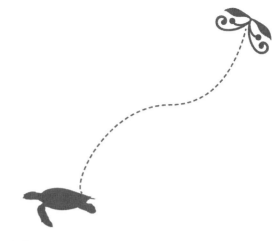

Chapter 9

Nest 75, Day 61

"I'm sorry I don't have a nicer view," Rachel McDowd said, smiling.

Tom turned from the window and the grim view of the Brunswick Detention Center. "It's not such a bad place," he said. "But I'd just as soon not go there again."

"Can't blame you for that." She motioned to the two chairs in front of the desk in her tiny office. The small space was crammed with filing cabinets and cardboard boxes overflowing with file folders.

Once Tom and Aubrey were settled, the public defender summarized the current charges against Tom.

According to the police report, Heather alleged that after Tom walked her to her car shortly before midnight last Monday night, he attacked and attempted to rape her, but she fought him off and escaped in her car. When she got home, she didn't wake her parents, but the next morning, her mother discovered severe bruises on Heather's arms and face. Heather refused to tell her mother anything. Mrs.

Carson kept Heather home Tuesday and wouldn't let her go to the turtle nest that night.

On Wednesday morning, when pressed, Heather told her parents this "big homeless guy at the beach" had tried to rape her, and they called the police. When the detective interviewed her, she first claimed she couldn't identify her attacker, just repeated that it was a "big guy." She finally broke down and said she didn't know the man's name or location, but he was the man who had been hanging around the turtle nest every night. She was sure he would be back at the turtle nest that evening because he was "stalking" Ms. Benson, the English teacher who volunteered there.

Tom sat in grim silence; they had both heard some variation of this story before. But Aubrey was compelled to speak.

"Tom wasn't stalking me," she insisted. "He was helping us at the nest. And he never showed any interest in Heather."

The public defender added that the police had matched his description with a man arrested weeks earlier for assault on a police officer, which is how they knew his name. At that point, they had obtained an arrest warrant for Tom.

"At this point," Ms. McDowd said, "Heather's case is a matter of he-said-she-said. While there's certainly physical evidence that Heather was attacked, there's nothing to prove Tom was her attacker. Except, of course, the fact that he accompanied Heather to her car that night, and none of you saw him again until the next day. When Tom was arrested Wednesday evening and taken into custody, he was examined at the detention center for any sign of a defensive attack. There were what appeared to be fingernail marks on his upper arms and back, *not* consistent with Heather's story, which Tom said he acquired elsewhere, but declined to be specific."

"I can be specific," Aubrey said. She blushed furiously, but added, "There are some new marks today from the same source."

Ms. McDowd leaned back in her chair and picked up a piece of paper. "Tom might not have been arrested, only questioned, except for this previous assault charge, which is still pending."

"There's a good explanation for that, too," Aubrey began.

"Yes, I know about that. I told Tom I don't think it will amount to much, but it gives Heather's accusation more credibility."

Aubrey made a scoffing sound, and Tom put his hand on her knee.

"When I was arrested," Tom said, "I couldn't figure who would have made that kind of accusation against me, Ms. McDowd. When they said it was Heather, I was blown away. I walked her to her car, stood by while she started up and drove off. Then I went back to my usual spot on the beach and bedded down. I never touched her, not even when we walked through the dunes where the sand is deep. I didn't even open her car door, just stood back while she got in, started her car and drove away. I've learned over the years that some women, especially young ones, are intimidated by my size, so I make of point of not looming over them, or touching them."

The lawyer looked at Tom's hand on Aubrey's knee, and he pulled it away.

Aubrey was indignant. "It's a little different with me, Ms. McDowd. I *like* Tom touching me, and he knows it."

"Aubrey ..." Tom soothed, and Ms. McDowd chuckled ruefully.

"Sorry, guys. That was reflex. I'm aware that you two have a close relationship. And that could work in our favor. Ms. Benson is a teacher and a respected member of the community." She looked directly at Aubrey. "On the other hand, a less than favorable outcome could damage Ms. Benson's reputation. Are you prepared for that?"

Tom made an involuntary movement, but Aubrey focused on the public defender. "Yes, I am, Ms. McDowd," she said. "But I'm *not* prepared for a 'less than favorable outcome.'"

The lawyer nodded. "At this point, the prosecutor's case is pretty weak," she said. "I expect to win. And I'd appreciate it if you called me Rachel."

The two women smiled at each other, but Tom's expression was troubled.

"If this goes to trial, would Aubrey have to testify?" he asked.

"Definitely," Rachel said. "If the prosecution doesn't call her first, I'd be calling her."

"And they could ask her anything?"

Rachel leaned forward, elbows on her desk. "Anything material. If it's not material, I would object, and the judge would rule their question out. Is there a problem, Tom?"

"I just don't want Aubrey dragged into this," he said. "I don't know why Heather lied, or who actually hit her, but Aubrey had nothing to do with any of it. She was just trying to help the sea turtles, and ended up helping me, too."

"Tom," Aubrey said, putting her hand on his arm. "It'll be okay. I don't mind. I'm proud of our friendship and proud of you."

Rachel spoke up. "I really don't think it will go to trial, Tom. I expect the –"

Tom interrupted. "I won't plea bargain. I won't say I hit that girl. I'd rather go to prison."

Rachel shook her head. "I really expect the D.A. to drop the charges for lack of evidence. Especially considering your exemplary military record. When the judge sees your list of medals and commendations, versus a hysterical sixteen-year-old, he'll make the whole thing go away. Of course, that still leaves the assault against the cop."

"But –" Aubrey began.

Rachel waved her off. "I know. There's a good explanation for that. I plan to talk to the officer myself." Brows lowered, she stared at Tom. "Meanwhile, stay out of trouble. It would be good if you could get a job."

"He's got a job," Aubrey said. "He starts Monday."

"Great!" Rachel said. "And it wouldn't hurt to get a psych eval on the earlier assault charge. Just someone to say that loud noises are a problem for you, and why that is. We'd get both reason and sympathy in our column with that. I'll call a doctor I know in Wilmington and get you an appointment."

"Whatever you think best," Aubrey assured her.

Rachel stood and walked around the desk. "Good. Then I'll let you two go. I have another appointment at nine, and a few calls to make first."

They rose to shake her hand, then left her office. Aubrey was buoyant, sure that Rachel McDowd would make it all work out in their favor. She squeezed Tom's hand and smiled up at him as they headed for the door, dismayed to see his expression once again troubled and dark.

"Tom? Aren't you excited? Rachel thinks this will all go away. You're starting work Monday. Things are looking up!" She shook his arm with both hands, and he smiled tentatively as he opened the office door for her.

"What?" she asked, holding his hand as they crossed the parking lot. "Don't you agree this is good news?"

He stopped and looked down at her, stroking her upper arm with his free hand. "Yes, Aubrey. Most of it sounds fine."

"Then what's wrong? Is it the psych evaluation?"

He shook his head and started walking slowly toward the car. She automatically pressed the remote to unlock the doors, but her attention was centered on his profile.

"I can stand the psych eval. I had a couple of those when I was still in the Army."

He held her door open while she stepped into the car. She started the engine and maxed the AC while he walked around to the passenger side.

In the car, he said, "I don't like the idea of you being questioned in court. I'll bet you never in your life had to do that." He jerked the shoulder belt across his chest and snapped it in place. "Not until I came along."

I'm thankful every day that you came along, she thought. Aloud, she said, "It probably won't come to that but, if it does, I'm not worried about it."

She started to put the car in reverse, but he put his hand over hers on the shift. "You're something else, Aubrey," he said softly. "I've never known anyone like you."

She flashed her most brilliant smile at him. "You just keep thinking that, soldier boy, and we'll get along just fine."

She waited until they were on the highway before she told him what she'd discovered that morning. When he went to make coffee, she had gone to her room and had found the contents of his backpack scattered across her bed, where she'd left them after locating the condoms the night before.

Among the items was a small leather case with what looked like jewelry spilling out. She opened it and found several medals and ribbons, along with a sheaf of papers. Too curious to resist, she had read two or three of the documents. Then Tom had shouted that the coffee was ready, and she hurriedly stuffed the papers and medals in the case and put it with everything else into his backpack.

"You're a hero, Tom," she told him as she drove. "Of course, all the men and women who serve over there are heroes, but those papers said that you saved a wounded man's life by refusing to leave a bombed-out house without him. And another one said you broke cover to shoot a sniper who had your men pinned down."

Tom shook his head. "I did what I was trained to do, Aubrey. Like you said, all the soldiers over there –"

"Damn it, Tom, you're a hero! Stop denying it!"

He grinned and reached over to squeeze her shoulder. "You just keep thinking that, teacher, and we'll get along just fine."

As they were letting themselves into Aubrey's house, her cell phone rang. It was Kate, letting them know they would excavate Nest 75 that evening. She asked Aubrey how everything was going, but Aubrey was reluctant to go into detail. She just said, "Not too bad." Kate seemed to understand and didn't press her.

Tom went outside to finish mowing the lawn, while Aubrey went to her room to change. She was in panties and bra when her phone rang again.

"Sunny! How are you, sweetie?"

"Hi, Mom! I'm great. There's no school tomorrow!"

It was an old joke between them – a cheer they would say to each other every night at bedtime during the summer break – and Aubrey laughed to know Sunny remembered it.

"We won't be able to say that much longer, Sunny-bear. How's everything going for you at your dad's?"

"Oh. Okay. I'm kinda looking forward to moving back in with you."

"Imagine that," Aubrey said, laughing. "Look, honey, I'm sorry if things aren't going so well. But you know you can move back home any day." She pulled the curtain back a little on the bedroom window. Tom was mowing the lawn, shirtless. She caught her breath, captivated anew by his physical splendor.

Aubrey was a tiny bit ashamed of the relief she felt when Sunny said, "No, that's okay. I'll wait until school starts."

"Whatever you want, angel."

"Hey, Mom, I asked Diane about that girl, Heather."

"Yes?"

"That football player she loves is Ricky Stout, from Boiling Spring Lakes. Like I said, he's a senior this year, and Diane says he's really nice."

Diane thinks every cute boy is "really nice," Aubrey was tempted to say. But boy-crazy Diane was Sunny's best friend, so she said only, "Well, thanks for letting me know, Sunny-bear."

They chatted for a few more minutes, then disconnected. Aubrey took pencil and paper from her bedside table and was writing "Ricky Stout, BSL" just as Tom came into the room.

"Tom," she said, "listen to this. Heather's nuts about a football player named Ricky Stout."

"So?" He stood behind her and lifted the hair from her shoulders to kiss the back of her neck.

"So, a football player would be a 'big guy,' right?"

"Mmmm." He unhooked her bra and slid the straps down her arms. "Well, *this* big guy just finished mowing your lawn."

"No, wait, Tom." She couldn't concentrate with him kissing her shoulders like that. "Maybe Heather really was hit by a 'big guy,' but the big guy who hit her was this football player."

The bra, unhooked, fell to the floor. "And maybe you didn't hear me," he said, slipping his hands around her to cup her breasts. He kissed her neck between words. "I. Mowed. The. Lawn."

"Hmm? What?" Aubrey wanted to talk about Ricky Stout, but she couldn't remember what was important about him. Not with Tom tweaking her nipples that way.

"And what do I get when I mow the lawn?" he reminded her.

She dropped the note onto the table and put her hands over his on her breasts. She leaned her head back against his chest. He smelled like sweat and gasoline and newly cut grass. Her knees felt wobbly.

"I should take a shower first," he said.

She turned in his arms and slid her arms around his neck, rubbing herself against him. "No, you should take *me* first." She kissed him, letting her head drop back as he bent into the kiss, his tongue making forays into her mouth. She felt his hands undoing the front of his jeans.

He drew back enough to whisper, "Where'd you put our little friends?"

She tapped the top of the bedside table. "Right here in the drawer. Handy."

He smiled. When she had bundled up the sheets from Sunny's bed that morning, she had informed him in no uncertain terms that he was to sleep in her bed from now on. Then she'd made a big show of once again distributing his belongings in her bedroom and bathroom, while he watched in amusement.

She shivered when she heard him slide the zipper down. Impatient, she knelt and pulled his jeans and boxers down. He moaned and swayed slightly as she used her hands and mouth on him.

"Holy shit," he whispered. "I am mowing that damn lawn every damn day."

As her ministrations grew more fervent, he kicked free of his clothes and shifted his feet to keep his balance. Finally, he bent and seized her under her arms, pulling her into his embrace. He hugged her tightly as he whispered, "I'm about to fall over, like a big old tree in a windstorm."

"Well, fall on me," she said.

He lifted her and settled her on the bed with him, stripping off her panties in one swift move. They were each becoming familiar with the other's bodies, as well as their preferences and the meaning behind the sounds each one made. He clearly knew she loved to stroke his arms and shoulders, and he allowed her as much time as she wanted to pet him. She knew he enjoyed suckling at her breasts, and the sensation aroused her as well. She loved the way he hissed in his breath when she drew her fingernails lightly along his rigid length. He had come to accept the sounds she made when he entered her as cries of pleasure, not distress.

And in the quiet time they spent together afterward, he let her rest on him, seeming content as long as she was comfortable. Aubrey delighted in rising and falling with each breath from his broad chest.

So, they talked, first about inconsequential things. Who was the better writer, Hemingway or Harper Lee? What is your favorite kind of music to listen to in the car? Did you have a pet when you were a child?

She told him about her worst year ever: four years ago, when her father had died, and she and Craig had divorced. She said, "Pop took us in when I left Craig, and it was such a blessing for all of us. When Pop got sick, I was there to take care of him, and Sunny spent a lot of time with *her* dad. A month after Pop's death, I got the final decree of divorce. Not Craig's fault – just the timing. I didn't regret leaving him, but I did feel like such a failure."

"That wasn't failure," he insisted. "That was courage."

Tom told her about growing up in Georgia with no father. His dad had died in a farm accident when Tom was five. His flighty mother, unable to manage the farm alone, had moved from one man to the next. "She never beat me, but she let them hit me whenever they wanted, and for any reason. I grew fast. Started hitting back when I was nine or ten. By the time I was twelve, I could give about as good as I got, and they mostly left me alone."

"Oh, Tom," she whispered. "I'm so sorry."

He went on to tell her how he left home at sixteen and worked in strawberry fields in north Georgia and on shrimp boats in the gulf until he was eighteen. He joined the service, intending it to be a career.

"Kate was saying that you'd make a good teacher," Aubrey told him. "And I agree."

He scoffed. "Even with the little bit of college I've had, what with working full time, it would take at least three years to get a degree."

"So?"

"So, in three years I'll be thirty-seven."

"And how old will you be in three years if you *don't* go back to school?"

He rolled her onto her back, and himself on top of her. "You're kind of a smartass, you know?"

"I know. It's one of the things I like best about me."

He kissed her. "Know what I like best?"

"What?" She held her breath, expecting something sexy or romantic.

"Your tuna sandwiches." He rolled off her and sat on the edge of the bed.

She pretended to be insulted. "Really? Tuna sandwiches? That's what you like best?"

He cocked his head to one side and appeared to be considering. "Well, now that you mention it, that's the *only* thing." He gave her a comically innocent look. "But they *are* really good."

She poked at him with her foot. He grabbed her ankle and kissed her arch.

"And I'm hungry," he said. "Why don't you fix lunch while I take a shower?"

She watched him walk away from the bed. "Mmmm," she murmured, thinking this was a view she could enjoy every day.

"Get your mind out of the gutter, woman," he said, closing the bathroom door.

Dressed in shorts and tee-shirt, she stood at the counter in the kitchen, mixing canned tuna, mayo, mustard, parsley, chopped celery and white pepper in a bowl. There was a brief sound at the side door, and a moment later, Sunny came rushing in.

"Mom! Hi!" She hugged her mother and peered into the bowl Aubrey was holding. "Yum! Tuna fish! Yours is the best."

Aubrey gave a shaky laugh. "So I've been told," she said.

"Hey, Aubrey," said Craig.

Aubrey turned, startled to see her ex-husband – although she knew *someone* had brought Sunny to Oak Island – and dismayed to see Craig's girlfriend behind him.

Fiancée, she corrected herself mentally.

"Hey, Aubrey," said Maya in that little-girl voice Aubrey found so annoying. She was dressed in white short-shorts and a coral halter top that exposed more than it concealed.

"We came to get my snorkeling gear," Sunny informed her. "Dad's taking us to the Keys next week."

Aubrey looked from Sunny to Craig, not sure how she was supposed to respond. Taking her daughter that far away was one of those things she had insisted Craig consult her about, before making promises to Sunny.

"Now, don't get all whiny about it," Craig said. "It came up unexpectedly. An old client invited us down, and I thought, why the hell not?"

She saw Craig's expression change, and turned to look behind her. Tom was crossing the open space between the hall and the kitchen. He was fully dressed, thank goodness, but his hair was still wet and his feet were bare.

"Well, what a surprise," Craig said, smirking. He introduced Maya and Tom, frowning when Maya began to gush over the big man, tossing her blond hair and posing with hands on hips. "Go get your gear, Sunny," he said to his daughter.

Sunny was staring at her mother, embarrassment plain on her face. She pulled free of her mother's arm and moved to sidle around Tom, who greeted her in a friendly tone.

"Hi," she muttered, scurrying past him toward the hall.

The four adults made awkward and trivial conversation for the few minutes it took for Sunny to return, snorkeling bag in hand.

"Bye, Mom. I'll call you." Avoiding eye contact, she flapped her hand at Aubrey and dashed for the door. Craig looked at Maya and jerked his head toward the exit. She gave one last lingering look at Tom before following Sunny.

"Craig, listen ..." Aubrey said, stepping toward her ex-husband.

"See you soon, Aubrey," he said, turning to the door.

She followed him through the utility room and down the steps to the carport.

"Craig, wait," she said.

He stopped and turned to her with a sneer on his face. "Congratulations," he said. "Glad you finally climbed off your pedestal to join the rest of us sinners."

It took all her will to keep her voice calm. "How is this situation any different from you and Maya?" she asked.

"Oh, it isn't," he said. "I have to say, I wouldn't have thought that monosyllabic Tarzan would be your type. But at least you no longer occupy that moral high ground you love to preach from." He turned his back and walked to his car, chuckling over his own wit.

Aubrey could do nothing but wave at her daughter as Craig backed his BMW out of her driveway and into the street. Sunny returned the wave without enthusiasm.

In the house, Tom was seated at the kitchen table.

"Sorry, babe," he said as she came in. "When I got out of the shower, I heard voices, so I got dressed and came out to see what was going on. If I'd known it was them, I'd have stayed in the bedroom."

"Well, they were going to find out sooner or later. Craig suspected already." She sat in his lap and put her arms around his neck. "It's okay. This will give Sunny some time to think about it."

He hugged her. "Every time something great happens ..." He shook his head.

She smiled. She'd been thinking along similar lines: that things had seemed fine and even their very serious problems manageable. Then Craig had come along to add to the tangle. But now, knowing

Tom's "something great" was *her* or, more accurately, the two of them together, she was buoyed up once more. A thought occurred to her. "Oh, my," she said. "Sunny used her key. We should just thank our lucky stars they didn't walk in an hour ago!"

She laughed, but Tom didn't seem to find it amusing. His frown deepened.

"Oh, come on, sweetie," she said. "Nothing all that terrible happened. Let's have some lunch." She gave him a little shake, which was a bit like trying to shake an oak tree.

She was determinedly chatty over lunch, and although he responded, she could see the effort it cost him. Finally, she asked what he wanted to do that afternoon. He said he'd spotted a few repairs around the house that he wanted to tackle. She made a face.

"That doesn't sound like much fun," she said. "Why don't we try to find Ricky Stout?"

"You mean, the football player?" He shook his head. "You need to stay out of the detective business, Aubrey."

"But, Tom, we might –"

"You're in enough trouble because of me." He stood and carried his plate to the sink. "What would the school think about you stalking a student in defense of a child molester?"

"Tom!"

"Well, that's how they'd see it. Especially if Ricky Stout's parents complain to the school about you."

Aubrey jumped up and ran to him, throwing her arms around him from behind. "Tom, this is too important. I'm glad Rachel thinks they'll dismiss the charges, but if we could find out –"

"Please, Aubrey." He gripped her hands and pressed them hard against his waist. "Please, just let Rachel handle it. Call her, if you want, and tell her about Ricky, but don't stick your neck out any farther than you already have."

She rested her cheek against his strong back and sighed. "All right," she reluctantly agreed. "I'll call Rachel."

He pulled her arms from around him and turned to look down at her, one big hand cupping her cheek. He gazed at her in silence for several seconds.

"Have you ever thought what you might do if some loud noise set me off?"

"I'm not afraid of you, Tom." She smiled. "Remember, the second night you stayed, the thunder gave you bad dreams. I wasn't afraid of you then."

He held her, resting his cheek against the top of her head. "Aubrey. You're such a loving woman. You want to fix what's broken in me." He held her away and looked at her solemnly. "But I'm not Sunny. You can't just apply patience and wait for me to grow out of it."

On the phone with Rachel McDowd, Aubrey explained her theory about Heather's story. "Maybe, on the night Heather was beaten, she met with Ricky and came onto him, to get him interested in her. Things got rough, and when she got home, she made up the story about an assault, then added Tom's name to make it more credible and get her parents off her back."

Rachel was dubious. "It's pretty thin, Aubrey. I'll keep your theory in my pocket, just in case, but I really think Tom's service record is what will make the difference."

Kate was only slightly more encouraging. They met at Nest 75 in the early evening. Kate wanted to wait for Brett, who was running late. While they waited for him to arrive, Tom went for a walk along the water's edge, and Aubrey explained her Ricky Stout theory to Kate, and told her about the somewhat embarrassing surprise visit from Sunny and Craig.

"Now he's gone all quiet again," Aubrey said, sitting next to Kate on the warm sand and watching Tom in the distance.

"I've never seen him any other way," Kate pointed out. "He was a little excited the night of the boil, but he doesn't usually say more than a few words."

"Oh, you'd be surprised," Aubrey said. "Lately, he's been talking in whole sentences. Sometimes he even strings three or four sentences together."

Kate feigned astonishment. "Good grief! He'll be running for Congress before you know it." They chuckled together. "Seriously, Bree. The man obviously cares about you, and he doesn't want your feelings for him to get you into trouble. He's got a point."

"I know. But I can't just stand by and wait for whatever's going to happen."

"Oh, believe me, kiddo, I know you better than that. And I think your Ricky Stout theory has *some* merit. Just be careful." She pointed along the beach. "Here comes Brett."

Tom had spotted him, too. Aubrey saw the boy overtake the ex-soldier and give him a brief nod as he passed. Tom followed, arriving just behind Brett.

Aubrey let the boy take her usual place beside the nest, while she and Tom readied the runway. Kate began digging the hole by hand. By the time Aubrey and Tom were ready, Kate had already uncovered live hatchlings. Tom and Aubrey shielded the little crawlers from the hot evening sun by holding up a beach towel as they walked along beside the runway.

A small crowd gathered and, because this was a daytime event, there were no rules about cameras or cell phones. Aubrey, in the lead with her corner of the towel, had to ask several people to move out of the way so they could get past. With the next turtle, she put Tom in the lead, and people were quicker to step back. She explained to a couple of people that, at that time of day, the little turtles might die of sun exposure without the shade afforded by the towel.

Aubrey was at the water's edge, guarding the seventh turtle, when Kate shouted that she had reached the bottom of the nest. Tom jogged to the nest, then back to Aubrey. Her eyes were focused on the dark little dot being pushed and pulled by the wave, when Tom came up behind her and put his hands on her shoulders.

"No dead turtles," he said softly.

Smiling, she touched his hand, her focus still on the final turtle, and said, "Thanks, Tom."

Moments later, she joined him in tearing the runway apart, coiling up the edging, and smoothing out the sand. Only a few people lingered to watch or ask questions. Kate and Brett were conferring over the shells piled into groups on the sand.

Tom put the rolls of edging in the cardboard box and moved up to stand behind Brett, who was still squatting by the nest to help Kate bury the remains of the hatching. Aubrey saw him freeze when Tom's shadow fell across him, but he said nothing.

When everything was buried and nest filled in, Aubrey used the broom to smooth the sand, then sprinkled a handful of dead leaves and dried bits of sea oats on top. Kate was writing in her journal, chronicling the count of turtles and eggshells.

"Now that's what I call a successful nest," she said with obvious satisfaction. "A hundred and fifteen turtles into the sea. Love it!"

She looked around at her little group, smiling. Aubrey saw that Brett was still crouched below where Tom stood about two feet behind him. Tom reached down and touched him on the shoulder. "Here, son, let me give you a hand."

Brett stared at Tom's hand for a moment, then took it and let Tom pull him to his feet. When he thanked Tom, and turned away, Aubrey was amazed to see what seemed to be tears in the boy's eyes. Tom glanced at her, and she gave a slight nod of understanding. Her look said, *I see what you mean. That boy feels just awful about something.*

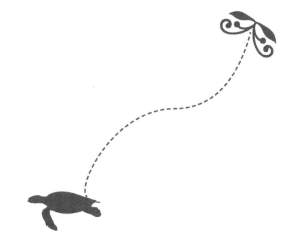

Chapter 10

Nest 75, Day 62

"Mom?" Sunny's tearful voice on the phone jerked Aubrey from semi-sleep to fully awake in an instant.

"Sunny? What's wrong?" The bedside clock read 12:17. Why was her daughter calling after midnight? She could feel Tom behind her, awake and alert, his arm protectively around her.

"Can – can you come get me?" Aubrey was already moving. Tom released her at once and vaulted out of bed after her, turning on the bedside lamp.

"Of course, baby. Where are you? Your father's? Are you all right?"

"I'm at a p-party. I'm not hurt, just scared." She gave an address in Southport and Aubrey repeated it as Tom wrote it down on the pad she kept in her bedside table.

"Stay on the phone, honey. I'm getting dressed."

Tom held her phone, listening silently, while Aubrey pulled shorts and a tee-shirt over her nakedness. She took the phone back from Tom, stepped into flip-flops and headed up the hallway.

"Are you at a friend's house?" She grabbed her handbag and car keys. Tom ran into the kitchen, fully dressed.

"No. Not really a friend. I'll tell you when you get here."

"Okay, honey. Just stay on the phone."

Tom mouthed the words, "Shall I come?"

Aubrey hesitated. If there was trouble, Tom would be a big help, but she wasn't sure how Sunny would feel about him being along. Tom clearly sensed her reluctance. He shook his head, mouthing, "Call me."

She nodded and hastened to her car. Tom watched from the door, waving reassurance. Once out of the driveway, she put the phone to her ear again.

"I'm on my way, baby." There was no response.

Aubrey experienced a few seconds of near panic, then a flood of relief as Sunny said, "Okay, Mom."

Eleven minutes later, Aubrey pulled up in front of a house on the outskirts of Southport, where every window blazed light and the sounds of a boisterous party resonated from within. There were a few teenagers on the lawn, pushing each other and laughing loudly. None of them were Sunny, and Aubrey's gaze probed the dark shadows for a glimpse of her daughter.

Just as she said, "I'm here, baby," into the phone, her passenger door was opened and Sunny flung herself into the car.

"Go, Mom. Just go," she sobbed.

Aubrey sped away from the house and drove for a couple of miles before she wheeled into the parking lot of a church. She shifted into park and turned off the headlights, but left the engine running. She gathered her weeping daughter into her arms.

"What is it, Sunny? What happened?"

"Oh, Mom. I was so s-scared!"

Aubrey took her daughter's face in her hands and held her away to look into her eyes. "Sunny, stop crying and tell me what happened. Are you hurt? Do you need to go to the hospital?"

Sunny shook her head and took a packet of tissues from the car's console. She blew her nose and dried her eyes, took a deep breath, and haltingly explained what had happened.

Devon, a "really cute" boy she had met at her dad's condo, had invited her to go with him to an end-of-summer party in Southport. He knew she was from the area and thought she would know many of the kids who were going to be there. Her dad liked Devon and thought it would be fine.

Aubrey knew right then that she was going to have a serious talk with Craig.

Sunny explained that when they met in the condo parking garage at eight, there were three other Wilmington teens coming along. Sunny didn't know the two boys and a girl, and she hesitated at first, but they seemed nice enough.

At the party house, she found a crowd of teens and a few young adults. Devon disappeared with the three other teens, and Sunny wandered around, nibbling at party food and trying to make conversation. She saw some kids she recognized from school, but none she really knew.

She was bored, and wanted to go home, but she couldn't find Devon. She texted her dad but never got a response, and then remembered that he and Maya had an event to go to. She found another girl her age whom she recognized as a cheerleader. This girl, Annette, was just as bored with the loud music and loud conversation. They found a relatively quiet spot at the top of some stairs and chatted for an hour or so. Then Annette called her parents and asked them to come get her. She offered to take Sunny home, too, but when Sunny told the other girl that she currently lived in Wilmington, Annette said her parents would probably not want to go that far.

By this time, it was nearly eleven, and Sunny was desperate to find Devon and get back to the condo. Could he possibly have left without her? But she had been in plain sight the whole time; he couldn't have missed her.

Aubrey interrupted her daughter's narrative. "Why didn't you call me, sweetheart? I could have brought you home for the night and taken you to your dad's in the morning."

Sunny bowed her head. "Well, you've got a boyfriend now. Dad said you want to be alone with Tom."

Mentally cursing Craig, Aubrey assured Sunny that being her mom always was and always would be the most important part of her life.

Sunny continued. "I went looking for Devon again. I opened a bedroom door, and there were two people having sex. I was so embarrassed. Then I went downstairs, and I needed to use the bathroom, but there were kids in there doing coke. One of them asked me what I wanted, and I said I was looking for Devon. They told me Devon was probably in the shed. I went out back, and I found Devon and some other guys sitting around this shed, drinking and smoking weed. Devon told the other guys he was b-babysitting me."

She started to cry again, and Aubrey cuddled her close, wiping her child's eyes and nose with tissue, just as she had when she was a toddler.

"I've never been so humiliated. They were all laughing at me. Then one of the guys said he wouldn't mind babysitting me, and how much did it pay. Devon said the guy would have to pay *him*, and how much would he give Devon to take me into the shed."

"*What?*"

Sunny nodded. "That's when I got scared. I told Devon I wanted to go home. He said he wasn't through partying yet, and it was time for me to grow up. He said – he told the others I'd been bothering him all summer, and that he finally –" More tears. "He finally took p-pity on me."

Aubrey held her daughter tight, wishing she could get her hands on this Devon. It was just as well that Tom hadn't come with her. On the other hand, she allowed herself a brief fantasy of Tom going all Rambo on their teenage asses.

"Is that when you called me?" she asked, kissing her daughter's forehead as she smoothed her curly hair.

"Not right away. I ran back inside, but the kids in there were so crazy. One guy pushed a joint at me, but I went around him. This mean-looking girl said she wanted my earrings. You know, the seahorse ones? So, I took them off and gave them to her. That's when I ran outside, in the front yard. There were boys pushing each other around, kind of fighting, I guess. I went behind a big tree and called dad again, but he didn't pick up. So, I called you. Oh, Mom, I'm so s-sorry!"

"You have nothing to be sorry about, sweetie. I'm just sorry I somehow let you believe I might not be available whenever and wherever you need me. I will always, *always* come when you call. No matter what else is happening in my life, or whoever else I might care about, you will always be my top priority. Got it?"

Sunny nodded against her mother's shoulder.

"Now, speaking of other people, there's a very nice man who is waiting and worrying about us. He wanted to come with me, but he thought you might want me to yourself. Mind if I give him a call?"

Sunny sniffed and shook her head, letting go of her mother just enough for Aubrey to reach her phone. Tom answered the house phone on the first ring.

"Hi. I've got her. We're fine. We'll be home in fifteen minutes."

"Okay. Thanks for calling."

"See you soon."

"Bye, Aubrey. Tell Sunny I said 'hey.'"

She started to say he could tell her himself in fifteen minutes, but he had disconnected. She stared at her phone, frowning.

"Is everything okay?" Sunny asked.

"Sure, baby. You can sleep in your room tonight, and I'll take you back to your dad's tomorrow. But I want you to call him to let him know where you are."

"He's probably not home yet." Sunny yawned, exhausted from the stress of the evening, as well as by the late hour.

"Well, we'll call him from home." She gave Sunny another kiss and a quick cuddle.

"Mom?"

"Yes, sweetheart?" Aubrey stroked her daughter's hair again.

"I don't like it at Dad's anymore. Can I come back home?" Sunny's plaintive tone made her sound about five years old again.

"Sunny-bear! Of course, you can come home. I've missed you like crazy."

"I mean, can we just go to Wilmington tomorrow and get all my stuff from Dad's?" She was starting to tear up again. "Tom won't be mad, will he?"

"Whatever you want, sweetie." She turned on the headlights and shifted into drive. "Tom won't be mad, I promise. He's not like that. Now, buckle up."

Sunny buckled her seatbelt. "Mom?"

"Yes, angel?"

Sunny's voice was so small, Aubrey could barely hear her. "I'm sorry for being kind of a brat this summer."

"It's all right, Sunny. It's been a pretty confusing time for you." She pulled onto the main road. There was almost no traffic this time of night.

"I try to be nice to Maya, but she's such a ..." Sunny struggled for the word and finally settled for shrugging her shoulders.

"You know what, baby? That's okay. You don't *have* to like anyone, and I know Maya can be hard to take."

"I always thought you were too strict, especially now that I'm older. But Dad isn't strict enough. He lets me get away with murder."

Aubrey laughed. "Well, we'll get you back on track, little girl. But tonight, you just go to bed and don't worry about anything."

A few minutes later, they got out of the car and went into the house to find no one waiting for them. There was a folded piece of paper on the kitchen table, with Aubrey's name. The note read:

> *You and Sunny need some time alone. It's a good night*
> *for sleeping on the beach, and I'll be fine. Call you*
> *tomorrow. Tom.*

"Is everything okay?" Sunny asked. Her face, under a too-heavy layer of make-up, looked tired.

Aubrey smiled and hugged her daughter. "Sure, honey. Tom is just giving us some time alone. Why don't you run along to bed? You still have clothes and pajamas here, and you know where we keep the extra toothbrushes."

"I thought you wanted me to call Dad?"

Sunny forced a smile. "I'll take care of that."

After Sunny went to her room, Aubrey dialed Craig's cell phone number. As when Sunny had called, there was no answer. She left him a terse message. "Craig, when you get around to checking your phone – on this night when our daughter went to a party with people we don't know – you'll find a couple of panicked messages and texts from Sunny. I hope they give you some bad moments before you get this one. It's 1:20 a.m. Our daughter is safe and at my house. She's ready to move back home. We'll call you later this morning."

Sunny was scrubbed and back in her own bed, tucked in by her mother with a goodnight kiss, and asleep in an instant, but Aubrey found herself unable to sleep. Just as she had lain awake and pictured Tom in a jailhouse bunk, now she pictured him on a deserted beach. She tossed and turned, grabbing brief snatches of sleep peppered with disturbing dreams.

As soon as the sky hinted at dawn, she rose and pulled on jeans and a tee-shirt. She left a text message for Sunny and let herself quietly out of the house.

At the beach, she went to Tom's favorite spot, and found him already awake and sitting on the sand, watching the endless rush of the surf. She sat beside him and he put his arm around her. They didn't speak for a long moment, while Aubrey fought a long and familiar battle with her pride. And finally won.

"I love you, Tom," she said.

He turned to look at her, searching her face, his eyes revealing a deep need to believe her words.

"I love you," she repeated, "because you are the best man I know. You have honor, and kindness, and a loving spirit. You're brave and smart and good. Life has kicked you around, but it hasn't left you bitter."

She turned her head and kissed the hand cupping her shoulder. "There's a word that's not used much these days, but it describes you perfectly. *Noble*. You're noble, Tom. And I am proud to say I love you."

She looked at him. He was watching the sea again, his lips parted slightly, his eyes wet. When he turned to her, the pink-orange light of dawn reflected on the single tear that slid haltingly down his unshaven cheek.

"Oh, Tom!" She threw her arms around his neck, feeling her heart might actually break. This good man ... this good and decent man ...

"I love you, Aubrey." His voice was rough, and his chest shook with emotion. "I love you."

They held each other for a long time, and might have gone on longer, happily locked in each other's arms, but the tide was rising, and when it crested Aubrey's flip-flops and wet her toes, she gave a startled squeak. They laughed, looking at each other with new eyes.

This is the man I love, she thought. *The man who loves me.*

They gathered his things and walked slowly to her car, holding hands and smiling at each other. On the drive home, he amused her by saying, "Wow. I'm glad we got *that* out of the way." Then surprised her by adding, "But, honey, I can't live with you, much as I want to."

"Why not?"

"Because Sunny is home now, isn't she?"

Aubrey acknowledged this with a nod. "But Craig and Maya –"

"Are Craig and Maya, not you and me. And Maya isn't an accused child molester." He held up his hand, forestalling her next objection. "I don't know where I'll go, but I'll find a place. If necessary, I'll go to the V.A. and see what they can do for me. But I can't live with you. And believe me when I tell you, there's nothing I'd like better."

She knew what it would cost him to ask the V.A. for help, so she said nothing more about his decision.

Sunny slept while they ate breakfast. Aubrey noticed that every time she and Tom were in range of each other, they touched. And when they couldn't touch, they smiled. She couldn't remember ever feeling this way before. She had loved Craig in the early years, but this peace leavened with euphoria was new to her.

Aubrey's cell phone rang, and the display showed the caller to be Rachel McDowd. She started to hand the phone to Tom, but he whispered, "Speaker." She answered and laid the phone on the table between them.

"Rachel, Tom is here, and I have you on speaker," she said.

"Good. I have some great news. The police officer who charged Tom with assault called the D.A. to say that he has reconsidered. Turns out he's a vet, too, and when he learned about Tom's service and the noise-related PTSD, he had a change of heart. He plans to testify that he believes Tom hit him accidentally."

Aubrey and Tom exchanged amazed looks. Aubrey said, "Rachel! That's wonderful!"

"Oh, it's huge," Rachel agreed. "When the D.A. calls me at eight on a Saturday morning to say they're dropping a charge, it's big. Don't be surprised if Officer Hanover stops by your place today to talk to Tom. He feels bad about the whole thing."

Her tone changed, "But don't forget, the child sexual assault charge still stands. And it's that case that would result in the more severe sentence."

Aubrey looked at Tom as she spoke. "But you still think those charges will go away?"

"With no more evidence than they have now, I'd say it's likely. Of course, first Tom will have a felony probable cause hearing in district court. If the court rules that the evidence is sufficient, it goes to a grand jury to evaluate the evidence and formally indict or dismiss the charges. I'm sure you've heard the saying that a grand jury would indict a ham sandwich, but at this point, I don't think it will even go to the grand jury."

"That's a relief."

"I could guarantee it, if Tom were willing to plead to a lesser charge, like simple assault."

Tom shook his head, jaw set.

"No, Rachel. Tom won't confess to assault or anything else against Heather. He literally never touched her."

"Well, chances are good the charge will be dropped, regardless.

If not, we'll cross that bridge down the road. Meanwhile, next week I'll call Ricky Stout and interview Brett Solingen."

"Good. And thanks for taking time out of your Saturday to call us with this great news, Rachel."

After they ended the call, Aubrey uttered a muffled scream of delight, and jumped up to sit in Tom's lap.

"One down, one to go!" she whispered excitedly. She did her best to control the vocal expression of her joy, aware that Sunny was still sleeping.

Tom returned her smile, but his eyes were troubled. "I wish the thing about Heather could be dealt with so easily. I'd have been willing to plead on the other assault charge. After all, I really did hit that cop. But I can't do that with the Heather thing."

"I know, honey," she said. "It's just not in you to lie about hurting Heather, any more than you could actually hurt her."

His hug said he appreciated her understanding. They were smiling contentedly at each other when they heard Sunny's door opening. In an instant, Aubrey was off Tom's lap and carrying their breakfast dishes to the sink.

The guest bathroom door closed behind Sunny, and they relaxed. Aubrey prepared oatmeal with cinnamon, Sunny's favorite breakfast, while Tom washed the dishes. When Sunny emerged, dressed in an old pair of shorts and a Panthers tee-shirt, her bowl of oatmeal was waiting next to a glass of milk on the kitchen table.

"Hey! Thanks, Mom," she said. She was polite and cheerful around Tom, but shy, which Aubrey considered normal.

Aubrey was sitting next to her daughter, chatting about nothing much, when her phone signaled a text. This was from Kate, to tell her they would have a third nest, number 105, in early September, and where it was located.

Aubrey read the text to Tom and Sunny. "Interested?" she asked.

"Sure!" Sunny declared.

"Why not?" asked Tom.

Aubrey texted Kate that she had three helpers. In a few seconds, her phone rang.

"Three?" asked Kate. "Does that mean ...?"

"Yep. Sunny's home."

"Great! I'll put you and me on the list, and Tom and Sunny can be unofficial. School will have started by then, remember."

"Well," Aubrey said, with an apologetic shrug for her daughter, "Sunny may not be able to join us every night, with school starting." She glanced at Tom. "And I assume Brett and Heather will bow out for the same reason."

"I'm not even calling them," Kate said. "They'll need to concentrate on their studies. There won't be so much for us to do, with the summer crowds gone. We can handle it."

"You bet."

"So, mark your calendar for September 10," Kate concluded. "That's when we'll prep. That will be in the late afternoon, so Sunny should be able to help with that. We'll probably start sitting on the thirteenth."

After the call, Aubrey, Sunny and Tom spent several minutes discussing sea turtles, including Tom's description of the boil of Nest 75.

"That was my favorite," he said, with a meaningful glance for Aubrey.

She smiled, remembering the amazing night that had followed that boil.

Sunny seemed oblivious to the erotic overtones of the conversation. She finished her oatmeal and took her dishes to the sink, where Tom took them from her with a smile.

"Thanks for the oatmeal, Mom. And thanks for washing my bowl, Tom." She looked at Aubrey. "Is it okay if I make some calls? I want to let Diane know I'm home." At Aubrey's nod, she bounded back to her bedroom and her cell phone.

"She's glad to be back," Tom observed.

"And I'm glad to have her back, except for the one thing." She smiled ruefully.

"I'll miss you, too," he said. "But it will all work out."

"Hey, that's *my* line," she said. She rose and crossed to where he stood leaning back against the sink. She wrapped her arms around his waist and rested her cheek against his chest, then jumped when her cell phone rang. "Goodness," she said. "Who's left to call?"

She looked at her phone and pressed the talk button. "Hello, Craig," she said coolly.

"Okay, let me have it. I'm a terrible father. I don't pay enough attention to her. I want to be her friend, not her parent. Blah, blah, blah."

"Thanks," she said, crossing the kitchen to sit down at the table. "You just summed up my closing arguments for me."

"Well, let me sum up something else. I'm dropping the custody thing. You win."

Aubrey took a deep breath. She wanted to say something sarcastic but reminded herself that this man was about to be Tom's boss. She settled for saying, "Glad to hear it. So, Sunny will need her things, except for the stuff she always keeps at your place. Shall we come pick it up?"

"I'll bring it – Maya's packing her stuff up now. And I still want to take her snorkeling next week, if it's okay with you."

"That's up to her. I won't interfere."

He snorted. "Is the boyfriend still living with you?"

"If you mean Tom, he does *not* live here, but he's here at the moment. Did you want to speak to him?"

"No. No, I just wondered. I would have to say I don't think it's appropriate for a strange man to be living in a house with a teenage girl."

"I don't consider you an expert on what's appropriate for a teenage girl, but it just so happens Tom agrees with you." She looked at Tom, still leaning against the counter. "That's why he doesn't live here."

"Good. Can Sunny wait until Monday for her things?"

"If she can't, we'll call and let you know when we'll be there."

"Fair enough. Okay, I'll see you Monday. Bye."

"Bye." She stuck her tongue out at the phone as she ended the call. Tom chuckled. "Very mature."

She returned to the sink to stand beside him. Glancing over her shoulder to make sure Sunny was out of hearing, she said, "It just irks me that he was fine living with Maya in unwedded bliss in the same home as his daughter, but it's not 'appropriate' for me to have *you* here."

"You've got to admit, it's different having your daughter around a strange man. It's not just about setting an example. It's about mitigating risk."

"Now you sound like Craig." She sighed. "Sure didn't take long to get used to having you in my house." She lowered her voice. "And in my bed."

He, too, glanced down the hallway before bending to give her a swift, hard kiss. "We'll find ways to be together," he whispered. "Knowing you love me makes all the difference."

"I do love you, Tom."

"And I love you."

They were grinning happily at each other when they heard the bedroom door close. Tom grabbed the kitchen sponge and began wiping an already clean stovetop. Aubrey strolled to the table and picked up her cell phone.

"Hi," Sunny said. "What are we doing today?"

"Well, Tom and I are expecting company," Aubrey said, "so we're going to hang around here. But that doesn't mean you have to."

Sunny brightened. "Great! Diane is visiting her grandma in Raleigh, so she'll be gone all day, but Kim wants to hang at the beach. We'll just walk there and back."

"Okay. You know the rules."

Sunny nodded. "And, Mom?"

"Yes?"

"We'll be gone all day."

Aubrey reddened. Was her daughter hinting that she and Tom would have the house to themselves? Then it hit her.

"Oh! You need lunch money." She got her bag from the little hutch behind the table and took a ten from her wallet. "This should work for the Dairy Queen or the Lazy Turtle."

Sunny took the ten, thanked her, smiled at Tom, and ran back to her room.

Aubrey looked at Tom and burst out laughing. "You thought the same thing I thought."

He laughed, too. "I didn't know what to say."

"Not that it's a bad idea," she said.

They were still smiling at each other when Sunny dashed through the kitchen, carrying a ragged denim backpack.

"Got my old swimsuit under my clothes," she said breathlessly.

She was out the side door almost before the adults had time to say goodbye. Aubrey watched through the kitchen window as Sunny ran up the street, stopped briefly to pet the neighbor's dog, then raced up the road in the direction of Oak Island Drive. Aubrey turned to look at Tom.

"What are you waiting for?" he asked.

She hurried into his arms and they kissed for a long moment. Then he scooped her up and carried her into the living room. On the big, worn sofa, he stretched out with her on top of him, still kissing wildly.

"It seems like a long time since last night," she said, when she could catch her breath.

"Was it only last night?" he asked. He slid his big hands under her tee-shirt, and she felt him suck in his breath when he found only her.

"I got dressed in a hurry this morning," she said against his lips. "I had something important to do."

"I remember." He tugged her tee-shirt up and, with his hands under her arms, slid her up along his body until his mouth found her breasts.

She braced herself on her arms, while he licked her nipples into hard little nuggets, then pinched one while he lightly chewed the other. She writhed on his body throughout the rising tension and release. Delirious, she ground her knee against his crotch and he cried out.

She swung her legs off the sofa and sat up on his thighs. "Did I hurt you?" she asked. He rose and carried her up with him.

"Oh, I'm hurtin'," he drawled. "But not like you mean."

"Bedroom," she said, although he was already heading for the hallway. "And lock the door."

Two hours later, showered, shampooed, and fully dressed, Aubrey stood at the stove, frying bacon. Tom stood nearby, slicing tomatoes and toasting bread. Every minute or two, they would turn to each other and smile.

Glimpses of him still had the power to take her breath away. In a light gray tee-shirt, his hair still wet, his jaw set in concentration, he moved gracefully from counter to fridge and back. He was, in fact, close to perfect, except for the deep scar on his back. Her heart ached a little every time she saw it, knowing what it had cost him in physical pain and emotional turmoil.

Things had to turn out right for Tom. The God to whom she prayed – often, if somewhat haphazardly – would surely know that Tom had suffered enough in his life. The loss of his father, the poverty and abuse, the trauma of war, had not made him bitter or callous. It had taken her some time to see past his wall of silence to the gentleness within, but she now knew him to be a wise and loving man.

"Bacon's ready!" she sang out.

"I put mayo on the toast," he said.

They gathered the makings of their lunch and sat at the table.

"Do you mind if I pray?" she asked.

"Aubrey," he said, "I don't know much about church. My mom never took me when I was growing up, although she sang hymns around the house a lot. I got some exposure to church in the service, and I said prayers whenever I was in trouble. I'd like to know more about it. I hope you'll help me with that."

"I will," she said. "Or at least, I'll introduce you to people who can."

She took his hand, gave thanks, and prayed for help with Tom's situation. He interrupted her "Amen" by saying, "And thank you for bringing Aubrey into my life."

After lunch, Tom began cleaning out and organizing the shed, while Aubrey went through some teaching materials for her upcoming classes. They were taking a break and enjoying some iced tea at the kitchen table when the doorbell rang.

Tom looked at Aubrey. "That must be him," she said. "None of my friends would come to the front door."

They went to the door together. Aubrey, suddenly nervous, took Tom's hand. He opened the door to a tall, slender, dark-skinned man with a shaved head, who was dressed in jeans and a white polo shirt. The man's wide smile broadened as they greeted him.

"Hey, there," he responded. "I'm Reggie Hanover. Remember me?"

Tom stuck out his hand to shake Reggie's and draw the man inside. "Come in," he said. "This is Aubrey Benson and I'm Tom Clayton."

"Oh, I remember *you*," the officer said, rubbing his nose and grinning at Tom.

"Listen, man …" Tom began, but Reggie forestalled him.

"Let's get this out of the way. What happened was an accident. When I found out about your service and your thing with loud noises, I understood what happened."

"Just the same, I'm sorry –"

"If I hadn't been about half out of it, with blood all over my best uniform, I'd probably have handled it different. My buddies who jumped you hustled you one way and me the other. I hope they weren't too rough on you."

Tom shook his head. "I've known rougher," he said.

Reggie looked at him appraisingly. "And handled it fine, I'm guessing," he said with a smile.

Aubrey stepped forward. "Won't you have a seat, Officer Hanover?"

"That's kind of a mouthful," said the young man. "Make it 'Reggie.'"

"There's iced tea in the kitchen," Tom said. "Aubrey makes great iced tea."

"Sounds good," said Reggie, following them to the kitchen. "It's already a scorcher out there. I finally got a Saturday off and I'm hell bent – pardon me, ma'am – on spending it outside. But it sure is a hot one."

Aubrey insisted the two men have seats while she poured the tea. When she served it, Reggie looked at her with a puzzled frown.

"Hey, aren't you a sea turtle nest parent, Aubrey?"

She smiled. "Yes, I am. And you look kind of familiar yourself."

"My girlfriend does some work for the *Pilot* as a stringer and photog. I go with her to some events. And, of course, I'm all over town in uniform."

Aubrey nodded. "Weren't you at last year's wrap-up party?"

He nodded. "That was me. Us, really. Carolyn was taking pictures."

"Well," Aubrey said. "I'll leave you guys to get acquainted."

Both men rose slightly from their chairs as Aubrey left the kitchen. "Nice meeting you, Aubrey," said Reggie.

She heard him ask Tom a question about where he'd been stationed with the Army, then she left them to manage this get-acquainted conversation on their own. They were deep in military jargon when she went through the living room and out the sliding doors to the backyard. She started digging weeds in the shadiest spots she could find. Nearly an hour passed before she heard the side door open and close, and Tom came around from the carport.

"Hey, honey," he said, kneeling beside her. "Don't work too long in this heat."

"I was just about to come in," she said, wiping her forehead with her arm. "I hope you left some tea."

"Barely," he said, grinning. He helped her up and kept both her grimy hands in his. "Listen, Aubrey. After I told Reggie about the situation here, he invited me to come stay with him. He was sharing a house with his grandfather, but the old boy died last year, and Reggie's looking for a new roommate."

Aubrey's spirits fell. She knew Tom had to leave, but it was happening so quickly. Then she remembered her prayer at lunchtime, asking God for help with Tom's situation. Here was the answer, and she shouldn't protest.

"That's ... very nice of him," she said quietly. *Don't cry,* she commanded herself.

"I was worried he'd get into trouble with the department for letting a suspect live in his house, but he thinks they'll be fine with it. Says I'll actually be less of a 'flight risk' this way. And he's willing to wait until I get paid to decide how much I should chip in for rent." He gave her hands a gentle shake. "Honey, don't look that way. This is a good thing, and it's all because of you."

She shook her head.

"Yes! Yes, it is." He wrapped her in his strong arms. "Things are finally going right for me, and it's all thanks to you. Even Reggie. Maybe he would have taken a second look at the situation and maybe he would have tracked me down on the beach and offered me a place to live, but you *prayed* for me. As far as I know, nobody's ever prayed for me before."

That did it. She sobbed into his shirt, her tears making dark patches in the pale gray. He squeezed her hard. "Damn, Aubrey," he said. "You know that just about kills me."

She nodded and loosened her grip on his shirt. She smoothed out the wrinkles left by her fingers and tears, afraid if she looked at his face she'd start crying again.

But he lifted her head with a finger under her chin and rubbed her tears away with the thumb of his other hand. Smiling, he said, "I can see I'm going to have to start packing a handkerchief."

By the time Sunny returned home an hour later, Aubrey's eyes were clear, and her mood had improved. Tom had been tender with his farewell, sincere in his promise to call her that evening, and utterly convincing in his claim about this being a positive thing for everyone.

After she'd waved goodbye to Tom and Reggie, she called Kate and had a long chat. Kate agreed with Tom that living in Aubrey's house was not the wisest idea.

"It'll be good for both of you," she said. "Things are pretty hot between you right now. This will give you a chance to cool down and think things through."

"I'm not sure I want to cool down," Aubrey said, then sighed. "But I get what you're saying. And maybe, with Tom working next week, I'll have time to puzzle out this whole mystery of why Heather would accuse him."

"Just be careful playing junior detective, Bree. The police won't approve of you messing things up. I got a taste of how crazy things can get when I talked to Heather's mom. That woman has *issues*."

"I just wish I'd been straight with Sunny before I involved her. Now I have to own up to it."

"Good luck, kiddo."

When Aubrey sat Sunny down on the sofa that evening, she explained about Heather and Brett helping with the nest alongside Tom, about Tom walking Heather to her car and his subsequent arrest for assault and attempted rape, and about her own firm belief in Tom's innocence.

"So, that's why you wanted to know about Heather," Sunny said. "It was nothing to do with her being a mentor."

"No. I'm sorry, honey. That was just a cover."

"It was a *lie*, Mom. And it was a really shitty thing to do."

Aubrey knew this was not the time to chide Sunny about her language. "I know, and I'm really sorry. I didn't want you involved in –"

"But you *did* involve me!" Sunny protested. "You had me spying for you, collecting information about a girl, without telling me the real reason. Without giving me the chance to say I didn't *want* to be involved."

Aubrey nodded, acknowledging all Sunny's accusations, and mutely seeking her forgiveness.

"You know, if *I* did that – if I asked for something from you and told you a lie about why I wanted it – you'd totally freak. I'd get grounded or lose my phone or something."

"Sunny, I know it was unfair. All I can say is that it seemed reasonable at the time, but now I know it was a mistake."

Sunny just shook her head. "Un-*freaking*-believable," she muttered. She stood up. "I have to think about this. Alone." She fled to her room, and Aubrey let her go.

Chapter 11

Nest 105, Day 30

"I'm just saying, I don't know why I have to go," Sunny said. Her crossed arms and protruding lower lip expressed her rebellious mood. She had clearly not forgiven her mother for lying to her.

"You know, we just heard a wonderful sermon about forgiveness. How about throwing a little this way, huh?" Aubrey glanced sideways at her daughter, then back at the road. "And I want you to go because I want you to get to know Tom. He's going to be part of my life from now on, and you're the *center* of my life, so I'm hoping you'll learn to like each other."

Sunny's face was turned toward the window, giving her mother few clues about the effect of her comments. Minutes later, they pulled into the parking lot at the Old Bridge Diner. Tom was waiting just outside the door.

"Are we late?" she called. She smoothed the skirt of her pale-blue summer dress as she got out of the car.

Grinning broadly, he shook his head. He held the door into the diner for Sunny, then swept Aubrey up in a huge bear hug that took her breath.

"God, I've missed you," he whispered.

"Same here," she answered. "Has it really been less than a day?"

"Something's wrong with all the clocks," he said. He released her and opened the door, watching her with frank admiration. Sunny was just inside the diner, waiting and pouting.

"Over here," Tom said, pointing to a big booth in the corner.

Reggie rose as they approached and gestured to the pretty woman next to him. "Carolyn, this is Aubrey and her daughter, Sunny. Carolyn is my fiancée." He held out his hand to Sunny. "Hi, Sunny. I'm Reggie."

Sunny shook his hand and greeted Carolyn. She and Aubrey sat in the round booth and scooted closer to Carolyn to make room for Tom. Aubrey extended her hand to Carolyn.

"Hi. It's so nice to meet you. We're so grateful to Reggie for all he's done."

Sunny remained mostly silent as the four adults got acquainted. Then Carolyn mentioned that, in addition to her part-time job with the newspaper, she also had her own interior design business.

Sunny perked up. "Really? That's what I want to do!"

Aubrey turned to her daughter in amazement. "You do?"

"Yes! Remember how much I hated Maya's idea for redecorating my room at Dad's? Well, I started sketching out some ideas for what I would do if I could choose. I really got into it. And I've always loved those decorator shows on TV."

Sunny was more animated than she'd been all day. Aubrey was so relieved to have Sunny acting like Sunny again that she wasn't about to question the sudden interest in decorating.

Carolyn smiled. "That's how I started, by decorating my own room. My parents had a wholesale fabric business, and when they had a surplus of this great print, I decided it would be a perfect covering for one wall of my room. Sort of like wallpaper. It looked great, all my friends loved it, and I was hooked."

The waitress brought their drinks and took their orders. They continued to chat about this and that, but right after their food arrived, Reggie turned to Aubrey and said, "Tom says you've been doing some sleuthing on his case."

Aubrey glanced at Tom, who frowned and shook his head. She decided to ignore him. "Not as much as I'd like to do." She went on to tell him what she'd learned about Heather's crush on Ricky Stout, and that someone certainly had beaten Heather, as proven by the bruises on her face.

"I have a friend with BSL PD," Reggie said. "I'll ask him what he knows about Ricky Stout."

Sunny spoke up. "My friend says Ricky's a nice guy, but what if he's on steroids or something?" She looked at her mom. "Well, I was thinking about it after we talked yesterday. I heard on TV that steroids can cause violent rages. And I read online that a lot of high school athletes take steroids."

Reggie smiled. "It's worth checking out. I'll let Tom know what I find out, and he can fill you in." He took a card from his pocket. "Meanwhile, this is my personal contact info. Let me know if you learn anything else, and I'll pass it on to the investigative team."

Tom groaned. "Jeez, Reg. Don't encourage her. I've been trying to keep her out of all this. And I don't think we should be talking about it in front of Sunny."

"Hey, I'm not a little kid," Sunny protested, around a mouthful of pancakes. She swallowed. "School will be starting soon, and I'll bet Heather's story will be all over the campus. I might hear something that would help."

"I think the public defender can handle everything fine," Tom said. "She's pretty sure of her case."

Reggie cleared his throat. "She *was* pretty sure. Like I told Tom last night, Southport P.D. contacted the D.A. yesterday afternoon."

"Reggie ..."

Just as Aubrey had done, Reggie ignored Tom. "Nothing official yet, seeing as how it's the weekend, but a tourist in Southport reported being assaulted and groped on June 30, when she took her dog out for a walk after dark. The perp tried to drag her into an alley, but her dog bit him and he ran off."

"Oh, no!" Aubrey said. "Not in Southport!"

Reggie nodded. "The tourist left town and the case kind of languished. Just no way to figure out who did it. They checked the local medical providers to see if anyone had been treated for dog bites, but no luck. All they know about the attacker –"

"Wait for it," Tom interrupted. "He was a big guy."

Reggie nodded.

Aubrey, aghast, dropped her fork in her plate. "So, now they think *Tom* did it?"

"Well, they heard we arrested a guy that fits that really vague description, and someone got to wondering if we had a serial rapist in the area. You know, violent crime is pretty rare around here."

Carolyn nudged Reggie and tilted her head toward Sunny. He clammed up, but Aubrey turned to Tom and asked, "Why didn't you tell me this last night?"

Their phone conversation the previous night had been brief but sweet. Tom had explained that he didn't like to tie up Reggie's phone, but he had wanted to wish Aubrey a good night. He told her he had missed her at dinner, and would miss her even more at bedtime, and had closed with "I love you."

At the time, Aubrey had been thrilled by his call, but was genuinely furious now. She had shown him in no uncertain terms that she was on his side. He seemed determined to push her away, to hide things from her and rely on Reggie and Rachel instead. Aware her feelings were petty, and that Tom's situation was not, she tamped down her ire and forced herself to smile at Reggie and Carolyn.

"See what I'm dealing with here?" she asked in a sweet voice that fooled no one.

They finished their meal in an uncomfortable silence punctuated by random and inconsequential remarks. Tom picked up the check with what Aubrey was sure must be the last of his cash reserve. Reggie made a small protest but was no doubt unwilling to hurt Tom's pride by insisting.

They all left together, and when Aubrey would have followed Sunny to her car without another word, Tom caught her hand and held her back.

"Aubrey, wait." He held her hand against his chest with both of his. "I'm sorry I didn't tell you about the Southport thing. I didn't see any reason to add to your worry. It'll probably come to nothing."

"You can't leave me out, Tom. We're in this together." She tilted her head to one side. "Aren't we?"

He dropped her hand and put his arms around her. "Sorry, babe. I'm used to handling things on my own. And I hate to see you worry about my problems."

My problems. "Tom …" Aubrey closed her eyes, fighting tears.

"I promise I'll tell you everything from now on. Just don't cry, okay?" He hugged her tight, and she nodded against his chest.

"All right. Can you come home with us now? I can take you back to Reggie's tonight."

He looked at the car, where Sunny stood waiting, impatience in every line of her frame. "I think you have some fence-mending to do with your girl. Maybe tomorrow." He released her.

She sighed and smiled up at him. "You're probably right. You usually are. I really hate that about you."

He laughed. "Tough, because I really *love* you."

He called her at bedtime. "Is this a good time to talk?" he asked.

"Of course. I'm just getting into bed."

He groaned. "Please don't tell me about it."

She laughed. "Guess what I found in the drawer beside my bed?"

There was a pause, then he chuckled. "I forgot they were in there. Not that I need them here."

"What's Reggie's house like?" she asked.

"A lot like yours, I'd say. Two bedrooms, two bathrooms. The closet in this room is still full of his dad's clothes but, as you know, I don't need much closet space."

"Now that you'll be working, you might need more clothes."

"I'm okay for a while. I've got my army boots for the construction site, five tee-shirts, and three pairs of jeans. What more could a man want?"

"Sounds like you're set. Does Reggie have a washer and dryer?"

"Yes."

"Oh."

He chuckled. "You sound disappointed."

"I was hoping I could get you over here to do laundry, at least."

"Baby, I'm going to be at your house every chance I get. I just don't want to intrude on your time with Sunny."

"If Sunny behaves as usual, she'll be gone more than she's here. Besides, I think she may be coming around."

"How do you mean?"

She hesitated. "I'm not sure I should tell you this, but as we were driving away from the diner, she said, 'I can see why you like Tom. He's hot.'"

"No shit." She heard him swallow. "Sorry. That took me by surprise."

"I agreed with her, then told her all the other wonderful qualities I admire in you."

"I do mow a mean lawn," he said.

"Hey, I paid you for that," she said.

"I'll say." Tom groaned again. "We'd better not talk about that. What did you and Sunny do with the rest of your day?"

"She wanted to go hang out at her friends', but I talked her into going to the beach. I haven't been to the beach, just for fun, all summer."

"Did you swim?"

"Off and on. We relaxed on the beach till we got too hot, then swam for a few minutes, then greased each other up with sunscreen and laid on the beach again. I read. She texted her friends. Probably about how boring her mom is."

There was long silence.

"Tom?"

"Hmm? Sorry. I was picturing you lying on the beach. Imagining what it would be like to rub sunscreen all over you."

She caught her breath. It took so little for this man to excite her. "I thought we weren't going to go there," she said shakily.

"Tell me about your swimsuit," he said.

Her heart rate kicked up a notch. "It's a green two-piece. Strapless top with double ties in the front. The bottom has double ties on the sides."

"I'll bet you're gorgeous in it." His voice was low and rough.

Aubrey couldn't suppress a shiver. "Oh, you know. It's a good style for a woman without much on top."

"Now you've got me thinking about *them*. And wondering how I'm going to sleep without one of them in my hand."

Her heart was racing now. "And now I'm thinking of your big hands, and what they do to me."

"And how soft your skin is, and the sounds you make."

She was almost too breathless to speak. "And how big you are. And how you feel inside me."

His groan this time was long and loud. "Baby. We have to stop. This is just about to kill me."

She rolled onto her side and curled up in a fetal position. "Oh, Tom …"

He was breathless. "Quick. Talk about … something else. Anything."

"Um. Craig said he's dropping the custody petition. Oh, I told you that last night."

"That's okay. Keep talking."

"Well, I told him he'd have to tell Sunny, but he said he never told her he drafted it in the first place." She could feel her heartrate slowing.

"Good. But I'm sure she wouldn't have gone along with it." His breathing was slower now.

She rolled onto her back. "I think she might have yesterday, but she's happier with me today."

"How could anyone *not* be happy with you? I love you, Aubrey."

She was glad he wasn't there to see the tears sliding past her temples and into her hair. She did her best to keep them from her voice. "I love you, Tom. So much."

"Good. Don't stop believing in me. Please."

"I won't, my love. I promise."

He took a deep breath and exhaled shakily. "Goodnight, Aubrey."

"Goodnight, Tom."

Chapter 12

Nest 105, Day 31

R eggie didn't have a land line, only a cell. Tom's call in the morning was quick, because Reggie was heading to work as soon as he dropped Tom at the construction site.

"Good luck!" she said, as he announced his arrival at the site.

"Thanks, babe. It'll be great."

The day passed slowly for her, but she was excited all day, knowing he was working at the job she'd helped arrange. She was dumbfounded when he called just after five and told her the job with Craig's company "didn't work out."

She asked him why not, and he said he'd tell her more later, but just wanted her to know he got an even better job, through Reggie. He had spent the day driving a truck for a flooring company owned by Reggie's uncle.

"I'm learning how to install, too," he said, sounding pleased.

"Can you come over for dinner?" she asked meekly. The news about his job had thrown her, and she felt unsure of herself.

"That would be great!" he declared. "Carolyn's coming over here this evening, so I'm sure they'd like the place to themselves."

She heard Reggie's voice in the background, and Tom's laugh.

"I'll pick you up at six," she said.

"I can walk."

"Don't be silly. It'll only take me a few minutes to drive there."

"Okay. Thanks, babe. I'll see you at six."

After they disconnected, she sat at the table, staring blankly at the schoolbooks, lists and other teaching materials spread out before her. Tom had a job he apparently liked and was staying with a good man in a nice place. She could see him every day, or nearly. So, why was she feeling so blue?

An image appeared in her mind of Tom in the back yard, telling her that every good thing that had happened to him was because of her. She'd protested, but he'd insisted, and the idea had pleased her. Now, he was receiving help from others – Rachel McDowd, Reggie, even Kate and Sunny – and he wasn't as beholden to her any longer.

With a sickening rush of shame, Aubrey realized what she felt was fear; that same fear of abandonment that had troubled her when she'd learned of Craig's infidelity, and when Sunny had wanted to live with her dad. And it all came from the fear that Tom was no longer in her debt.

She stood up, grabbed her purse and stepped into her sandals. Sunny was at the movies with a couple of girlfriends and wouldn't be home until suppertime. Aubrey needed to talk, and Kate would understand better than anyone.

"Don't beat yourself up," Kate insisted, pouring Aubrey's second glass of iced tea. "It's natural to want to help the people we love, and just as natural to feel a little discarded when they don't need us as much as they once did."

"I didn't know I was that selfish."

"It's not selfish. We all need to be liked and like to be needed. Remember how you felt when Sunny was a toddler, and you went back to work? You resented her perfectly nice day care because they did such a good job and Sunny was happy there."

Aubrey shrugged her shoulders. "I suppose I did, at first. But –"

"But then you realized that Sunny was getting a real benefit from being socialized to other adults and children. And then, when she started to school, and when she fell in love with her third-grade teacher, and –"

"You're right," Aubrey said, laughing. "You're right. Guess I've always been selfish."

"No," Kate said sternly. "That's not selfish. Those parents – you've seen them yourself – who bring their little ones to day care and then torture them by lingering, they're the selfish ones. They're gratified by their children's frantic, demonstrated need of them. You taught Sunny that she could be away from you and still be safe, still function."

"But, as Tom pointed out, he's not my child. He's a grown man, and he comes with all kinds of baggage. Some of his problems may not be fixable. And maybe I don't even have the right, or the ability, to fix the ones that are."

"So, you come with this need to be needed. Is that so awful? Did you *object* to Reggie's help, or to the public defender doing her job?"

"No," Aubrey admitted.

"Then give yourself the same breaks you give Tom. Your feelings are your feelings. Long as you're not giving in to resentment, you're doing fine." She gave her friend a hug. "Tom's lucky to have you on his side."

It seemed Tom agreed with Kate. When Aubrey pulled up at the address on Reggie's card, Tom was waiting on the front porch, and hurried to the car. Once in the passenger seat, he held her face between his hands and gave her a long, lingering kiss.

"Wow, I've missed you." He kissed her again. "You look good, you smell good, and you sure do taste good."

"Mmmm. You, too." She slid her hands behind his neck and drew him down for another kiss.

He slipped his hands inside her thin, sleeveless shirt to caress her back. "You feel good, too." One of his hands wandered to the front of her shirt and under her bra to cup her bare breast.

She felt the stir of heat between her legs. As hungry for him as he was for her, she pressed her palm against the hard ridge that bulged the front of his jeans.

"Damn," he said. "Damn." His hand left her breast and he pulled her fingers from his crotch. "I'm as horny as a teenager with no place to take his girl on prom night."

She laughed, refitting her bra. "Maybe when it gets dark, we'll just park someplace and do it in the backseat."

"Don't tempt me." He squirmed uncomfortably. "And take your time getting home. I need to, uh, *calm down* before we see Sunny."

"Oops! And she'll be home by the time we get back. I'll drive around the block a few times if I need to."

He shifted in his seat and stretched his legs as much as he could. "Just try not to look so damn sexy for a few minutes."

"I will if you will."

He had himself under control by the time they drove into the carport. When they entered the kitchen, Sunny was setting the table, without being told.

"Hi, sweetie," Aubrey said. "Thank you for doing that."

"No problem," she answered breezily. "Hey, Tom."

"Hey, Sunny. How are you?"

"Good, thanks. How'd the job go?"

Tom caught Aubrey's eye, unsure what to say. Aubrey gave him a go-ahead nod.

"It was great. The guys are good to work with. I think it'll work out."

Sunny sat at the table and crossed one leg over the other. Looking and sounding very grownup, she said, "I'm sorry the job with my dad didn't work out."

Aubrey stared. "How did you know?"

"Dad texted me. Said he wanted to tell me before you did. He said Tom's arrest meant he couldn't work for him. He also told me Tom is probably a child molester, and I shouldn't be alone with him." She looked from Tom to her mother and back again. "I told him I didn't believe for a minute that Tom hurt Heather or anyone else, and I thought firing him – and not even letting him know until he showed up at the worksite – was a shitty thing to do."

"Sunny!" Aubrey remonstrated. "Your language is crude, and you need to show your father more respect."

She glanced at Tom. He was sitting with his elbow on the table and his hand covering his mouth. She could tell by the expression in his eyes that he was struggling not to laugh. She couldn't help grinning in response.

"Even when he's being shitty," she added, and they all laughed.

Dinner was pleasant. Tom ate three helpings of spaghetti with meatballs, two servings of salad and half a dozen slices of toasted garlic bread. Sunny was talkative and funny. Her description of the movie she'd seen that afternoon had her mother and Tom laughing out loud.

Tom went into more detail about his new job, describing the two fellows he worked with, and the three installations they'd handled that day. "Bobby says installing is hard on your back and knees, and it'll be even tougher for a guy my size. But I don't have to do this forever."

"Do you have something else in mind?" asked Sunny, pulling apart a slice of garlic bread.

"I was sort of thinking about going back to school." Tom glanced at Aubrey. "Maybe get into teaching."

She smiled, and their gazes held for several seconds. It occurred to Aubrey that she was very happy just sitting at the kitchen table, eating spaghetti with her child and the man she loved. And she loved listening to him plan his future.

After dinner, while Tom and Aubrey began washing the dishes, Sunny put the food away.

"I've got some calls to make," she announced. "I'll probably be in my room for an hour or more."

As she hurried down the hall, Tom and Aubrey looked at each

other in astonishment. He said, "Did she mean what I think she meant?"

Up to her elbows in suds, Aubrey nodded slowly. "I think so." Sighing, she added regretfully, "But I'm afraid we can't. Not with her in the house."

"I know," he said, taking a clean dish from her hand to rinse and dry it. "But I think it's a good sign that she said that. Like she accepts us as a couple."

When the dishes were put away, Aubrey and Tom moved to the living room and sat on the sofa to watch TV. Tom's arm was around Aubrey's shoulders, but they didn't dare risk further contact. Still, Aubrey enjoyed sitting quietly in Tom's embrace as they watched a quiz show and two situation comedies.

At nine, Tom suggested it was time for him to leave.

Wanting to make Sunny aware there was nothing amorous happening, she called out, "Sunny! Tom's leaving!"

Sunny rushed into the living room, clearly surprised to see the television on and her mother just standing beside Tom, holding his hand.

"So, goodnight, Tom," she said. "It was nice to see you."

"Goodnight, Sunny. Thanks for the movie review."

Aubrey followed Tom to the car, calling over her shoulder, "I'll be back in a little bit, sweetie."

At least it was dark when they pulled into Reggie's driveway and parked right behind his car. They turned toward each other.

"Well," Aubrey said. "Can you come over again tomorrow night?"

"You don't have to feed me every night, you know."

"I like to. And I think Sunny really enjoyed your company tonight."

Tom smiled, looking down at their joined hands. "She's a great girl, Aubrey. You've done a helluva job there."

"Thanks. I like her, too. Most of the time."

"Have you ever thought of having more kids?"

Aubrey felt her heart kick up a notch. "Sure. The doctors say there's no reason why not. But it would have to be soon." She hesitated. "Do you want to be a father, Tom?"

"I never really thought about it, until lately." In the darkness of the car, his gaze lifted to hers. "I can't really think about anything … permanent. Not until this whole crazy business is over."

"It will be. I'm sure of it."

"You're incredible, Aubrey. When I'm with you, I feel like anything's possible." He lifted her hands and kissed the knuckles. "Goodnight, baby. I love you."

"I love you, Tom. See you tomorrow."

Chapter 13

Nest 105, Day 35

"A date? Really?" Aubrey smiled at the phone as if it were Tom in person. "I'd love that."

"Well, it's the least I can do. I've eaten your food every night this week. And this paycheck is burning a hole in my pocket."

"What did you have in mind?" Aubrey asked. "Dinner? A movie?"

"How much time do you have?"

"Well, Sunny also has a date tonight. Her curfew is eleven, so I should be home by then to make sure she's on time."

Tom said, "Then let's make it dinner. You'll have to drive. Reggie told me I can use his car when he doesn't need it, but he's taking Carolyn out tonight. If you don't mind, we can go to your house after dinner and wait together for Sunny to get home."

"That sounds great," Aubrey said. "I'm so excited!" After she'd hung up the phone, she danced a little jig of happiness, giddy as a teenager.

She dressed with great care that evening. She had a deep blue dress of a slinky jersey material. Sleeveless, it tied at both shoulders and the A-line skirt swung at mid-thigh. She had purchased it last year for a faculty party, then decided it was a bit too sexy for a school function. She rubbed lotion on her legs, and stepped into a pair of silver designer heels, picked up at a consignment store years ago. Craig hadn't liked her to wear them because the extra three inches they gave her made her his height. She added curl to her auburn hair and pulled some back from the crown into a silver filigree clip in back. Her only jewelry was a pair of silver earrings in the shape of tiny sea turtles.

"Wow, Mom!" Sunny declared. "You look like America's next top model!"

Aubrey laughed and kissed her daughter before applying dark red lipstick.

"You look very nice, too, sweetheart." Sunny was dressed casually in white crop pants and a hot pink tee-shirt emblazoned with "Oak Island" over a palm tree. She and her date – a boy her own age whom Aubrey knew – were going to the movies.

The doorbell rang and Sunny squealed. She still hadn't finished braiding her hair.

"I'll get it," Aubrey said.

Carl, Sunny's date, stood on the front porch. A tall skinny boy with an unfortunate haircut, Carl greeted her with, "Hey, Ms. Benson! I'm –" He got a good look at her then, and his jaw dropped.

Aubrey laughed. "Come on in, Carl. I'll get Sunny."

As soon as Carl and Sunny drove off, Aubrey carefully made her way down the steps from the side door, thinking these shoes would take some getting used to.

At Reggie's house, Tom was waiting on the front porch, wearing a black tee-shirt and his best jeans. When he got in the car, he whistled, looking her up and down.

"I don't deserve this," he said, gesturing to dress and hair. "I mean, you always look great, but this is over the top."

"I just wanted you to see that I don't always look like a teacher or a beach bum."

He looked closer at her dress, and Aubrey knew the second he realized she was not wearing a bra. He squeezed his eyes shut and shook his head. "Oh, man," he whispered. "I'm in a lot of trouble."

At the restaurant, a reasonably priced seafood place on the beach, he asked her to wait while he loped around the car to open her door and take her hand. As she stood, he whistled again.

She kissed him lightly on the corner of his mouth, then wiped away the lipstick smudge with her thumb. Inside, she tried not to notice the frankly admiring male stares that followed her.

At their table overlooking the water, they ordered drinks and talked about his new job. "I got paid today. The boss let us stop at a bank at lunchtime, so I could open an account. And after work, Bobby – you know, he keeps the truck at his house – stopped at Walmart so I could buy a cell phone." He handed her a piece of paper with a phone number. "It's nothing fancy, but now we can talk for as long as we want."

Aubrey tucked the slip of paper in her bag. "I'm glad you like your job so much, sweetheart. Really glad." She realized she meant it and was proud of herself.

"It's not what I want to do forever, but it's a steady job and the pay is decent. I crunched the numbers, and if I'm careful and continue living with Reggie, I should be able to start paying you back in a couple of months. How's five hundred a month for six months?"

"Tom, I'm in no hurry to –"

"I know, honey, and I love you for it. But it weighs on me, so let me do that. I can get along without a car until my insurance comes through. Then, maybe this fall, I can start taking some night classes at the college."

"That's so exciting!"

He smiled, and his expression was contemplative. "I never thought about being a teacher until you put the bug in my ear. Now it's what I think about most, next to you."

She put her hand over his on the table. "I'm so proud of you, Tom."

Tom started to reply, then his attention was caught by looks he was receiving from a nearby table. A heavyset man dining with a woman was staring at Tom and whispering something to the server, who looked around at Tom with a shocked expression.

"That a guy's a cop," Tom said quietly.

Aubrey, who had watched the interplay along with Tom, asked, "How do you know?"

"See that bulge in the back of his jacket? That's a gun in a belt holster."

The server approached their table and stood near Aubrey. Without a smile or eye contact, she asked for their order, wrote it down and left without another word.

Aubrey looked questioningly at Tom. "What's going on?"

His expression was bleak. "I think I know." He sighed, staring into his glass of tea. "Let's try to ignore it. Tell me about your mother, back in Baltimore."

Anxious to appear unaffected by the odd scene she'd just witnessed, she launched into a story about her mother, who was remarried, and whose husband was difficult for Aubrey to tolerate. "Just kind of a blowhard," she admitted. "Always telling me what I ought to do about almost everything."

While she spoke, Aubrey observed their server at a couple of other tables. At one, she jerked her head in their direction and the two patrons turned to look at them. At the next, she actually pointed to Tom and the four diners openly stared.

Aubrey stared back, and when one of the women pursed her lips and shook her head with a shame-on-you expression, Aubrey stuck out her tongue. The woman gasped and turned red.

"I'm sorry, baby," Tom said, turning the hand she held palm up to clasp hers before releasing it. He put both his hands in his lap. "I never thought this would happen. I'm guessing the cop recognized me – I'm easy to spot, after all – and he clued in the waitress. Now she's spreading the word that there's this bad dude in the place."

His expression was filled with sadness and regret. She reached under the table to take his hand and return it to the surface, then held it in both of hers.

"It's not fair," she said. "But stupid, gullible people are everywhere." She raised her voice a notch. "So, screw 'em."

"Do you want to leave?" he said.

"If you're good, I'm good," she assured him. "But promise me you're *not* leaving a tip."

Despite her bravado, Aubrey found it difficult to enjoy her meal. Tom kept his eyes mostly on his plate, with an occasional rueful glance at her. They ate their meal and asked for the check, which was brought to them by the sullen waitress. Rather than enjoy a leisurely cup of coffee, as they would have preferred, Tom paid the check, *sans* tip, and they stood to go.

Aubrey started toward the cop, but Tom grabbed her hand and said, "Let it go."

"I just want to find out who he is," she protested.

"*Please*," he said, and she gave in.

However, on the way out, the *maître d'*, who was apparently the only one not informed of Tom's identity, asked if they'd enjoyed their meal. Aubrey couldn't resist saying, "Not at all. The food was good, but our server was terribly rude. We won't be back."

He started to apologize, but Tom just held up his palm in a gesture of dismissal and ushered Aubrey ahead of him out the door.

In her car, he leaned his head back against the headrest and closed his eyes. Aubrey's heart ached for him. She knew he'd been looking forward to this date, and now he felt humiliated.

"How about a walk on the beach?" she asked. "Still plenty of daylight."

He chuckled. "Sure. Why not? Maybe no one will recognize me there."

She drove to the next beach access and parked the car. Tom jumped out and came around to open her door, while Aubrey slipped off her shoes. With his arm around her waist, they took the path through the low dunes and beach vegetation to the open beach. Dozens of people were walking, playing, swimming, or just sitting on the sand in the golden evening light.

On the windy beach, Aubrey had to gather her skirt in one hand

and pull it tight to keep the wind from blowing it above her waist. Tom walked along with his arm around her shoulders and his head bowed.

"Tom, you can't let ignorant people make you feel bad about yourself. That cop and the waitress and the other people – they don't know you. Like too many people, they're ready to judge you without knowing anything about the circumstances."

"They were ready to judge you, too, Aubrey, just for being with me. Aren't you worried that this is how it'll be from now on? I don't exactly blend in, you know. Even if the charges are dropped, who will know that? I'll always be the guy that attacked that little girl."

She stopped and turned to face him, smiling encouragement. "We'll take out a full-page ad in the paper. 'This man innocent of all charges!'"

"Aubrey, let's face it. I'm a marked man. As far as the world is concerned, you're the girlfriend of a child molester. Are you sure you can take that?"

She put her free hand on his chest. "Yes. I'm sure. Like I'm sure you never hurt Heather. Like I'm sure this will all work out in the end. Like I'm sure I love you."

"Even with all this," Tom said, smiling gently down at her, "I still feel like the luckiest man in the world."

"Good. Now let's go before this wind pulls my skirt out of my hand and everyone on this beach learns what color panties I'm wearing."

He grinned. "Then, by all means, let's scram. I'm the only one authorized to receive that intel."

He took her free hand and they hurried back to the car, laughing together.

The sun was just setting when they arrived at Aubrey's house. Both eager, they wasted no time getting out of the car and into the house. She tossed her keys and bag on the kitchen table and they raced to the bedroom, where she locked the door and threw herself into his arms.

His mouth came down hard on hers and he held her so tightly

she could barely breathe. Between kisses, he said, "Babe, it's been so long."

"Too long," she agreed. With her arms locked around his neck, her feet were just clear of the floor. She kicked her shoes off.

He backed toward the bed and sat down, pulling her across his lap, still frantically kissing her. She skimmed his tee-shirt over his head and ran her hands over his back and shoulders. The feel of the ridges of muscle under his skin made her weak.

"Aubrey! I don't know if I can … take it slow."

"Don't even try. If we hurry, we might … have time for another."

He slid the narrow straps of her dress off her shoulders and pushed the top down to expose her breasts.

"Oh, yeah. There they are." He kept one arm around her while he caressed her breasts, his hands rough against her soft skin. Her nipples tingled and rose to hard little points. "Oh, baby," he whispered. His mouth moved from her lips to her breasts.

She bucked in his lap when he captured each nipple in turn between his teeth, lightly biting and tugging. "Yes, Tom. More. *More!*"

She felt his hand slide under her skirt to stroke her thighs. He hooked a finger around the crotch of her panties and whisked the tiny scrap of lace down her legs and off. The hand returned, and she felt his fingers penetrate. Her back arched and the room spun like a top.

Above the sound of her own harsh breaths, she heard Tom say, "I gotta get these jeans off while I still can." Lifting her, he stood and settled her on the bed. He shucked his jeans and shorts while she tugged her dress over her head and tossed it aside.

He jerked open the drawer of the bedside table and grabbed a handful of foil packets. She took one from his hand and opened it. He stood by the bed, groaning, as she sheathed him. She pushed herself back on the bed, opening her thighs and holding out her arms to him. "Hurry, baby," she said. "I want you."

He knelt between her legs, positioned himself, and thrust fully into her. Aubrey had thought herself accustomed to his size by now, but the suddenness of the impact generated a muffled shriek through her clenched jaws. Her traitorous hips rose to take him deeper and she sobbed with mingled pain and passion. But when he, seeing her discomfort, would have withdrawn, she wrapped her legs around his hips and clutched at his ribs.

"Aubrey!" he cried hoarsely.

"It's all right," she whispered, panting. "Just give me a minute to adjust."

An hour would not have been enough time to adjust, and a minute was too long for her to wait. In seconds, she was rotating her hips, coaxing him to thrust. With her body and voice, she demanded he satisfy her, demanded he spend himself. In only a few minutes, he did.

Soon after, they lay side by side, breathing hard and laughing.

"Wow," she said.

And he replied, "Wow."

"We really needed that."

He pulled her against his side. "I've been thinking about this all week. Coming up with different scenarios of how we could get time alone in a private place."

"Yeah?" she said, ruffling the damp curls on his chest. "What did you come up with?"

"You don't want to know." He cupped her breast and caressed her nipple with his thumb. "The most sensible one involved Bobby leaving the flooring truck with me, and you and me parking in some deserted area and doing it on the rolls of carpet in the back."

"Hmmm. Very romantic."

"It got kind of ... *uncomfortable* carrying rolls of carpet back and forth. I kept checking to see which was softest. Then I'd picture you on that carpet, and me on you, and, well, you get the idea."

"I believe I do. Maybe we'll try that someday."

He pulled her across his chest, and she reveled in the feel of his hair against her breasts. His hands squeezed her buttocks as she explored his mouth with her tongue. She slid down his body by pushing against his upper arms.

"Good grief," she muttered. "Your arms are bigger around than my thighs." She squeezed the muscle, or tried to. "And apparently carved out of stone."

He chuckled. "Feel free to explore, ma'am."

She did. Learning the curves and angles of his impressive body was an activity of which she never tired. The chest where she now rested her head was solid as oak, but she knew where the tender places could be found. The hard little points of his nipples in their nests of curly hair drew her mouth like a butterfly to a flower. She scraped one sensitive peak with her teeth, drawing it into her mouth to suck, while probing the other with her fingernail.

He uttered one breathless little "oh" and "ah" after another, his ribs rising and falling beneath her. When the nipple in her mouth grew plump and red, she moved to the other and gave it the same attention. Then slowly, deliberately, she trailed her tongue down his chest and belly to his navel, while her hand crept between his thighs to fondle the softest flesh on his hard body. Moments later, her mouth followed.

"Aubrey!" he cried, gasping. His hands trembled in her hair and his thighs went rigid with tension. When she felt he couldn't take any more, she kissed her way back up his body, and reached across him for the condoms on the bedside table. Again, she covered him, while he watched with fevered eyes.

She straddled him, and with those massive arms, he lifted, lowered, and slowly impaled her. Their gazes locked, their fingers intertwined, and they moved together, their cries of passion mingling.

Aubrey grew limp with gratification, and only Tom's powerful grip kept her upright. Later, when his own climax overtook him, he seized her buttocks and pulled her forward, his hips arcing high and his face twisting in a grimace of pleasure. With a small shriek, she dropped onto his wide chest and lay sobbing and laughing helplessly.

"Holy shit," he said. "How're we gonna top that?"

It took her a moment to respond. "We can't," she whispered breathlessly. "All we can do now is … shake hands and part friends. I don't know about you … but I'm joining a convent."

"I don't think they'd take me." He rolled to his side and carefully withdrew from her. The sound she made was a cross between a whimper and a sigh. "You okay?" he asked, smoothing her hair back from her face.

"Big man," she said, "I've never been more okay."

He chuckled. "As soon as some blood returns to my arms and legs, I'll shower and get dressed. I can't see the clock from here, and I don't have the strength to turn my head."

She rolled her eyes toward the bedside table. "Mmmm. It's a little after ten. We're okay for a while. But wake me if I fall asleep."

"No problem. But who's going to wake *me*?"

He pulled her into his arms and held her gently. Wrapped together, they dozed for several minutes. Tom roused first and carefully eased away from her, stood and walked to the bathroom. One of Aubrey's favorite things was to watch Tom walk away from the bed, but she lacked the energy to open her eyes. She heard the shower come on and was just wishing she had the strength to join him, when she felt his arms beneath her, lifting her up.

He maneuvered her carefully through the bathroom door and stepped past the open shower curtain. The warm water was soothing and reviving at the same time.

"Are you going to carry me around until Sunny gets home?" she asked.

"If you want me to," he said.

"No," she decided. "I can do this. Step one." She pulled his head down and gave him a long, lingering kiss. "Step two." She squirmed in his arms and he gently lowered her feet to the tub floor. "Step three." She unwound her arms from his neck and stepped back into the rushing water.

When she opened her eyes, he was watching her with so much love and tenderness in his smile, it caught at her throat. She put her arms around his waist and pressed against him. "I love you, Tom."

He hugged her tightly, bending his head close to her ear. "There aren't enough words to tell you how much I love you, Aubrey. You've given me a whole new life."

She swallowed past the lump in her throat, then gave his bottom a playful smack and stepped back a few inches. "Now, Tom. We both know I have a crying problem," she said. "If there were a 'Weepers Anonymous,' I'd have to go to meetings for it, especially if you're going to be saying things like that."

Smiling, he leaned down to kiss her. "Don't start now. You may have noticed I don't have a hankie."

They had just finished dressing when the doorbell rang.

"Who could that be?" Aubrey wondered.

"Maybe Sunny forgot her key," said Tom.

"She wouldn't come to the front door."

Aubrey yanked open the door just as Tom came up behind her. Two uniformed police officers stood on the porch. Aubrey's heart leapt into her throat. Had something happened to Sunny? She couldn't speak; just stared at them with eyes wide and mouth gaping.

"Ms. Benson?" one officer said. She nodded. "We have information that Tom Clayton might be here."

So, not Sunny. She breathed a sigh of relief. Tom stepped up beside Aubrey.

"I'm Clayton. What's this about?"

One officer put his hand on the weapon in his holster, the other brought forward a pair of handcuffs.

No, thought Aubrey. *This cannot be happening again.*

"Mr. Clayton, you're under arrest for sexual assault of a minor." The officer with the handcuffs stepped through the doorway. "Please turn around and put your hands on your head."

Tom looked at Aubrey with a stunned expression, then did what the officer said.

"Wait a minute. This can't be right," Aubrey said. "He's on bond for that charge."

"Can't help you there, ma'am," the other officer said. "We have a warrant for his arrest, issued today." The officer holding Tom's arm nudged him toward the door, and Tom, with one last despairing look at Aubrey, stepped onto the porch.

"Tom! I'll call Reggie," Aubrey shouted after him. "It'll be okay!"

The officers put Tom in the back of their vehicle and drove away. Aubrey, clutching a porch post, lowered herself to the step and sobbed aloud.

No, she told herself. *I can't let go. I've got to pull myself together.*

She rose and stumbled through the open doorway. She grabbed her cell phone from the kitchen table, selected Reggie's number and waited for an answer. When his recorded voice spoke the greeting, she nearly broke down again. At the tone, she fumbled through an explanation of what had happened, ending with, "It must be a mistake, Reggie. Please call me. *Please!"*

When Sunny came home a few minutes before eleven, she found her mother pacing the living room, arms folded and eyes red.

"Hi, Mom. How was your –" She paused, looking closely at Aubrey's face. "What's wrong?" She glanced at her watch. "I'm not late. What happened?"

"It's Tom," Aubrey said. "He was arrested again. Less than an hour ago. They wouldn't say why. Same charge as before, but –" She broke down, dropping into a chair and sobbing.

"Mom!" Sunny ran to Aubrey and knelt in front of her. "It's got to be a mistake." She wrapped her arms around her mother and hugged her tightly.

"Oh, God, Sunny! I don't know what to *do!"* Her sobs were loud and harsh.

Sunny rocked her back and forth. "It'll be okay, Mom. You'll see. It's some kind of mistake. Just a stupid mistake. *Please,* Mom."

Aubrey knew she was scaring her child, so she fought to get herself under control. While Sunny ran to get a box of tissues, Aubrey swallowed the sobs that threatened to rise in her throat, gripping her thighs so tightly her fingernails left red crescents in her skin.

When Sunny returned, Aubrey was able to nod and give her daughter a tremulous smile. "I'm sorry, sweetie. It was the suddenness of it. I just never expected –" She broke off, wiping her eyes and blowing her nose.

"I understand, Mom. I can see you really love Tom. I've never felt that way about anybody. I've had a few crushes that seemed real at the time, but they weren't, or I wouldn't have got over them so quick."

She sat on the floor in front of Aubrey's chair and rested her head against her mother's knee.

"*Gotten*," Aubrey responded automatically, then sighed and stroked her daughter's hair. "I hope someday you really love someone, my angel."

"I'm not sure I want to." Sunny's voice held a little quaver that touched Aubrey's heart.

"You haven't seen much of the happy side of being in love, have you? Between the divorce from your dad and these troubles with Tom, it must seem hardly worth it." She leaned forward and wrapped arms around Sunny's shoulders from behind, pressing her cheek to the top of Sunny's head. "But it *is* worth it, honey. When it's good, and when the person you're fighting for is the right one, it's *so* worth it."

"But how do you know when he's the right one?"

"That's a hard question to answer." Aubrey thought for a minute. "The one you love has to be right for you, but also a good person in his own right. If you're the only one who sees the goodness, you have to wonder if you're fooling yourself. It's important not to be willfully blind to someone's faults, just because you *want* him to be good."

"And you think Tom is a good person?"

"Yes, I do. And I'm not the only one who sees it. Kate and Reggie think he's solid, and they're not easily fooled. And his public defender, a very smart woman, believes Tom is innocent of hurting Heather."

"I think so, too," said Sunny.

"That's why it hurts so much to think about him being in jail, and to know we can't help him. Not tonight, anyway."

They were quiet together for a long time, then Sunny spoke up. "I don't want to be an interior designer, after all."

"No?"

"I want to be a lawyer and help people who are falsely accused. I think maybe there's nothing worse than being accused of something you didn't do, especially something like Heather is saying Tom did."

"I love you so much, baby girl," Aubrey said. She kissed the top of her daughter's head. "I'm so proud to be your mom."

Sunny turned in her mother's arms and hugged her. "Thanks, Mom."

Later, Aubrey lay in bed, her little devotional in her hands. She was stunned when she opened it to a page that quoted Romans 12:9-10. She read it twice silently, then aloud. "Love must be sincere. Hate what is evil; cling to what is good. Be devoted to one another in love. Honor one another above yourselves."

Chapter 14

Nest 105, Day 36

Tom's image flickered onto the screen in the visitor's booth at the detention center.

"Aubrey! I couldn't believe it when they told me you were here," he said.

"Hi, sweetheart," she answered. "How're you holding up?"

"I'm okay, but they won't tell me anything. I don't know what's going on."

"Brace yourself." Aubrey took a deep breath. "Reggie called me last night, after he got my message. All he knew then was that a new warrant had been issued for your arrest, and they couldn't find you at his place. Then one of the local cops reported having seen us together at that restaurant."

Tom nodded slowly. "And so, they came to your house."

"He called back this morning to tell me what he found out. It turns out that another girl from the high school reported that you attacked and groped her, but she got away without injury."

"*What?*"

She nodded. "She says this happened the night after you supposedly attacked Heather."

He thought for a moment. "The night of the boil. That's the night we – the night I came home with you."

"Exactly. But I didn't see you until about eight that night. Reggie wasn't able to find out what time this bogus attack is supposed to have happened. He's going to find out. If it was any time after eight, you have a solid alibi."

Tom leaned his elbows on the table and lowered his head into his hands, running his fingers through his hair. *He needs a haircut,* Aubrey thought tenderly, if irrelevantly.

She went on. "Reggie called his uncle first thing this morning to tell him what happened, and to let him know he believes you're innocent. His uncle is going to hold your job for you."

Tom looked up at the camera. "Well, that's something," he said with a brief smile.

"And as I was leaving to come here, Sunny told me to tell you she believes in you, too. You have a lot of people on your side, Tom."

She watched the play of emotions across his face – despair, hope, confusion and, finally, determination. He squared his shoulders and sat back in his chair with his hands in his lap.

"Okay. So, what's next?"

"I'm afraid there's more. Reggie found out that another female, an adult tourist, is saying she was attacked by a 'big guy' on the beach Thursday night. Assaulted and … raped."

He looked flabbergasted. "You mean, night before last?"

She nodded. "She didn't identify anyone. Just said –"

"Yeah, yeah," he said. "Big guy." He grimaced. "Sorry, babe. I'm just getting tired of hearing that."

"But, Tom, listen. She says she was attacked about ten. The guy grabbed her and dragged her into the seagrass, beat and raped her. Horrible. But you and Sunny and I watched that movie that ended at ten, and then I drove you to Reggie's, and we sat in the car a while."

He shrugged. "Yeah, for a few minutes."

"But it was well after ten when you got out of the car. So, you have an alibi for that attack."

"Yes. That's good. But what with that Southport tourist in June and three attacks in Oak Island – and this last one an actual rape – the authorities have got to be thinking there's a serial rapist on the loose. And I fit the description, so no way are they going to set a reasonable bond."

"You're probably right. But the rapist left DNA, and once that gets tested, they'll know it wasn't you. Reggie doesn't think you'll even be charged. But I'm afraid bail is out of the question."

He nodded. "God only knows how long it'll take to get the results of the DNA. It's hell to be locked up when I haven't done anything."

She longed to touch him, to put her arms around him and offer him comfort. "I hate this for you, sweetheart. And I miss you so much. But I'll be back tomorrow, and we –"

"You don't need to be driving here every day, babe."

"If I want to see you, I do. Their online system is still out of service. And I do want to see you." She smiled. "Lucky for us, the admissions officer is a former student. One of the ones who actually *liked* me."

Tom took a deep breath and squared his shoulders again. "Well, it's not exactly the army, but I do get three hots and a cot, and plenty of time to read. The worst of it, Aubrey, is how I've turned your whole life upside down."

"Together we'll get both our lives right side up again, Tom."

She was pulling into her carport when Reggie called with more information. He said the teenager alleging Tom assaulted her said the attack took place around eleven the night after Heather's assault.

"*Ha!*" Aubrey said. "Tom and I were together from about eight that night, and right around the clock until he was arrested on the beach."

"Anybody else with you?"

Aubrey turned off the engine and sat in the car. "Yes! Four volunteers with the program – Kate, Brett, Lynn and Bernie, and several onlookers. I remember Lynn saying she had to get home because it was after eleven."

"And then?"

"Kate, Brett, Tom and I went to the Lazy Turtle to celebrate. We were there until almost midnight. Then Tom and I went to my house. And we were together last Thursday, when that poor woman was raped on the beach."

"I'm sure the judge will dismiss the charge involving the other girl, and it's unlikely Tom will even be charged in connection with the rape of the tourist. Just the same, the authorities are freaking out. You know this kind of crime is practically unheard of in this area, and nobody wants to scare off the tourists, so I doubt any judge would set bail for him now."

"That's what Tom said. I left a message for Rachel McDowd, but I expect he'll just have to wait it out." She swallowed the lump in her throat. "I hate that for him. He's not a criminal. He's a hero."

They exchanged a few other comments, then disconnected with promises to keep in contact. Aubrey was getting out of her car when she was startled by the sudden appearance of her daughter at the side door. Sunny was smiling and bouncing with excitement.

"What is it?" Aubrey asked.

"I found out some stuff today! Hurry up!"

Aubrey rushed into the house with Sunny on her heels. "Tell me!"

"Diane knows this girl Robyn, who always knows *everything* that's going on. I asked Di to ask Robyn about Heather. Robyn told Diane the other girl who said Tom attacked her is Danielle. She's like Heather's BFF. And – you'll love this – Heather also asked this *other* friend, Arlene, to accuse Tom. Arlene told another girl, who told Robyn, that when she told Heather she couldn't lie to the police like that, Heather got all hysterical and said Arlene wasn't her friend anymore."

"Oh, Sunny! I got lost in there somewhere, but I think you're saying that Heather asked Arlene to lie about Tom, Arlene refused, and Heather ended their friendship. So, Danielle, who *did* lie about Tom, must be doing it out of loyalty to Heather. Have I got it?"

Sunny, grinning, nodded vigorously. "Isn't that great?"

Aubrey hugged her daughter. "Baby, that's terrific! Tom already has an alibi for the time Danielle was attacked, but now we know that Heather has been asking her friends to lie about Tom. We need to let the public defender know about Heather's conspiracy right away. I hope she calls me back today."

She released Sunny and sat in a kitchen chair to reflect. "So, we know why Danielle lied, but I still can't figure out why Heather lied in the first place. And she didn't lie about being hit, just about Tom. Why? She must be protecting someone. Ricky Stout?"

"Mom, I don't really know Ricky," Sunny said. "But he's a senior now. I can't see him having anything to do with an underclassman like Heather."

"But he is a *big guy* in Heather's life."

Sunny sat opposite her mother at the table. "So, who says the one who really hit her had to be a big guy?"

"I don't know," Aubrey said, putting her hands to her cheeks. "It's all so confusing. The other accusers have all said it was a big guy, so I guess I just had it in my mind that she picked Tom to accuse because he's physically similar to the one who *really* hit her. But maybe she only chose Tom because he was briefly alone with her, and to her he seems … *expendable*."

Sunny shook her head. "That's awful. Nobody's expendable. Especially not Tom."

Aubrey reached across the table and took her daughter's hands in hers. "Thank you, baby girl. You really boost my spirits."

With Sunny's companionship, Aubrey made it through the rest of that day. But everything she did, from eating meals to taking out the trash to talking to Kate on the phone, reminded her that Tom was confined to a small cell in an unfriendly place.

At bedtime, still not having heard from Rachel McDowd, Aubrey knelt by her bed – something she had not done since she was a child – and prayed for God to keep Tom safe and at peace until the whole puzzling mess could be resolved. Then she got into bed, although sleep eluded her.

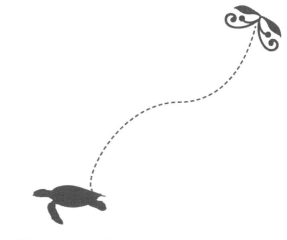

Chapter 15

Nest 105, Day 37

It was another hot Carolina day. The relentless sunlight reflected off the water of the Intracoastal Waterway like the flash of a knife blade as Aubrey and Sunny drove across the Swain's Cut Bridge over the Intracoastal Waterway.

Finding Ricky Stout was easier than Aubrey had expected. Against Tom's wishes and Reggie's advice, Sunny and her mother had set out as soon as Aubrey returned from visiting Tom. Aubrey had pondered the ethics of using her access to the school's computer to locate Ricky's address. Sunny had rolled her eyes and Googled the information on her phone in less than a minute.

"I hate to say this," Sunny declared, "because I know all this is really serious. But I like playing detective with you."

Aubrey smiled. "I get that. It's nice working as a team again, even though we're not happy about the need for it."

In less than half an hour, they were cruising into the community of Boiling Spring Lakes. Sunny consulted her phone's GPS and guided her mother through the series of turns leading to Ricky's home. Aubrey was nervously rehearsing in her mind a script to offer anyone who opened his door but, as it happened, she didn't need one. When they pulled up along the grass verge in front of his house, a young man appeared from a side door, holding a leash attached to a fat, lively, golden retriever puppy. The boy smiled as they got out of the car and approached.

"Are you Ricky Stout, the football player?" Sunny asked.

"Yeah, that's me," he answered, struggling to rein in the rambunctious pup. Just then the collar slipped over the puppy's head and he bolted for the street. Sunny, however, was quicker, grabbing the pup around his chubby middle until Ricky could stoop and pick him up.

"Thanks," said Ricky. "He's a handful. Mom said she thinks I really brought three pups home, because Beau moves so fast it's like he's everywhere at once. I'm trying to leash-train him."

Sunny stroked the puppy's ears and let him lick her face. "His name is Beau?" she asked, looking up at Ricky with a tilt of her head and a sideways glance that Aubrey found amusing. She had a front row seat at a demonstration of her daughter flirting, and it was resounding hit. Ricky smile showed he was captivated, his eyes never straying from Sunny.

"Yeah. Actually 'Beaufort.' After the town up the coast where my dad was born." He shifted the puppy to his other arm. "You look familiar. Do you go to South?"

Sunny looked down with a show of bashfulness, which Aubrey knew was faked; Sunny had never known a bashful day in her life. "Yes, but you wouldn't know me. I'm just a sophomore this year, and I'm not a cheerleader or anything."

Ricky's grin widened. "You should be," he said. He looked over at Aubrey. "Are you here to see my mom?"

"Your mom?"

Aubrey stepped forward. "Hi, Ricky. I'm Ms. Benson, and this is my daughter, Sunny. Why would we be seeing your mom?"

"Oh, no reason, ma'am. Mom's a bookkeeper, and she does the

books for a lot of small businesses around here. I just thought you might be a client. You look familiar."

Aubrey managed not to chuckle. She had been teaching at South Brunswick long before Sunny started school there, but she clearly didn't look familiar to Ricky. "I'm a teacher," Aubrey answered. "We actually came to talk to you."

"Really?" He hefted the wriggling pup into both arms. "Let me put him on the porch, and I'll –"

"I'll take care of him," Sunny offered.

"You sure?"

Sunny nodded. Ricky set the puppy on the ground and handed Sunny the leash. She moved away from the car and into the front yard, baby-talking the eager dog.

"Would you like to sit on the porch, Ms. Benson?" He gestured to the house. "Can I get you a glass of iced tea?"

"Thank you, Ricky, no." Aubrey was impressed by his good manners. "I'll only keep you a minute."

"Yes, ma'am. That's fine. What can I help you with?"

She leaned back against the fender of her car. "Can you tell me how well you know Heather Carson?"

"Heather?" Aubrey's heart raced as she saw color flood into Ricky's face. "Why? What'd she say about me?"

"Nothing, as far as I know. But a lot of people believe she has a serious crush on you."

He shoved his hands in his pockets and hunched his shoulders. "I keep hearing that, but I don't remember even talking to her. Maybe I did, but I talk to lots of people I don't know. I never touched her or asked her out or anything. I don't want to get her in trouble, but she's driving me crazy, Ms. Benson."

Despite herself, Aubrey found she liked this young man, and hoped he wasn't the one who had hurt Heather. "How do you mean?"

"Someone keeps pushing notes through the vents in my locker. You know … love notes." He blushed again. "Real mushy stuff. They're not signed, but the handwriting looks the same on all of them. The rest of the team's been giving me a hard time about it. I don't know for sure it was Heather, but one time when I found one in my locker and was reading it, I looked up and saw her watching me."

"I'm sorry you're having this problem, Ricky. We have an anti-harassment policy in school. Have you considered reporting her?"

He put his hands in his pockets and looked away. "That's what Mom said I should do, but she left it up to me. I don't want to hurt Heather's feelings, especially now. And, like I said, I can't *prove* it's her. I just wish she'd stop. Anyway, maybe she will now that she's got a real boyfriend."

"She has? Who?"

"I don't know the kid, but I saw them at McDonalds in Southport a couple of days ago. They were having this real intense conversation."

"Do you have a girlfriend, Ricky?"

He ducked his head. "Not really. I've been out a few times. But I never know what to say to girls." He glanced at Sunny, on her knees in the grass, playing with Beau. "*Most* girls."

"You said you didn't want to hurt Heather's feelings, 'especially now.' So, you heard what happened to Heather?"

"Well," Ricky said, "I heard rumors. I don't know how much is true."

"Someone hit her. Two weeks ago, tomorrow. I hate to sound like a TV detective, but do you remember where you were that Monday night?"

"I'm usually home Monday nights. I have a job at – Wait! I remember! I was at Tanner Jones' house watching the Olympics until after midnight. My mom let me 'cause Tanner has a big-screen."

Aubrey felt a mixture of disappointment and relief. She thanked Ricky and motioned to Sunny, who brought the puppy, walking calmly beside her, over to Ricky.

"Hey! You're good," Ricky said. "I wish I had your knack with Beau."

Sunny smiled. "Call me sometime and I'll come back over and help you with him."

Ricky beamed. "Okay. I'll call you."

They were opening their car doors when Ricky shouted, "Hey, Ms. Benson!"

She turned. "Yes?"

"I just wanted to say that I thought of something I know about Heather's boyfriend. I don't know his name, but I remember he was the equipment manager for the boys' soccer team when I was a sophomore."

"Thanks, Ricky," Aubrey called, waving.

"He's cute," said Sunny as they drove away.

"Ricky? Yes, I'd have to agree with you. But he seems very shy."

Sunny cocked her head. "I like shy guys. I don't know why, but I do."

Aubrey had to laugh. "Probably because they let you do all the talking." She sighed. "I wonder how we can find out who handled the equipment for the boys' soccer team year before last."

Sunny snapped her fingers. "The yearbook! I don't have the one we need because last year was my first. But you have your teacher's copy."

"Wow," said Aubrey. "Ricky was right. You *are* good."

He was easy to find in the section titled "Cougar Athletics." There was the photo of the boys' soccer team with a caption that identified the skinny boy on the end as "Equipment Manager." But Aubrey didn't need to see the name that followed. Brett Solingen hadn't changed much in two years.

A minute later, she was on the phone with Kate. After explaining the situation, she asked, "Do you think Brett would meet us at the new nest if you asked him?"

"I don't see why not. If Brett has nothing to hide, he won't mind answering some questions. And if he is somehow tangled up in this mess, he needs help finding his way out. What time should we meet there?"

"You don't have to come, Kate. I'm already asking too much, just having you mislead Brett."

Kate's voice was firm. "Brett needs a ride and you need a witness. What time?"

They had arranged to meet at seven, and Kate texted that she was bringing Brett. Aubrey arrived a little early and was sitting on the sand when the other two arrived. She stood up as they reached the nest.

"Hi, Brett," she said, brushing sand from her shorts.

"Hey, Ms. Benson." He looked around nervously.

"Oh, our other helper, Tom, will be here soon," she said.

"No, he won't!" Brett blurted out. "He's in jail!"

Aubrey narrowed her eyes and leaned slightly toward the boy. "How did you know that, Brett?"

He didn't answer.

"Did Heather tell you?" Aubrey took a step forward. "Did she tell you she got one of her friends to tell the same lie about Tom that *she* told?"

Brett pressed his lips together and looked at the sand.

Aubrey's voice gentled. "In spite of what you and Heather may think, Tom is not expendable, Brett. He was a soldier, like your dad. He saved the lives of other soldiers. He was wounded, almost killed. He's good man, Brett. Not a throwaway. And you know he never hurt Heather."

Brett looked up and Aubrey was startled to see tears on his cheeks. He turned and looked past Kate toward the ocean. It was a long moment, and as Aubrey took a breath to speak again, Brett broke his silence.

"You're right, Ms. Benson. Tom didn't hurt Heather." He turned back to look at her. "I did."

"*What?*" Kate and Aubrey spoke in unison.

Brett nodded. "That's right. She's been after this football player. It makes me mad that she likes him, and I'm right here, and she treats me like I'm her kid brother."

"So, you hit her?" Aubrey still couldn't believe it was going to be this easy.

"That's right. After Ms. Mitchell dropped me off at my house, I ran to Heather's. She was just getting home. I talked her into going for a drive. We came to the beach for a walk, and got in this big fight, and I hit her." He squatted on the sand with his knuckles pressed to his eyes. "I was so mad! Why does she treat me that way?"

Kate and Aubrey knelt together to put their arms around the sobbing boy. Over his bent head, Aubrey looked a question at Kate, and Kate shrugged. They helped him stand, and Kate gave him a tissue from her bag. When he was calmer, they walked him to Kate's car.

"Are you going to take me to the police?" he asked, his voice expressionless.

Kate answered for them both. "No. I'm going to take you home and talk to your mother. Then we're going to call the police about what you told us. They'll figure it all out."

Reggie was astonished. "Are you really telling me that Brett Solingen assaulted Heather?"

"I'm only telling you what Brett said," Aubrey answered. "I don't know if his mother has called the police yet. If she's smart, she'll call a lawyer first."

"And you believe him?"

Aubrey shifted the phone to her other hand. "I don't know, Reggie. Brett was certainly sincere about being angry with Heather. I don't know if he hit her. I only know Tom *didn't* do it, but he's the one sitting in jail. Mostly because he looks like a guy who could beat up anyone he chooses. But I know he never would."

"I know that, too, Aubrey. Listen, you did good detective work with that kid, and with Ricky Stout, too. But now I wish you'd go back to teaching and let us handle it. I'll let the team investigating this string of assaults know about Brett, and they'll get to the bottom of all this."

"Thanks, Reggie. But tell them to hurry. Okay?"

Chapter 16

Nest 105, Day 38

"I don't believe a word of it," Tom said. "I don't care what he says." He shook his head, looking straight into the camera. "Brett may have a crush on Heather, but I don't think he's a kid who would fly into a jealous rage and beat a girl."

"Tom, I know it seems unlikely. But maybe Brett's confession will at least give the judge something to think about when setting your bail." She felt her eyes fill. "I just want you out of here."

Tom leaned back and ran his fingers through his hair. "I know, baby. And I want out, too. But you can't afford to pay any more bond money. And I'm fine in here. It's okay. The guards are nice and the food's not bad." He winked. "Not as good as your tuna fish, of course."

"Tom ..."

"Aubrey, honey, I know you just want to help, and you *have* helped. Maybe, because of you talking to Brett, we'll find out why Heather lied. Everything will work out in time. The last thing I want is you getting in trouble with the school or the law."

"I miss you," she said. The tears spilled over, and she saw how that distressed him. "I'm sorry, Tom. You're right. Everything will work out." She wiped away the tears with her fingers.

"I miss you, too, baby. You can't know how much. And it's knowing how you feel that keeps me from going goofy in here."

Following another restless night, Aubrey fell into a dead sleep about dawn, and was wakened by a text from Sunny.

> *Mom don't forget I'm going with Diane to volunteer at freshman orientation at 8. Diane's mom driving. Get some rest and tell Tom hi for me. Love you!*

She marveled at the loving tone and at the recent change in Sunny. She rolled over with the intention of getting a bit more sleep when her cell phone rang.

"Hi, Reggie! Good news?"

"Not very, I'm afraid. Brett recanted his story about hitting Heather. And lawyered up."

Aubrey sighed. "Tom's convinced Brett didn't do it. To be truthful, I can't bring myself to believe it either, even for Tom's sake. So, I guess this doesn't help our case."

"You're right," Reggie agreed. "Tom's not going anywhere for a while. But hang in there, Aubrey. It's just a question of when."

She visited Tom, wishing as always that she could see him in person, maybe even touch him. She babbled about this and that – school, turtles, and so on. He described the book he was reading about the Apollo space missions. He was still upbeat, at least with her, but she could see the stress in his face.

She had never imagined hating a child, but she was beginning to hate Heather for what Tom was going through. The two main issues of the whole case were *why* Heather blamed Tom, and *who* had really hit her. Added to that, why had Brett offered his false confession? Aubrey was convinced the solution to one would provide the key to the others.

Desperate for some answers, she went to see Heather. She hoped that if she were able to talk to the girl, she could convince her to tell the truth.

It was a nice house in a good neighborhood, but nothing fancy, and she wondered what the Carsons did for a living. She vaguely recalled that Mrs. Carson didn't work outside the home. She couldn't remember whether Heather had mentioned having siblings, but she recalled a rather ominous remark Heather had made regarding the loss of a parent as being "maybe not the *worst*" thing that could happen. And Kate had said that the mother seemed a little unstable.

She climbed the two steps of the concrete porch, rang the doorbell and heard the distant chimes within. She waited for a couple of minutes, and was about to ring again, when the door opened barely a foot, and a dark-haired woman peered at her from behind it.

"Mrs. Carson? I'm Aubrey Benson, from the high school. I just stopped by to see how Heather is doing. Is she at home?"

The woman stared at her for a few seconds, then craned her neck to look back over her shoulder into the room behind her.

"No. Why do you want to see her?"

"I don't want to see her, necessarily," Aubrey lied. "I just wanted to find out how she's doing after her … accident."

"She's some better," said her mother. "But this time it wasn't an accident."

This time? "Yes, so I heard." Aubrey shook her head sympathetically. "It's hard to imagine anyone being angry enough at a child to want to hurt her that way."

She half expected Mrs. Carson to say that it wasn't about anger, but instead the woman narrowed her eyes and looked Aubrey up and down with suspicion.

"Who did you say you are?"

Aubrey felt a momentary panic. Would Heather's mother call the school and report that a Ms. Benson was harassing her family? If Mrs. Carson didn't grasp Aubrey's connection to the incident, someone at the school would surely have heard about it by now.

School offices and faculty lounges were prolific rumor mills, and the advance preparation for the school year had already begun.

She deepened her southern drawl. "Oh, I work at Heather's school. I was just concerned about her. Such a *sweet* girl. I can't believe she has an enemy in the *world!*"

"Enemy?" Mrs. Carson was scornful. "Whoever you talked to didn't tell the whole story. Some homeless pervert tried to rape my little girl. Not that she wanted us to know. She knew her daddy would take a scalpel to the bastard's balls if he found out. First she told us she fell down helping with those damn turtles."

Aubrey was sure she looked appropriately shocked, although it was the woman's language and attitude that stunned her.

"I kept at her until she told me the truth about almost getting raped. Then I told her daddy, and he forced her to admit it was this big homeless guy tried it." She leaned toward Aubrey, lowering her voice only slightly. "I told her not to mess with that lesbian teacher and her bunch of do-gooders. She didn't listen, and almost paid the price."

At the woman's foul breath and fouler words, Aubrey automatically backed up a step. The stench of alcohol and tobacco was so strong, she half expected the woman's breath to be visible.

"Well, uh, you tell her I said *hey.*"

Mrs. Carson took a step through the door and onto the porch as Aubrey backed down the steps. "I will if you tell me your name."

"That's okay. I'll see her in school before long. Bye now!"

When Aubrey reached her car, she glanced back at the Carson's porch. The door was closed, but she detected movement at the curtain covering the front window. She got into her car and left.

Despite being the week before school started, always a very busy time for Aubrey, the next six days dragged by. For one thing, Sunny had been in the Keys with her dad for four days, and the house had been emptier than ever.

Usually Aubrey was excited by the first day of the school year, but on this day, she was subdued, aware that she now had to wait until afternoon to visit Tom. When she had explained that to him the day before, he had told her not to visit him every day.

"You have enough to deal with," he'd said. "Let Rachel handle all this business. I love seeing you, but I'm okay."

"Maybe you can get along fine without me, but that doesn't mean it works the other way," she had replied, trying and failing to sound light-hearted.

"When this is finally over and I'm back at Reggie's," he'd asked, "will you want to see me every day?"

Aubrey had paused for a moment, enjoying the dream of Tom on the outside, working a regular job and seeing her when he could. "Maybe every now and then I could get by with just talking on the phone," she'd said. "Meanwhile, the only way we can talk is this way, and I'm not missing any opportunities."

On this, the first morning of her sophomore year, Sunny looked gorgeous, tanned and healthy, with sun streaks highlighting her curly auburn hair, and wearing a carefully casual new outfit bought especially for her first day of school. She kissed her mother's cheek before hopping out of the car in the teacher's parking lot.

"Love you, Mom. Have a great day!"

Aubrey thought again how much Sunny had changed from the restless and defiant teen of early summer to this sweet girl so much like the one Aubrey remembered. She spotted her across the campus once in the mid-morning and was delighted when she rushed into Aubrey's homeroom at lunchtime.

"Mom!" Sunny lowered her voice. "Quick, you gotta see this!"

Hurrying to keep up, Aubrey followed her daughter to a remote corner of the campus, where she could see a girl and boy sitting side-by-side on a bench by the aquaculture pond. Sunny motioned her back into the shadows as they drew closer to the pair, whom Aubrey now recognized as Heather and Brett. Even from this safe distance, Aubrey could see Heather was crying, and Brett was trying to comfort her.

"Sure wish we could hear what that's all about," Sunny whispered.

Aubrey took a deep breath. "Poor kid. She's really upset about something."

Sunny looked at Aubrey with a trace of the old scorn. "Come on, Mom. 'Poor kid,' my butt. Heather's probably just having an attack of conscience. And she deserves it." She put an arm around her mother. "Don't forget, while she's here boo-hooing, Tom's sitting in jail."

Aubrey gave Sunny a quick, hard hug. "I never forget that, angel. And I love that you're on Tom's side. There's nobody I'd rather have standing with me."

They turned and walked slowly back across the campus, heading for the cafeteria. Sunny surprised her by commenting. "You know, Mom, you've really changed."

Aubrey stopped, staring at Sunny in amazement. She'd just been telling herself Sunny was the one who had changed. "I have?"

"Big time. Since you met Tom, you've become a lot – I don't know – *softer* somehow. A couple months ago, you were biting my head off at the least thing. Maybe you were just lonely."

Lonely and scared, Aubrey mused to herself. *And scared of being lonely. Scared of feeling my daughter slipping away from me.* But she couldn't say it aloud without tears, and Sunny would be horrified if her mother cried in front of the school population. *Here I go again, Tom,* she thought wistfully. *And not a hanky in sight.*

Bemused, Aubrey thanked her daughter and said goodbye. She grabbed a yogurt from the cafeteria and headed back to her room. While she ate, she used her computer to look up Heather's last class of the day, which turned out to be Art History.

The students in Aubrey's own last class of the day were delighted to be dismissed five minutes early. She hustled over to the art classroom just as the students were leaving. Heather came out, head down, clutching a small stack of books to her chest. Aubrey touched her arm, and Heather jumped, staring.

"Ms. Benson!"

"Sorry to startle you, Heather. I just wanted to know how you're doing." She smiled at the girl. "Here. This room's empty. Let's have a chat." She drew her into the next room and patted an empty chair.

Heather was clearly reluctant, but no doubt accustomed to obeying her teachers. She sat down, resting her books in her lap and letting her backpack slide from her shoulder to her elbow. She kept her eye on the open door.

"I've got to catch my bus."

Aubrey consulted her watch. "You have ten minutes. I'll make sure you make it. So, how are you?"

Heather shrugged. "I'm okay, I guess."

Aubrey looked closely at Heather's face. "Looks like the bruises are all gone. Just in time for school." She smiled, but Heather was looking at the floor. "And how's your friend Danielle? I understand she was hurt, too."

Heather looked around, as if hoping to be rescued. "I – I don't know."

"But you knew someone attacked her, right?" She leaned toward the girl, who seemed ready to panic. "After all, aren't you the one who told her to tell that lie?"

"No!" Heather jumped up, spilling her books and dropping her backpack. "I don't know what –" She knelt and began gathering her books.

"What I'm talking about? Come on, Heather. We all know Danielle made up that story. Like we know you told her to do so. I know. So do the police. And Tom." She knelt by Heather and put her hand on the book the girl was trying to pick up. "Remember Tom, Heather? He's the man you falsely accused. The man locked up because you won't tell the truth."

Heather looked up, her face twisted with emotion. "You don't understand! My family – my mom –"

"What about your mother? Did she put you up to this?"

"*No!*" Heather broke down, sobbing, her hands over her face. Aubrey felt her heart wrenched with pity but steeled herself against her instinctive sympathy.

"You'll have to tell someone, sometime, Heather. For your own sake, you need to tell the truth."

"You don't understand!" Heather wailed. She blubbered something unintelligible. Aubrey only caught the word "family."

Aubrey put her hand on Heather's shoulder. "What are you saying, Heather?"

Heather looked up at Aubrey, her face blotchy and streaked with tears. "My mom's never worked in her life. Dad makes good money as a P.A., so she never had to be out there. She gets real nervous around people."

Aubrey shook her head, baffled by this outburst. "I don't understand. What does your mom have to do with the lie you told?"

Heather shook her head, sniffling, and Aubrey felt compelled to pick up the girl's books and help her to her feet. When Heather snatched the books and bolted for the door, Aubrey let her go.

Tom was as mystified as Aubrey about what Heather's false accusation had to do with her mother. Then he insisted on changing the subject and asked about her first day at school. Knowing he wanted to enjoy a normal conversation, she made her stories as amusing as possible.

"… So, the kid just sat there for fifty minutes, staring at me while I talked about exploring the similarities of *Oliver Twist* and *The Merchant of Venice*, and when the bell rang, he came up to me and said, 'So this isn't Basic Geometry?'"

Tom laughed much more heartily than the story deserved, but Aubrey was pleased to distract him.

"Aubrey, talk about what we're going to do together when I get out of here."

She raised her eyebrows and gave him a wicked smile.

Tom chuckled. "Not *that*. I don't let myself think about that. Just ordinary stuff."

Aubrey thought for a minute. "Well, once the tourist season is over, we really should take the ferry to Bald Head Island and have lunch and explore a bit. We could rent bicycles. And the three of us could spend a few hours at the aquarium at Fort Fisher. Sunny loves it there."

She rambled on for a few minutes about the various things to see and do between Wilmington and Myrtle Beach. She finished with holiday plans.

"You'll have Thanksgiving on the beach with Sunny and me – it's our own tradition. I cook a turkey and apple turnovers the night before and, on the day, we pack a lunch of turkey sandwiches and turnovers, and we picnic at the beach. Sometimes Kate joins us, if it's warm enough for her."

"Sounds great. Is Sunny always with you for Thanksgiving?"

"Yes. Her choice. Craig has a big Thanksgiving party for his friends and Sunny hates it."

"Does she spend Christmas with him?"

"We trade. Last year it was Christmas Eve with me, opening gifts. Then I took her to his place first thing Christmas morning. This year it'll be the other way around."

"So, will you spend Christmas Eve with Kate this year?"

She shook her head. "Kate spends all of Christmas break with her family in Connecticut. It's the only time she sees them." She smiled. "Usually, when Sunny's not with me, I just have a sandwich, watch TV and go to bed early. But this Christmas Eve, I'll have you. Shall I cook, or will we eat out?"

The way his face lit up brought the forbidden tears to her eyes.

"You shouldn't be doing that alone," Aubrey said.

She was standing in the weight room at the high school gym, a few feet from where Brett Solingen straddled the bench press, flat on his back. He tilted his head back and rolled his eyes up to see her.

"Ms. Benson," he said, with a note of defeat. He clearly struggled to inject defiance into his next sentence. "I can handle this."

"Seriously, Brett. There's a sign above the weight rack that says students are never to lift weights alone. Can't you get someone to spot you?"

He released the grip of the barbell he had been about to lift and, with a twist of his slender frame, sat up with his back to her.

"Are you going to report me?" he said woodenly.

"I don't need to," she said. "You're going to quit this until Coach Rigert gets back from lunch."

"I am?"

"Yes. First, because you're the kind of young man who follows the rules and, second, because you're going to talk to me for a few minutes."

He swung one leg around to sit sideways, but still avoided looking at her. He nervously unfastened and refastened the Velcro strip on his weight gloves. Aubrey folded her arms, prepared to wait until he was ready. It was her free period, and she had plenty of time.

"I don't think I should be talking to you," he said.

"Why? Did your lawyer tell you that?" He shook his head, so she asked the obvious question. "Why did you tell us you attacked Heather?"

No answer.

"Are you protecting someone?"

No answer.

"Or maybe you did hit her, just like you said. Only your mom got a lawyer who told you to take it all back. So, did you really hit Heather? Did you punch that little girl in the face?"

"No, I didn't! I'd *never* hurt Heather. I just – I got scared when the police told me about the tourist who was raped. I was afraid they'd think I did that, too. So, I had to admit I lied to you and Ms. Mitchell."

"Didn't the police tell you that the tourist was attacked by a large man?"

He turned to look at her, disbelief in his eyes. "No. If they'd told me that, I'd –"

"You'd have stuck with your lie about hitting Heather. But, Brett, please tell me why you thought falsely confessing to assault could possibly help Heather. Any more than Heather's lies will help *her* in the end."

He jumped to his feet, his face red and his eyes angry. "Adults always think they know everything. But you can't even see what's right in front of you!"

Aubrey automatically took a step back as Brett advanced on her.

"You all think you have the right to do anything to a kid. Lie to them, trick them. Even beat them if you want to!"

Aubrey knew pain when she saw it. Rather than retreat, she moved toward the angry boy and put her hands on his shoulders. "Brett. Maybe I don't see everything I'm supposed to see. I'm just a person, like you." She kept her voice low and soothing. "And like you, I'm just trying to help somebody in trouble. Somebody I care about."

She dropped her hands to his wrists and pulled him back to the bench. When she sat, he sat, too. She squeezed his hands.

"Brett, I understand how frustrating it can be, trying to help the person you love. I know you love Heather. And I love Tom. Tom has done nothing to deserve being used this way. He's a good man who served his country bravely. He's not a throwaway person. No one is."

Aubrey couldn't tell if the drops on Brett's cheeks were sweat or tears. He slumped on the bench, defeat in every line of his body.

"I know. I like Tom. And I know Heather lied. I thought if I said I hit her, they'd let Tom go. And maybe Heather would appreciate me for –"

Brett was interrupted by the strident bell announcing the end of classes. He pulled his hands free and got to his feet.

"I – I'll talk to Heather. Maybe we can straighten it all out."

"Brett –"

"I've got to go." He fled to the boys' locker room, where she dared not go.

Just as Aubrey reached her classroom door, a familiar voice called to her.

"Hi, Bree!"

She turned to see Kate approaching. "Oh, hi, Kate."

"How're you holding up, kiddo?"

Aubrey shook her head. "It's hard to say. I know they'll have to let him go eventually. Even if Danielle won't admit she lied, Tom has an alibi for the time she says she was attacked."

"That's right. He does. I agree with his lawyer. I think they'll drop that case like a hot rock."

"And even the case involving Heather is pretty weak, especially since Brett just confirmed that she lied. But –"

Kate put her arm around her friend. "But you miss him, and you can't stand to see him spend one more day in jail."

Aubrey nodded, too touched by Kate's understanding to speak.

"Listen. In a couple of days, it will be time to get Nest 105 set up, and I predict Tom will be free to help us. So, you just hang in there and see if I'm not right."

Aubrey shared Kate's prediction with Tom later that day and told him about her conversation with Brett. Tom said Rachel McDowd had been to see him, and she was still convinced it was all going to fall apart, and the D.A. would have no option except to release him uncharged.

"Once the DNA results of the rape are in, I'd have to be released on the bond you paid on Heather's case."

"Yes, but *when?*"

"Aubrey, I know you're frustrated." He ran his fingers through his hair, a gesture she had learned to recognize as a signal of his own stress. "Look, baby, just think about your classes and your students and Sunny. Hell, think about those damned turtles! But don't worry about me. I can be patient, just knowing you're out there living your life, and waiting for me."

Chapter 17

Nest 105, Day 48

M om don't forget I won't be home for dinner cuz I'm eating and studying with Diane. Be home by 10. Luv u!

"Well, crap." Aubrey put her phone down. She had forgotten all about Sunny's plan to study her Spanish at Diane's that evening. She took out the cling wrap and covered the bowl holding the half-mixed meatloaf, then turned off the oven.

She didn't know quite what to do with herself. She should look over tomorrow's lesson plan for her class in Advanced Literature, but she had already reviewed it twice and couldn't work up any more interest. She thought about calling Kate for a chat but knew Kate would probably be going over her own lesson plans. Nor was she hungry enough to fix herself anything to eat alone.

Alone, alone, alone. Before she had met Tom, she had enjoyed the occasional evening on her own. And once he was free, she might someday be glad of rare moments to herself. But his enforced solitude made her own unbearable. She wished Nest 105 were closer to hatching; a night on the beach would soothe her nerves.

Of course, nothing said she couldn't go for a long walk on the beach, turtles or not.

Unencumbered by her turtle bag, she jogged to the beach. Despite the warm evening, it wasn't crowded during the dinner hour. She ran on the hard-packed sand close to the water's edge, from 67th Street to the pier. There she stopped to catch her breath, turned and ran back the other way. On the return dash, she was hailed by friends sitting on a blanket, and stopped to chat for a few minutes. Then she encountered other nest parents gathering at their assigned nests for the evening and stopped to "talk turtle" for a while. By the time she left the beach and jogged back to her house, the sun was setting.

Aubrey was exhausted by her run, but she felt more at peace. She checked her watch; Sunny would be home in two hours. She fixed a peanut butter sandwich and sat at the kitchen table to go over her lesson plans. A few minutes later, her cell phone signaled another text message. Maybe Sunny was ready to come home and Diane's dad couldn't bring her.

But the text was from Kate, saying there was a "problem at 105," and asking her to come quickly. Concerned about whatever the problem might be, but glad for the distraction, she grabbed her handbag from the counter and her turtle bag from the laundry room.

She jumped in the car and drove to the same 67th Street parking area she'd left only an hour earlier. This time, however, the small lot was empty, and the beach was dark. She locked her handbag in the car, put her keys in her pocket, and climbed over the low ridge of dunes between patches of sea oats. It was dark on the ocean side of the dunes and she turned on her flashlight.

She headed west; opposite the direction she'd taken earlier. In just over a minute she was at Nest 105 and saw that she'd managed to beat Kate to the spot. She ran her light over the squared-off nest and saw nothing marring the sandy surface. She'd expected to find that foxes had been digging, or human vandals had disturbed the nest, but it looked fine. She snapped off the flashlight and squatted by the nest to wait.

It was a lovely night. The air, filled with a salty tang, was considerably cooler than when she'd been on the beach before sunset. The beach was deserted; not a single person could she see, nor the beams of any flashlights. The full moon was intermittently hidden by swiftly moving clouds. In the flashes of light from the distant lighthouse, she could see the little ghost crabs scuttling along near the waves.

Come on, Kate. What's keeping you?

She took out her phone and checked Kate's text again. She saw her own hurried response – *On my way* – and nothing after that. She looked around, hoping to see her friend or Kate's light coming toward her, but she detected no movement, and the roar of the incoming tide covered any sound that might have reached her on the night air.

She looked at the texts on her phone again, started to type *I'm here – where are you*, when she sensed rather than saw movement beside her. She started to rise, half-blind from the lighted screen on which she'd just been focused. Before she could straighten, an arm came around her from behind, drawing her up and back in a painful choke hold. Off balance, she fell against her attacker, and he dragged her backward, into the dunes.

He threw her to the ground, knelt over her and gave her a vicious punch in the stomach that knocked the breath from her body. He was a large man, with an odd, almost medicinal smell. His legs straddled hers, and he pinned her arms above his head, his face near hers.

"Been asking lots of questions, haven't you, bitch? Bothering people. Digging up secrets. Well, teacher, this will teach *you* to mind your own business."

He shifted his grip to hold her wrists in one hand in an unbreakable grasp. Over the noise of the surf, she heard the sound of his zipper and thought, *Oh, God, help me, I'm about to be raped.*

The horror moved her to fight. She thrashed and twisted against him, screaming. In the back of her mind, she knew that no one more than a few yards from her would be able to hear her cries. She heard him grunt with pain as one of her kicks landed, and his grip loosened slightly. She wrenched a hand free and raked her nails across his face. He threw sand in her mouth and she choked, feeling her strength wane. While she struggled to breathe, a brutal hand yanked her tee-shirt up to her chin, undid the snap in the front of her cutoffs and tugged at her zipper.

Then, just as suddenly as he'd grabbed her, she felt his body being lifted away. She rolled to her side, spitting and coughing. In the faint flashes of the lighthouse beam and the glow of the moon, she saw two men struggling above her.

It was over by the time she staggered to her feet. One of the men lay on the trampled vegetation, groaning and barely moving. She heard a voice she knew cry, "Aubrey!" and she fell into Tom's arms, sobbing and calling his name. He lifted her like a child, holding her against him.

"Aubrey. It's okay, baby. I've got you."

Her face was pressed against his neck, her eyes closed, but as he carried her from the sea oats onto the bare sand, she felt the rush of someone going past them into the dunes. She heard Reggie's voice in a commanding tone she had not heard from him before.

"Put your hands behind your head!" There was a choked reply, and Reggie spoke again. "Yeah? Well, you're lucky he didn't *kill* you. Now, hands *behind your head!*"

Tom walked toward the water, cradling Aubrey and murmuring to her, now and then kissing her brow, the top of her head. She locked her hands behind his neck and leaned back to look at him.

"Where did you come from? How did you find me?"

His face was set in lines that seemed carved from stone. He stared into her eyes for a long moment before saying, "The judge dismissed the new charge because Heather admitted to the D.A. that she lied, and forced her friend to lie, and her friend confirmed it. Reggie was at the courthouse about another case when he heard I was being released, and he hung around through a few hours of paperwork to bring me home. We thought it would be fun to surprise you."

He bent his head to press his forehead against hers. "It was almost the worst mistake of my life. If I'd called you first, you might have been home instead of here."

"But how did you know –"

"We saw your car was gone, and I told Reggie I'd wait there for you. I knocked on the side door, hoping Sunny was there to let me in. I saw through the window that your turtle bag was gone. I caught Reggie and had him drive me to the beach."

Aubrey was feeling stronger. "Tom. Put me down."

He shook his head. "Not just yet." He shifted her weight in his arms and hugged her to him. "I knew the nest was west of 67th. We saw your car was the only one in the lot, and I just had a weird feeling. Reggie said he'd wait while I checked on you. I think –" He swallowed hard. "I think he wanted to give us a few minutes alone. When I got to the nest, I saw your turtle bag, and your phone lying in the sand. Then one of your pink flip-flops."

He took a deep breath. "I've seen a lot in my day, some of it not very good. But that was one of the worst moments of my life. Then I heard you."

"Hey, guys." Reggie approached, interrupting them. "Aubrey, you okay?"

She nodded, not trusting her voice just then.

"I called for back-up. They're on the way. Meanwhile, I'll let the skeeters entertain our friend back there."

"Who is he?" Tom asked. "Do you know?"

Reggie nodded. "I've got his wallet. License shows he's Michael Carson. His address is the same as Heather's, so I assume he's her father. He's not talking yet." He did his best to look Aubrey over in the dark. "Do you need to go to the hospital, Aubrey?"

She smiled. "No, Reggie. He gave me a good punch in the stomach, but nothing's broken."

Tom made a strangled sound and tightened his hold on her.

From her perch in Tom's arms, Aubrey saw the emergency lights and heard sirens beyond the dunes. In the faint light, she saw four officers emerge from the gap in the vegetation and rush in their direction. Reggie waved and then lead them to the captive.

"If you feel like you just *have* to get down, I'll let you," Tom said.

"I'm good if you are," she answered. She rested her head on his shoulder.

He rocked her gently from side to side. "Oh, I could do this all night," he said.

As it turned out, it was only for the few minutes it took Reggie to return, then Tom put her down so he could gather her things and help her on with her flip-flops. Holding her possessions in one hand, he kept his other arm around her as they followed Reggie to his car.

"If you're sure you're okay, Aubrey," said Reggie, "we'll go straight to the station."

Tom helped her into the passenger side of the front seat, then climbed into the back. He reached through the gap between the front seats to hold her hand.

"Oh!" Aubrey said as they turned onto the main street. "Kate! How could I forget?"

"What about Kate?" Tom asked.

"I got a text from her, telling me to meet her at the nest, but she never turned up. Could he have attacked her, too?"

Reggie called to have a car sent to Kate's, and Aubrey gave him the address. Meanwhile, Aubrey texted Kate from her phone, hoping to hear back. She also texted Sunny to say she was out for a time but would be home soon.

At the station, Tom walked into the reception area with his arm around Aubrey, and Reggie right behind. In the bright light, Tom noticed bruising along Aubrey's jaw, and on her hands and thighs. Cupping her face in his hands, he said, "Now I wish I'd been rougher on him."

"You were rough enough," Reggie said. "He says you body-slammed him into the sea oats, picked him up and slammed him again."

"I wanted to make sure he wasn't going anywhere." Tom asked, still looking at Aubrey.

"Good work," Reggie said, grinning.

Aubrey was taken to a private room and examined by a female

officer, who took pictures of the darkening bruise on her stomach where Carson had punched her, as well as her other cuts and abrasions. They photographed and took scrapings from under her fingernails. Delayed shock and the station's air-conditioning gave Aubrey the shakes. The kind officer found a blanket to wrap around her and escorted her back to Tom and Reggie.

Tom guided her to a chair and pulled another beside it, then sat with one arm around her shoulders and the other holding her hand. Reggie brought her a cup of coffee.

"There you go. Cop coffee. If that stuff doesn't wash the sand from your mouth, nothing will."

Between the blanket, the strong, hot coffee and Tom's arm around her, solid as a steel bar, Aubrey soon stopped shaking.

Reggie told her Kate had been found unconscious in her apartment. She was going to be fine, he assured her, but had a concussion and would be in the hospital for a few days.

"She says Carson – although, of course, she didn't know it was him – came up behind her when she was entering her place, pushed her inside and knocked her out. She was just coming around when our officers got there."

"Did he – was she …" Aubrey put her hand to her mouth.

"*No.* He just knocked her out and stole her phone. I'm guessing he knew he could lure you out with a message from her phone. Looks like he read the message about your nest, so he texted you with Kate's phone, then waited in the dunes for you to show up. You were his prime target. He hasn't had much to say, but he called you a nosy bitch and said he just wanted to scare you."

"Well, he sure did that," she said. "Poor Kate."

A plain-clothes officer came into the station, talking loudly. Aubrey recognized him as the one who'd identified Tom to the waitress at the restaurant the night Tom was arrested again. He stopped talking in mid-sentence and stared at them. Aubrey gave him her fiercest look and watched as he turned to a uniformed officer nearby and spoke quietly, jerking his thumb in their direction.

"Ignore that jackass, Aubrey," said Reggie. "There's one in every cop shop, and he's ours."

The officer in question turned his face back to Aubrey and Tom, his stunned expression saying more than words. Head down, he hurried off.

Reggie and another officer took Aubrey's statement. When they were through, Reggie offered to drive them home.

"Can't I go see Kate at the hospital?" she asked.

"She's in the ER, Aubrey, undergoing tests. Then I'm sure they'll want her to rest." Reggie smiled. "It'd be better for y'all to wait until daylight." He checked his watch. "Which will be here soon."

Tom and Aubrey had only been inside her house for a minute when Sunny came into the kitchen in her pajamas, blinking and rubbing her eyes. Her eyes opened wide when she saw Tom, and she squealed with excitement.

"Tom! When did you –" She stopped when she saw her mother's face, and the way Tom was supporting her as they crossed the floor.

"Mom?" Sunny's twinkle vanished and her eyes filled with concern.

"It's okay, Sunny-bear. Help me get these sandy clothes off, and I'll tell you about it."

Tom hung back while Sunny helped her mother down the hall and into her room. She alternately gasped and cheered as Aubrey told of the false text, Tom's release, the attack on the dark beach, and his timely rescue. Her eyes went wide with astonishment when Aubrey named her attacker.

"Heather's *dad?*" she said, standing by as her mother got into the shower to wash away the remains of the sand and the feel of Michael Carson's hands on her.

"I'm sure there's a lot we don't know yet," Aubrey called over the noise of the shower.

When she got out, Sunny had a big towel waiting for her, and her favorite tee-shirt and old plaid robe were laid out on the bed.

"Feel better?" Sunny asked.

Season of the Turtle

"Much. Where's Tom?"

"In the kitchen," Sunny told her. "He made a pot of coffee."

"Bless him. That coffee at the police station was like used motor oil, only not as tasty."

While Aubrey dressed in her night clothes and ran a comb through her wet hair, she told Sunny about Kate's injuries, and her plan to visit her in the hospital in the morning.

"I can skip my first two classes. The intern will handle them. I'll be there for the rest of the day."

"Mom!" Sunny was aghast. "You were *attacked* tonight! I think you can stay home tomorrow."

Aubrey decided not to argue. She hugged her daughter and thanked her for her help. "Now, you'd better get back to bed. You *are* going to school tomorrow."

Then she went into the kitchen. Tom stood up as she came in and pulled out a chair for her. She sat, and he kissed the top of her head. "I'll pour your coffee," he said.

Aubrey closed her eyes. "I feel as if I'm a hundred years old."

"You'll be better after you sleep," he assured her. "If you don't mind, I'll stay here tonight. I can sleep on the sofa."

"Thanks. I'd like that." He set her coffee in front of her, then put both hands gently on her shoulders. She leaned her head back against his stomach. "With all that happened, I haven't even had a chance to say how thrilled I am about you getting out. Or to thank you for pulling that creep off me."

"I should be thanking you. Rachel said Heather and Brett decided to tell the truth about me because of what you said to them."

"Did they? I'll have to thank them when I see them. That was very … very brave …" Aubrey trailed off, too tired to continue. Too tired to lift her cup or even open her eyes.

The next thing she knew, Tom was lifting her in his arms again. She felt herself being carried down the hall and into her bedroom. Still holding her, he managed to pull down the bedcovers and place her, robe and all, in her bed. She felt his lips against her forehead, then she fell into sleep like dropping into a well.

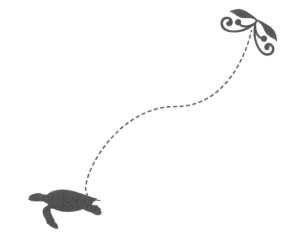

Chapter 18

Nest 105, Day 49

Tom hadn't slept on the sofa, after all. When daylight poked its intrusive fingers through the gaps in her curtains and annoyed her into wakefulness, Aubrey opened her eyes to find him slumped in the bedroom chair a few feet from the bed.

She smiled to see him there, but he looked as uncomfortable as she felt. When she stretched, she discovered the strain of fighting off her attacker, not to mention the blows she'd suffered at his hands, were more painful this morning than the previous night.

She groaned, cursing the man who'd thought he had the right to abuse her. She hoped he felt just as stiff and sore today from her defensive strikes and Tom's more damaging blows.

At the slight sound she made, Tom woke up and smiled. "Hey, baby," he said. At the same moment, Sunny opened her own door and crossed to her mother's open doorway.

She smiled and nodded at Tom. "Hi, Mom. How do you feel?"

Aubrey winced. "A little sore. I was never in a fight before, but

I fell down the stairs when I was eleven." She sat up. "Feels kind of like that felt the next day."

Sunny glanced from her mother to Tom. "Well, I think you've got this covered, Tom. I need to get in gear, or I'll miss the bus."

After a long and very hot shower, Aubrey was dressed and sitting at the table drinking her coffee and being served eggs and toast when Sunny came tearing through.

"Gotta run!" she said.

"Sunny! What about breakfast?"

The girl grinned. "Tom fed me while you were in the shower. He's pretty good with scrambled eggs." She leaned down to kiss her mother, then rushed out the side door. "Bye, y'all!"

Aubrey smiled. "She likes you."

He grinned. "The feeling's mutual. You've done a great job with her, Aubrey. She's polite, thoughtful and fun."

Aubrey nodded. "I can't help thinking about Heather and wondering how she got to be the way she is. Not that she's a bad person – but the fear, the lying. What brought that on?"

They learned more about Heather's life while visiting Kate at the hospital. Tom drove Aubrey in her car to Reggie's, where he showered and shaved. Then they drove to the hospital together.

Kate looked a little frail, but insisted she was fine. The doctors wanted to keep her through the weekend, just to make sure the concussion wasn't going to present major problems for her.

"But the doctors say no exertion of any kind for at least two weeks," Kate said. "That means I need you to set up 105 tomorrow. Can you do it?"

Aubrey looked at Tom, who nodded. "Sure, Kate. We got this. You just take it easy."

They were leaving her room when Reggie showed up. After greeting Kate, he took Aubrey and Tom to the cafeteria to have coffee and tell them what he had learned.

"Heather and Mrs. Carson came to the station shortly after y'all left," Reggie said. "Mrs. Carson was pretty useless – hysterical, shouting accusations against us, against you, even against Heather. But the girl gave us the true picture of life with her dad."

Reggie said Heather's father had been beating her and her mom for years. Heather had long been suspicious about why her dad was so often gone at night but had been afraid to confront him directly. On her way home after Tom walked her to her car that night, she spotted her father's car in a beach hotel parking lot. Terrified but intrigued, she pulled in and got out to see what he was doing and caught him peering into a hotel room window. He was furious with her for "spying" on him. He dragged her back to her mother's car and punched her. Heather had then driven to a secluded spot to try to pull herself together before going home to her mom.

"Oh, that poor kid," Aubrey said. She instantly forgave Heather for the trouble she'd caused.

Heather's mother had ignored Carson's abuse of her daughter for years. She'd convinced herself that she was the primary target of his rage, and that the times she saw him hit Heather were times when the child needed "discipline." But that night, when she saw Heather's terrible bruises, she became hysterical. Carson was still out, and she ranted about getting away from him and going back to her family in New Jersey.

Heather knew her mother was incapable of sustaining them both and, in addition, Heather didn't want to leave the area because she was in love with a boy at school. So, she told her mother she had been attacked by a stranger as she was leaving the beach. Later, when pressed by her parents and the police, she had chosen to blame Tom.

Despite her pity for the girl, Aubrey couldn't help being bitter. "Because he was some 'homeless guy' no one would care about."

Reggie nodded. "That was part of it. Also, because Tom had walked her to her car, so he'd have had opportunity. And it worked." He took a drink of coffee. "Before you lose all sympathy for Heather, you should know the rest. The Carsons moved here from Atlanta. On a hunch, we called Atlanta P.D. this morning. They've got a string of unsolved rapes starting about four years ago and ending about the same time the Carsons moved to Oak Island. The rapes always took place in the dark, and the only consistent description was that the attacker was large."

"Like Carson," Tom said.

"Yup," said Reggie. "He's five inches shorter but several pounds heavier than you. A 'big guy.'"

"So, Heather has been living with an abusive father who's also a rapist," Aubrey said. "That's rough."

"And don't forget," said Reggie. "She's also had a mentally unstable mother to cope with and protect." He put his cup down. "We got DNA from Carson to send to Atlanta. All the cases where they were able to get DNA were a match for each other but didn't match anyone in the database. I suspect they *will* match Carson."

"Oh! And so will the DNA from the tourist raped on the beach." Aubrey exclaimed, horrified.

Reggie nodded.

"What about Brett?" asked Tom.

"They're talking to him this morning," Reggie said. "But, according to Heather, Brett took the blame for her beating because he knew she didn't want the truth to come out. Apparently, Brett didn't know the whole truth, but he didn't want Tom blamed for it any longer. Then he got scared that we might link Heather's attack with the rape of the tourist, so he thought better of it and recanted."

"So, in his own fumbling way, Brett was on Tom's side," Aubrey mused.

"Yeah," Reggie continued. "He muddied the water for a minute, but he was doing his best to help Tom, while trying to earn Heather's gratitude."

Tom and Aubrey exchanged looks, and Tom shook his head. "I think I need to spend some time with that kid. He's got the right spirit. He just needs a little help with his judgment."

"Anyway," Reggie concluded, "between the dog bite on his leg – which he treated himself, by the way – the DNA from the tourist and the Atlanta cases, not to mention Heather's statement, we have enough evidence to send our friend Michael Carson away for a long time." He shook his head. "Talk about an arrogant bastard. He and

Heather both knew he was the one who hit her, but he had the audacity to insist – in front of her mother – that she identify her attacker."

"He knew she wouldn't say it was him." Aubrey leaned back in the booth. "I do feel sorry for her, but her careless attitude about Tom caused us all a lot of grief."

"Not to mention sending us on a wild goose chase," said Reggie. "You're the one who changed her mind, Aubrey. After you shamed her and Brett, they got together and decided they needed to free Tom from their lies. That's what got Tom out of jail."

"And then Tom saved *me*." Aubrey wrapped both arms around Tom's bicep and rested her cheek on his shoulder.

"From what I saw, you were doing a pretty good job fighting him off," said Tom. "At least you slowed him down until I got there."

"One thing I don't understand," said Aubrey, relaxing her grip on Tom. "Why the elaborate ruse to get me to the beach? Why didn't he just break into my place like he did with poor Kate?"

"We're not sure," Reggie admitted. "He's not talking, of course, but Heather told us he asked a lot of questions about you in the last few days. My theory is that he was targeting you for vengeance for what he considered messing with his family. He knew from Heather that you had a daughter who might be around to mess up a home invasion. And since, as we know, he prefers to strike in the dark, he attacked Kate and stole her phone to lure you to the beach."

"It almost worked," Aubrey said. "The first part *did* work. But he didn't count on Tom."

Tom turned to her, smiling broadly.

Kate was out of the hospital and at Nest 105 when it boiled. She was restricted to sitting in her beach chair next to the nest to oversee, but she made her presence known.

"Bree! Tom!" she shouted. "Get the edging. Here they come!"

Tom grabbed the extra rolls of edging and handed one to Aubrey. "You okay to do this, honey?"

She smiled. After what they'd been through, she could hardly believe they were together on the dark beach, helping with Kate's turtles again. It seemed so *ordinary*. "Sure. I'm on top of the world."

Her life, in fact, was so filled with joy, she wondered how things could get any better. A few days after Tom's release and Carson's arrest, Carolyn had written an "inside story" that had been featured on the front page of the weekly paper, along with a large photo of Tom and two smaller photos: Kate in her hospital bed and Aubrey and Tom standing together in the sea oats at the spot where Aubrey had been attacked.

The article had made Tom something of a local hero, and over the past few days several people had approached him, wanting to shake the big man's hand and express their admiration. He was embarrassed and touched by the attention, but handled it with grace and patience, knowing it would, mercifully, fade in a month or two.

A bit more tangible was the check he had received from his car insurance company. The first thing he did was to deposit it in his new bank account and write a check to Aubrey for the bond money she'd paid for him. Then he made a down payment on a used car. Reggie, sitting at Aubrey's table, told Tom he was delighted to have him remain as a tenant.

"For as long as you need a place," he said. "Which I think won't be all that long."

The men had grinned at each other, while Aubrey got busy making coffee and pretending she hadn't heard.

At Kate's announcement, Sunny, thrilled the boil was happening on a Friday night, when she could participate, grabbed the clickers and handed one to Brett and the other to Ricky Stout. Aubrey enjoyed watching Sunny and Ricky make eyes at each other as much as she enjoyed watching Tom be fatherly with Brett. Brett was back to his usual level self after a few days of despondency following Heather's move with her mother to New Jersey.

Tourist season was over, so there were only a handful of watchers for this boil on the moonlit beach. Aubrey could hear Sunny reciting Kate's litany to forgo using lights of any kind, and to stand behind the line that paralleled the edge of the surf.

Brett began shouting out the numbers as they crossed his line. "There's the first three! Uh-oh. Number four is turning back – no, there he goes. Here's number five, and six. Wow! Look at number seven go!"

Most of the little turtles didn't seem in a hurry to get to the water, but Number Seven was moving fast. It caught up with the first hatchlings by the time they reached the end of the edging and the start of the trench. Tom and Aubrey, opposite each other at the trench and moving with the turtles to the water, exchanged smiles every few steps.

When all seventy-eight turtles were safely in the water, and a careful inspection of the surf line indicated none had washed back, the watchers and crew cheered their success.

"We'll probably get a few more when we excavate," Kate said.

At Tom's nudge, Brett offered his arm to Kate and escorted her to Aubrey's car, while the others rolled up the extra edging and gathered the other equipment. The onlookers drifted away, shouting back congratulations and praise for the team.

"Sunny," asked Tom, "would you mind keeping Ricky company, while I have a minute with your mom?"

Smiling in the glow of her flashlight, Sunny nodded, grabbed Ricky's hand and ran with him up the dark beach.

Aubrey, standing near the water, pulled off her latex gloves and stared out to sea, still looking for the dark dots of turtles on the moonlit surface. "Thank you, Lord," she whispered. "For the turtles, for my beautiful daughter, and for giving Tom back to us."

Tom came up behind her and put his hands on her shoulders, and she leaned back against him.

"Happy?" he asked.

She sighed. "Yes. So happy."

For the first few days after Michael Carson had attacked her on the beach, she had suffered brief but powerful nightmares. After the first one, Sunny had slept in her bed, and having her daughter curled up beside her had helped.

Over breakfast on the fourth morning, Aubrey had told her daughter she could go back to sleeping in her own bed.

Sunny had given her an exasperated look. "I don't know why you don't just ask Tom to move in here," she'd said. "Dad's girlfriend lives with him, and I'm okay with that."

Aubrey thought for a moment. "I'm not sure you should be," she'd answered. "But, frankly, it's not just my decision. Tom doesn't think it's a good idea either."

"But they've dropped all the charges against him."

Aubrey shrugged, smiling. "That's just Tom, honey. He has his own code. I wouldn't change him. Would you?"

There was no question that she missed having Tom beside her at night but, despite his return to the flooring job and the extra hours he'd been working, they had found a couple of occasions for intimacy in the week following Tom's release. She smiled, remembering how tender he had been with her the first time after Carson's attack, not wanting to evoke any traumatic memories for her. She had reminded him that Carson had been unsuccessful in his attempt, largely due to Tom. And that she was, in fact, eager to make love to Tom after their weeks of enforced separation.

Tonight, leaning back against his warm, broad body, she felt only gratitude that things had worked out as they had. If Carson hadn't attacked her when he did, he might have been successful another time; if not with her, then with someone else. Now he was safely locked up and awaiting trial.

"We'd better get going," she said. "The others are waiting for us."

"Hang on a minute," he said. He turned her around and, holding her gently against him, he stared into her eyes in the moonlight. "I have something to say."

Her heart began to race. She suspected what was coming, and the dark beach, with the moon, the boom of the surf and the scent of salt spray in the air, was the perfect setting.

He took a deep breath. "Back when I hit thirty, I figured finding a nice girl and having a family was just not in the cards for me. I thought love was ..." He swallowed hard. "Just something you told somebody to make them stay. I never thought I'd feel this way. Hell, I didn't know anybody could feel about *anybody* the way I feel about you."

She watched in wonder as he knelt on one knee on the damp sand.

"Aubrey, I don't know why you love me, but I know you do. And I don't know why you'd want to marry me, but I hope you will."

As she began to cry, he reached into his pocket. "I know I should have a ring, but we can choose one together. I thought we'd need this more."

He held out his hand and offered her a handkerchief.

Epilogue

Nest 105, Turtle Number 7

She was so small, the currents pushed and pulled at her like the wind tosses a leaf. It seemed an impossible task, to swim hundreds of miles through the ocean, surrounded by every kind of threat, but she was a sea turtle, and this is what she was born to do.

Without a backward look to the place where she'd just hatched, she moved her tiny flippers and headed into deeper water, constantly on the lookout for predators, as well as for the floating mats of sargassum algae that would shelter her while she grew.

The instinct of ages had helped her endure the long climb through the sand to the night air, given her the will to make the arduous crawl down a dark beach to the water, and kept her swimming when her siblings were being devoured by predators. That same undeniable force would bring her back to this very beach in a pair of decades. On the way here, she would mate, and in the deliberate manner of her species, she would find the right place to crawl ashore and begin the cycle anew. But before that happened, she would live a life of danger and freedom in the vast oceans.

And she would survive.

Made in United States
Orlando, FL
26 August 2024

50785617R10140